I0589227

A Plot To Die For

A Ghostwriter Mystery
(Book 2)

C. A. LARMER

Larmer Media
ISBN: 978-0-9871872-6-0
Cover design: Stuart Eadie

To my sisters,
Michelle and Simone

ALSO BY C.A. LARMER

CONTENTS

ACKNOWLEDGEMENTS

I'd like to thank my sisters for begging me to create bedtime stories from an early age, and for encouraging me to keep telling my stories into adulthood. Your enthusiasm is my inspiration. I'd also like to thank Christian, Nimo and Felix for offering me the time and space to head off on another wild adventure with Roxy.

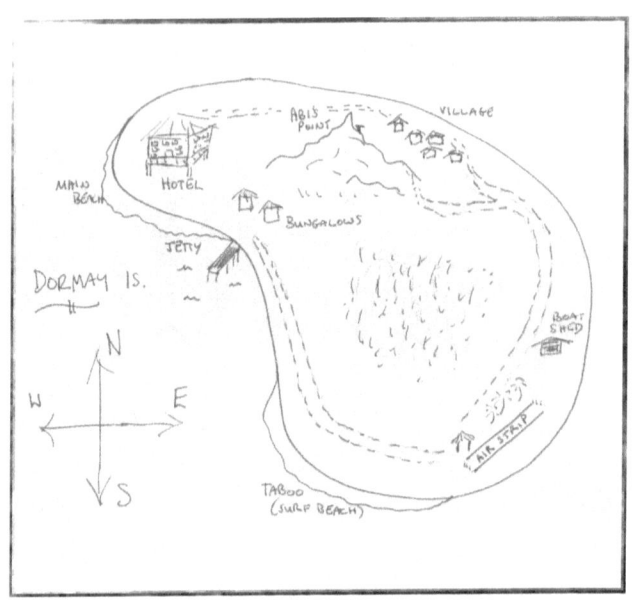

PROLOGUE

From a distance it looked like little more than an old coconut perched on the fringes of the beach, its husk tufting up in all directions. Upon closer inspection, however, it proved to be a human head, a woman's, her long hair poking out in every direction while crabs scuttled over the skull, devouring what remained of her flesh. Roxy would have screamed if she could find her voice. Instead, she stared mutely, shaking, knowing only too well whose head it belonged to and wondering, somewhat oddly, where the body had got to.

CHAPTER 1

The rattling, single-engine Cessna 182 tipped precariously to one side and Roxy gulped back her anxiety as she saw the tiny island of Dormay wing into view. From this height, it was breathtaking. Jelly-bean in shape and carpeted in thick rainforest, it had a lush hill soaring up at one end and a vibrant green valley sweeping down on the other. And all around it was a trimming of achingly white sand leaching into a fluorescent aqua-blue sea. Beyond the shallows were random clumps of darkness, boasting, Roxy assumed, more candy-coloured coral reef than she'd possibly have time to explore.

She spotted the resort instantly, propped as it was just below the cliff face at the most westerly point of the island, its verandas strategically positioned to take in that exquisite view. Directly below the veranda was a small patch of greenery that quickly turned to sand and then to sea. And at every glance, toothpick-like coconut trees stood to attention, waving in the breeze. As the plane flew overhead, Roxy could just make out a small jetty directly south of the hotel, jutting out of a rocky bay, and to the north, a cluster of traditional-style grass huts.

But where is the airport? She wondered momentarily. The plane straightened up suddenly then swept down towards the valley at the other end of the island, and that's when she spotted it, a light green mat etched into the darker, longer grass.

"Hold on!" the young pilot yelled back to her, his only passenger. "We're going down!"

She assumed this meant they were landing and tried not to panic as they did indeed start to descend towards that dodgy looking patch of grass.

What have I got myself into? She thought, swallowing her fears and thinking back to just 10 days earlier when the bizarre letter had arrived in the mail. She'd taken it straight to her agent, Oliver Horowitz whose offices were wedged in a dark and dusty part of inner-city Sydney.

Roxy read the woman's elegantly handwritten note aloud: *'I'd like you to tell the story of my life and the life of Dormay Island before I go. Please find enclosed the necessary details. I look forward to seeing you at your earliest convenience. Abi.'*

"It's slightly odd, don't you think?" she said, throwing it across to Oliver.

He sucked the oily remains of a doner kebab from his fingers and then picked it up, reread it and shrugged.

"Odd schmod. You're getting a free trip to Dormay Island. Christ, you know what Kate Moss and her lot pay for that privilege?"

Roxy considered this for a moment. Seated in a ratty old armchair in front of her agent's desk, books piled up beside her and a stack of posters at her feet, she had to agree that Abi's Retreat was beyond both their budgets combined. She was a relatively busy writer, he a relatively successful writers' agent but they still mixed in very different circles to Abi's clientele. She picked up one of the posters and unrolled it to reveal a zany looking guy with tufts of white hair and a lurid zebra-print suit.

"You're representing Sir Laugh-a-lot now?"

He scrunched the kebab wrapping up and tossed it towards the bin. He missed.

"Yeah, Larfy's putting a book out—*Lotsa Laughs with Laugh-a-lot.*"

She winced.

"Hey, don't knock it! He's one of the country's top comics. Makes more money in an hour of stand-up than you and I make in a month. Now, he could afford Abi's."

"Yes, but would they let him in? That's the question."

"Ouch. With that attitude they'll welcome you with open arms. Wanna a coffee?"

"Christ no, I have taste buds don't I? Listen, I'm serious about this. Abi's invite is great, sure, but it's slightly ominous, don't you think?"

"Bloody hell, here we go again."

Oliver sighed, leaning back in his creaky leather chair. In his late 40s, he was not exactly an attractive man—his slightly greying hair was greased and swept back, almost Elvis style, behind his ears, he had a trademark 1950's bowling shirt on (this one read *Tex*, whoever the hell he was), and these days he seemed to gain weight by the week— yet Roxy adored him nonetheless. She had worked with him for over a decade. She liked him, she trusted him. That was all that mattered.

"What's so ominous about it, Rox?" he was asking, his stubby eyebrows raised wearily.

"Well, for starters, the woman's extraordinarily private. I know this because I tried to do a freelance interview with her many moons ago for *Glossy* magazine. She never returned my calls. It's well-known, she doesn't want to be... *well-known.*"

In fact, Abigail Lilton had spent her entire life avoiding the spotlight, choosing instead to establish herself and her boutique resort in the heart of the vast Pacific Ocean on the remote Dormay Island. It was one of a handful of islands that made up a small, independent Pacific nation, clustered on the edge of an expansive coral atoll, equidistant from Australia and Papua New Guinea.

The resort, Abi's Retreat, was an aging yet still majestic colonial Queenslander. It featured wide wooden verandahs and crisp white shutters, friendly local service and secluded, shell-strewn beaches, and was a favourite amongst the rich and famous as much for its isolation as its unique holiday experience. Stressed out executive types, celebrities and bored heirs alike could book the six-bedroom place all to themselves or share it, begrudgingly no doubt, with other deep-pocketed individuals assured of privacy, anonymity and genuine adventure.

Abi's Retreat was famous, worldwide, as the smallest, most sought-after, ramshackle hotel in the tropics. And while it was kept in good nick, it had barely changed since Abigail renovated the original plantation house 35 years ago. Nor had her 'no-press policy' which was not the only reason why the invitation in Roxy Parker's hands had the young writer stumped.

It was the hastiness of it.

The elderly hotelier had suddenly decided it was time to tell her life's story and wanted Roxy for the job. Okay, that part made sense. Roxy Parker was a writer of some repute. Sure, she wasn't being invited to literary festivals every week or swapping tweets with Salman Rushdie just yet, but she was known in the industry as a very good ghostwriter. She could help almost anybody turn their life story into a pretty entertaining 'autobiography'. They got the credit, she got to pay off her credit card. It was a win-win.

Yet most of Roxy's clients came to it slowly. They mulled over the idea for a long time, took a little coaxing—should they really spill all? Wasn't that a little arrogant? Then, sufficiently coaxed by family, friends or financially motivated agents, they met with Roxy in person, chatted, often for many hours (in one case many months), to see if they really could work together and were on the same page, so to speak. Once that was agreed, they signed on the dotted line and began the complex process of synchronizing their insanely busy schedules.

Not Abigail Lilton. She didn't just want Roxy, a ghostwriter she'd never even met, she wanted her *pronto*. And, assuming the answer would be yes, had already included a cheque for airfares and a detailed description of when to come, what to bring and how to get there.

"So, she's changed her tune. It happens," said Oliver.

"Yes, but why the hurry? And what about the line 'before I go'? Seems a bit, I dunno, strange. Where's she going? Exactly? Is she running away? About to cark it? I just wonder why the rush?"

"Maybe the poor old duck's got cancer, that's why she finally wants to break her silence. She realises her time is running out. Does it make any difference?"

Roxy snatched the letter back from him, scowling at his paw prints.

"She's told me exactly when to come, what flights to get on, and she hasn't even left me a phone number so she's just assuming I'm going to show up."

"And aren't you? What have you got keeping you here?"

"Hmmm, let me see." Roxy held a hand up and began counting on each finger. "Tortuous lunches with my mother, Lorraine; cheesy articles for *Glossy* magazine; *Sex & The City* re-runs all by my lonesome at home..."

"So you haven't kissed and made up with Max yet?"

Roxy frowned and looked away. *Now why did he have to bring that up?*

Max Farrell was a talented local photographer and one of Roxy's best friends. Roguishly handsome and quietly cool, he had more mates than he had time for but it was to Roxy that he had offered his heart. And she had trampled on it superbly, insisting they should remain 'just friends'. You can imagine how that went down.

Roxy still regretted the way she had reacted, but she was angry, too, angry at him for placing his heart in her path. She hadn't asked for it, and she didn't want it, and she had told him as much. They had been such great mates, she was determined to remain that way. But of course, once trampled, the heart swiftly erects barriers, and it was their friendship that was now struggling to break through. They hadn't seen each other in weeks.

"I think he's moved in with that Sandy chick," she said, trying to sound as though it hadn't cut her to the core.

Oliver could see straight through Roxy, of course, but let the subject drop. "You're going, then? To Dormay?"

She relaxed considerably. "Of course I'm going, it's just so out of the blue. Excuse the pun."

Now it was Oliver's turn to wince. He shook his head at the writer sitting before him. Roxanne Parker was an attractive woman, early 30s, thick black hair, groovy Rayban-style specs. He liked her, had enjoyed representing her for the past decade, but, apart from commitment issues, she also had an annoying penchant for making mountains out of molehills.

"You've always got to think the worst, don't you?" he said. "Your business is ghostwriting other people's stories; she wants you to write her story, so just do it. Take the money and run. Besides, I reckon it'd be a juicy one, what with all the celebrity guests who've supposedly passed through. Rumour has it, royalty go there to bonk their mistresses stupid. This could be bestseller stuff, Rox. Might even end up a film deal."

"Let's not get too carried away."

"Just go, have fun, do the interviews and come back. It's that simple."

"Fun? Moi?" Roxy bat her eyelids at him then laughed. "I'm going, I'm going already. Just wanted to pass it by you, get your perspective, that's all."

She reached for her oversized, brown, leather handbag and got to her feet.

"So, I guess I'll be out of your hair for a while."

"Great, couldn't be happier, bugger off," he said. "But, hey, take your mobile in case you need to call me, and leave me a contact number for the retreat. You know, in case something 'ominous' happens..."

He did the wiggly quotation mark thing with his fingers (a pet hate of Roxy's if you must know).

She scoffed. "Now who's being dramatic?"

She swept in and planted a kiss on her agent's stubbly cheek. "Besides, what could possibly go wrong?"

CHAPTER 2

A sudden bump broke Roxy's thoughts as the Cessna landed on the grassy airstrip once, twice, then spurted skyward again before settling finally on terra firma and roaring to a halt. She peered outside her window and saw nothing but swaying palm fronds yet the pilot was already turning the plane about and heading towards a small grass hut.

The airport I assume, thought Roxy as she tried for a smile. She wondered how the rich and famous handled this kind of arrival, and made a mental note to ask Abigail.

Perhaps it was all part of the 'experience'.

The pilot, a jovial Australian bloke called Davo, had met her at the international airstrip on the main island, Beela, a place the locals simply referred to as 'the mainland'. She'd flown in directly from Cairns in far-northern Australia that afternoon and was thankful she didn't have to overnight at Beela. It was a pretty shabby capital as far as capitals went, with one or two half-decent concrete buildings and a few blinking neon signs standing somewhat incongruously beside shanty style shops and dusty market stalls.

Davo brought the Cessna to a shuddering halt beside the hut, switched the engine off, unhooked his seatbelt and stepped through the cabin to unlock the exit door. As he did so, a blast of hot air rushed in and Roxy felt as though he'd just opened the door to an enormous furnace.

"You'll get used to it," he said, noticing her discomfort, then helped her out and into the hut.

She grappled for her prescription sunglasses and swept a hand through her black fringe, which was already sticking, clump-like to her forehead. At that moment, Roxy could hear another engine roaring and she looked around to see a muddy, white four wheel drive crashing through what appeared to be thick jungle at one end of the strip.

"Right on time as usual," Davo said, then walked back towards the plane.

The vehicle creaked to a halt outside the hut and a man in his mid-30s, in Bermuda shorts and a white cotton shirt, came bounding out. He was of mixed race with the dark skin, short, wavy hair and chocolate brown eyes of a local, but when he spoke, his accent was authentic Australian. He sounded more ocker than she did.

"Roxy Parker? Hey man, welcome to Dormay. I'm Joshua, General Manager." His teeth gleamed white as he smiled widely and grabbed her hand to shake.

"Hi Joshua," she replied.

"Flight okay?"

"Yeah, well, not a great selection of inflight movies and the drinks trolley was a bit scarce but it did the job."

He laughed. "Your first small plane, then, eh?"

Before she had a chance to answer he took off towards the Cessna and was back in seconds, holding her small suitcase and laptop bag.

"You travel light."

"Sorry, no six-piece Louis Vuitton luggage for me."

"Hey, don't apologise. It makes a welcome change."

He placed her things into the back of his car, opened the passenger door and motioned her inside. "It's air-conditioned, much more comfortable. I'll just be a sec'."

Roxy settled into the back seat gratefully as Joshua

returned to the plane to help the pilot unload what looked like a bulging mailbag and boxes of supplies. They loaded them together into the back of the 4WD, then returned to the Cessna.

After several minutes, Roxy looked back to see Davo hand Joshua a brown paper bag, the kind you get from pharmacies. Joshua glanced inside and then said something to the pilot whose smile instantly deflated. He grabbed the bag and rummaged through it while Joshua rubbed one hand through his hair. They spoke for a few minutes longer, Joshua growing increasingly agitated and the pilot clearly trying to placate him, when the latter spotted Roxy. He said something to Joshua who swung around to her. He smiled widely, retrieved the bag without another word and returned to the car.

"Sorry about that," Joshua said, slamming his door. "Ready to go?"

Within seconds he had backed up and was charging off down the grass, away from the airstrip. Roxy glanced behind her in time to see the pilot steering his own craft in the opposite direction for take off. They clearly weren't into long goodbyes on this island.

"So, it's your first time on Dormay. What brings you here? Rest? Recreation?"

Roxy paused and, realising he expected an answer this time, didn't quite know what to tell him. It was clear from the general manager's question that he didn't know about the ghostwriting assignment, or if he did, he'd forgotten. Either way, she wasn't about to spill the beans. Abigail hadn't mentioned confidentiality in her letter, but then she hadn't mentioned much at all and, knowing how private the woman could be, Roxy opted for caution.

"Bit of both I hope," she said.

He caught her eye momentarily in the rear-view mirror.

"So, have I got the place to myself?"

"Not quite, no, but it's not our busiest season either. Mixed bunch this week. You'll meet 'em all at pre-dinner drinks. It's on the main veranda, every evening from 6pm. You got a cocktail dress, right?"

He gave her another quick glance and she was glad she'd remembered to pack a few fancy numbers for just such an event. But would her op shop vintage frocks be a match for the designer couture of her richer fellow guests? She cringed at the thought.

The drive from the strip to the hotel took about 20 minutes and was as much a white-knuckle ride as the plane journey, traversing thick rainforest, crunching over coral-edged rock faces and roaring past endless coconut trees bulging with nutty missiles. Joshua was clearly a man of few words but she forced the conversation anyway, desperate for a distraction.

"Are you from here? Originally?" She was wondering about that Aussie accent.

He caught her eye again. "I'm local, if that's what you mean. But I went to boarding school in Australia for my high school years. Then I did a hospitality course in Cairns before coming back to help Abi out."

"So you've known her a while then?"

"Abi? Yeah, she's like a second mum to me. Practically brought me up. My own mum used to work for Abi before she passed away." He paused. "So, yeah, she was the one who put me through school, all that. Anyway, enough about me. I should be giving you the rundown on the place."

He promptly launched into what she assumed was his usual tourist rant, complete with history, geography and climate details. He explained that while it had been pretty dry lately, this was, traditionally, the wettest time of the year and most guests, particularly those from Europe and those wanting to scuba dive, came between April and November when they could be assured of drier more consistent weather.

"Although they still find plenty to complain about," he said with a slight chuckle.

"So this is wet season?" Roxy squinted up towards the

cloudless sky.

"Yeah, gets really humid this time of year. Cyclone season, too. But it's been a good year so far."

"Well thank God for that."

"Oh you'll be right."

"Ever had a bad one?"

"Cyclone? Oh, we've had a few scary moments, man. Lost one of our jetties about 12 years back, a few workers' huts 'nother time. But no, luckily it's never been bad enough to tear the old house down. Touch wood!"

He tapped the side of his head with a laugh.

Roxy had already Googled the island so had some of the information he was telling her, but not everything. There was not a great deal on the internet about Dormay and absolutely nothing about its owner that didn't appear to be third-hand and contradictory. She was variously described as 'eccentric', 'shrewd', 'industrious' and 'sweet' and it was hard to form a true picture of the woman. Perhaps that was intentional, thought Roxy. In any case, it was clear from Google and her own experience that Abigail Lilton didn't do interviews, and Roxy wondered why. It was not a particularly good omen for the book.

She was about to ask Joshua when he yelled back to her, "There's the jetty!"

She noticed the dirt road turn to gravel and, through the coconut trees spotted a bleached wooden pier with a white railing reaching out to a small, protected bay. There was a gleaming white and blue yacht tied up at one end with its mainsail down and several sprightly seagulls perched atop the mast as if they owned it; and at the other end, a freshly painted wooden shelter, no doubt for guests to impatiently tap their toes while the staff prepared their vessel for boarding.

He didn't stop, continuing on for a few metres more until the scrub gave way to manicured lawn and the coconut trees to brightly coloured bougainvillea and hibiscus. There were two bungalow style huts under shady mango trees and what looked like a gardening shed, and between each one was a pebbled pathway that meandered across the lawn and towards the main house.

The house itself was just coming into view behind an enormous fig tree, and it really was a majestic sight. Standing on rickety legs, three-stories tall, it featured decorative arches around its three-quarter verandas and purple-flowered vines drooping down at intervals. Behind the house was that lush, green hill, so steep in places that all that survived were a few ferns clinging on to the sheer rock face.

Joshua slowed down and parked just below a small veranda at the side of the hotel where a staircase lead up to the main door and a large white sign read 'Reception: Welcome!' A bright yellow frangipani flower had been painted beside it.

As Roxy stepped out of the car, she spotted a woman, also in her 30s, descending the stairs. She had a mop of crinkly, auburn hair that had been chiselled into a chic bob above porcelain skin and emerald green eyes. She was wearing a light green top over white linen trousers and Roxy wondered how she managed to look so cool in this heat.

The woman darted Joshua a quick glance, her eyebrows raised skyward as though offering a silent question, and Joshua shook his head very slightly, as though the answer to that question was a tentative no. A brief flicker of something—was it anger, annoyance?—flashed across the woman's face but when she turned to Roxy her smile was firmly in place.

"How do you do, I'm Helen Lilton. Abigail's daughter." She gave Roxy a quick, curt handshake. "Mother's tied up right at this moment but she'll meet you for cocktails later. I assume Josh has filled you in on the schedule?"

"Yes, he has, thank you."

"Good." Helen threw Joshua another look before saying, "Come with me please and we'll get you checked in."

They followed her up the steps and while Joshua continued inside with her bags, Roxy was lead to a corner of the veranda and into a cushioned wicker chair that was facing towards the ocean. This was clearly not the main veranda but was small, shady and intimate. Roxy felt instantly relaxed.

"Please, just wait here while we get you settled in. I know those plane rides can be a little bumpy. I understand from my mother that your visit is... complimentary." She paused, her smile slipping slightly. "But I'll still need your credit card if you don't mind."

Roxy handed it over and, as Helen disappeared, spotted a jug of iced lemongrass tea and a glass that had been placed on a matching wicker table. She poured herself a drink, taking a long refreshing gulp before settling back to admire the view.

What a lovely way to check in! Roxy recalled her last holiday, waiting in a seemingly endless queue in a stuffy Melbourne hotel foyer to retrieve her room keys. No such annoyances here. The view was spectacular and the breeze that wafted in from the ocean was cool and revitalising. From this vantage point, Roxy could just catch a glimpse of the main beach and she noticed a blonde couple alighting a rubber dinghy. They had full diving gear on and what looked like a spear each. A local man was running down the beach to help them.

"The Zimmermans," Helen said returning with some forms. "They're here on an adventure."

There was something in her tone that made Roxy look up but Helen's expression was perfectly neutral. She handed the papers over.

"Just fill in the details and we'll have you in your room in no time."

"No hurry. I could sit her all day!"

"And, indeed, some people do." She smiled but there wasn't a lot of humour in her eyes.

She disappeared again as Roxy filled out the requisite information. One question, however, had her stumped: Purpose of visit? It was clear Helen knew she wasn't a normal, paying guest, but at the same time, she had to wonder how much she had been told. It was likely Abi had informed her own daughter about the book, how could she not? Yet Roxy wasn't taking anything for granted. Part of her contract routinely involved complete and unequivocal confidentiality. The whole point of using a ghostwriter, and not a co-writer, was to keep the real writer's identity ghostly or hidden. No one was to know that Roxy Parker had written the book, not the person whose name was etched in the largest font possible across the front cover. In many cases Roxy's clients hadn't even told loved ones they'd hired her, and it wasn't her place to say. She was the ghost in the machine, and she had to remain that way. It seems like a raw deal, especially if you have an ego, but for some reason—mostly financial—it didn't irk Roxy at all.

She decided to leave the line blank for now.

Less than ten minutes later, she was being escorted back through the lobby for a quick tour of the hotel. It wasn't air-conditioned and it clearly didn't need to be, its tall ceilings, plentiful open windows and large fans working wonders with the ocean breeze. There were traditional local artefacts at very glance—grotesque face masks hanging on the walls, crude wooden statues perched in corners, and a decoratively painted front desk where Joshua was now tapping away behind a computer.

"This is an old plantation house that's being constantly restored by my mother," said Helen, "despite the best efforts of sun, sea and cyclone. Through there—" she indicated a large veranda that faced directly West towards the sea—"is the main entertaining area."

Roxy noticed the wide, shaded deck had an assortment of lounge chairs and wicker furniture with a bar at one end and a set of stairs at the other leading down to the beach.

"You can hang out there anytime you like," said Helen. "The staff will bring you refreshments. And if you feel like going fishing or diving, we usually launch the Zodiacs from the main beach just below this veranda. They're stored under the house. But, please, ask Joshua to organise a skipper for you. We don't recommend guests take them out alone. The water's pretty flat here but it can still be tricky launching off the beach."

She gave Roxy the once-over as if to determine whether in fact she would do something so silly.

Roxy held her hands up defensively. "Oh I don't think you'll find me doing anything too tricky while I'm here. I don't even know what a Zodiac is."

"Well that's a relief. I can't tell you how many of our guests turn into Action Heroes the minute they hit Dormay. But just so you know, a Zodiac is an inflatable dinghy. We have several on the island."

"Sounds scary."

"Glad to hear it. The yacht might be more your scene." Again, the once-over. "That's also available most days should you want to have a sail around the island or take a trip to Beela. Again, just speak with Joshua. Okay, then, through here—" Helen's hand moved across to the room directly behind the lobby and leading out to a veranda on the other side of the hotel—"is the dining room where most meals are taken. You'll notice a set of stairs at the far right, they lead out to a small patio should you want some peace and quiet."

She turned and walked them past the dining room to the library. It was in the north-easterly corner of the hotel and was blocked off from the main lobby by a large bamboo screen painted with pictures of local fish.

"Our library is very small, but it should suffice."

Roxy poked her head around the partition and spotted a tiny antique wooden desk with a computer and telephone on top, and beside it a bookshelf that contained what looked like an assortment of pulp fiction and classics. A plush lounge chair had been placed in the corner with a side table overloaded with glossy coffee-table books.

"And here," Helen continued, leading her back to the main room, and to the bottom of a wide set of stairs, "is the way to your room. At the top of these stairs, on the first floor, turn right. Number 5. Your bag is already up there and Mary will help you unpack."

"Oh that won't be necessary."

"Suit yourself. As you know, drinks are in an hour on the main veranda, and dinner after that."

She gave Roxy one of those smiles that didn't quite reach her eyes. "I'll see you at dinner."

"You don't do the cocktail hour?"

Helen shook her head. "Not really my thing, but I suspect you'll enjoy it."

Once again, it felt like a slur but Helen's smile was still firmly in place, and Roxy gave her a curious look as she thanked her and made her way to her room. Helen was clearly a cool customer, Roxy decided. She'd better tread carefully with that one.

Roxy's room was easy enough to find. There appeared to be six rooms on the first floor—three at the front, facing the ocean, and three at the back looking out towards the cliff face—and Roxy's was one of the back ones, directly above the library. She stepped inside to find a young local woman with the blackest of skin and the meekest of smiles waiting for her. She bowed her head politely.

"Welcome, Missus!" she said in a singsong, melodic voice. "I unpack your bags now. *Tenkyou.*"

"Err, no, actually that won't be necessary," Roxy said and the younger woman's smile dropped. She looked confused. Clearly no one had ever rejected her services before.

"No offence or anything," Roxy rushed in. "It's just..." she pointed to her small suitcase. "There's not much to unpack. I'll be fine."

Still looking doubtful, Mary left and Roxy shut the door behind her. Then she glanced around the room and stifled a shriek of delight. It was simple yet stunning, and so utterly, blindingly white, she felt like she had been dropped into the middle of a snowflake, a glorious, luxurious, straight-out-of-Vogue Living snowflake. The wide wooden floorboards had been painted white, as had the wooden walls, the high ceiling and the shutters. In the centre of the room was a white four-poster bed draped with a white mosquito net and plumped up with an odd assortment of cushions—almost the only colour in the room, some light pink, some floral, one or two red and white checked. In front of the bed was a rustic, white wooden chest on which were placed several light rugs, a small turtle carving, some shells and a vase of fresh bougainvillea. Beside the bed stood an antique wooden cupboard where her suitcase and computer bag had been placed. On the other side were a small table and two wooden chairs. Again, all white. Above the lot was a crystal chandelier that hung down like an elegant spider's web.

One wall featured two large shuttered windows, and Roxy crossed to them now and opened the shutters wide. The sun streamed in, still bright at this hour, and she glanced out. Her room looked down to a small paved area that was shrouded in hibiscus trees and a myriad of ceramic pot plants. That must be the peaceful patio Helen mentioned, she thought.

There was a small bathroom at one end and a white cupboard that opened to reveal a well-stocked mini-fridge. A note above the fridge read, 'Compliments of Abi'. She glanced over the contents: assorted soft drinks, miniature bottles of liquor, brightly wrapped chocolate bars. All your basic nutritional requirements. She grabbed one of the bars, peeled it open and threw herself onto the bed with a whoop.

How could she ever have given this job a second thought?

CHAPTER 3

An hour later, freshly showered and donning a red and blue striped cocktail dress she considered far too skimpy for her untanned limbs, it was Roxy's turn to give herself the once-over. She stared at her reflection. Yes, she was obscenely pale for the tropics—she had considered using fake tan for, oh, about two seconds before deciding she just couldn't be bothered. It wasn't her style. She'd never been much of a beach babe, had always preferred a good book and a cosy lounge somewhere snugly indoors over a sweaty towel on a crowded beach. Still, this place wasn't exactly crowded, she decided, and she could probably stomach a little sunshine between interview sessions. Perhaps she could set up her tape recorder on a sunny deck somewhere and multi-task? She ran one hand through her black, now jaggedly cut bob, straightened her fringe down, readjusted her wide-rimmed glasses and contemplated. Something was missing. Ah, yes. She reached for her make-up bag and retrieved her matt red lipstick, then applied a thick layer that instantly added colour to her Icelandic face. Much better. She dropped it back in the bag, grabbed her room key and headed downstairs to the lobby.

A small crowd was already gathering on the main veranda when Roxy arrived and she was about to join them when a local waiter with greying hair and a tray of champagne appeared at her side. As she scooped up a glass, he smiled widely, revealing dirty red teeth, which would have shocked her if she didn't know better. Part of her internet research had revealed that the people in these parts—all over the Pacific region in fact—enjoyed chewing something called *betel nut* which left them in a kind of stained-tooth stupor. She wondered if it was worth it, and whether she'd be craving the stuff after a night with this lot.

Roxy glanced around the veranda. Billie Holiday was belting out a mournful tune on a hidden stereo somewhere but she needn't have bothered, she could barely compete with the crashing of the ocean just metres away. A gust of fresh, salty air slapped against Roxy's face as she stepped out towards the crowd.

"Roxy Parker!" roared a husky voice from one side and she turned to see an elderly woman hobbling towards her, one bejewelled hand holding firmly onto an ornate walking stick, the other clutching onto a large glass overloaded with ice and lime. The woman was short and round, her ample body wedged into a bright floral *meri* blouse, and had a large red hibiscus poking out from one side of her long, grey, frizzy hair. She placed her drink on a table and grabbed Roxy's hand firmly in hers.

"Hi, Abigail," Roxy guessed, "great to meet you at last."

"Please! Call me Abi. If it's good enough for Charles and Camilla, I reckon you can manage it!"

She roared with laughter then scooped her drink up again. "Sorry I couldn't come fetch you at the strip, love, it's been a bugger of a week. Just the usual staff problems, and then, to make matters worse, some of the crayfish spears have been nicked! What the hell that's about I cannot tell you. But I intend to find out."

She turned to the assembled group and quickly added, "Please, don't panic, anyone! We still have plenty of fresh seafood to go around."

She took a sip of her drink and then lowered her voice a little. "So glad you could make it, love. And at such short notice. Joshua pick you up from the strip okay?"

"Yes, thank you he was right on time."

"Oh, he's a good boy my Joshy. And Helen get you settled in alright?"

"Yes, Helen was great, too."

She snorted at this. "Not sure we're talking about the same Helen, then!"

This brought another stream of husky laughter from the old lady, then she leaned in and lowered her voice again. "Look, we've got lots to yak about, I've go so much to tell you, but I'm not gonna overload you on your first night. Let's just have a bit of fun, eh? Come on, I'll introduce you to the madding crowd."

Abi lead Roxy towards a 40-something man with a thick, black goatee who was deep in conversation with a painfully thin, much younger woman dragging on a cigarette. They pulled apart as Abi approached.

"Right, this is Luc Bermont, our resident artiste extraordinaire. Luc, this is Roxy, writer from Sydney."

The artist bowed his head slightly and flashed her a seductive smile. "'Ow do you do? Welcome to Dormay." He had such a thick French accent it was almost farcical.

"Hello," she said, restraining her smile.

It wasn't just Luc's voice that was cliché. He was strikingly good looking with the chiselled jaw and oily black hair of your stereotypical French man. He had a black fedora on his head and a crumpled white shirt that was unbuttoned enough to reveal a tanned chest beneath bead necklaces. His wrists were also covered in beads and he was wearing thick, black-rimmed glasses that on any normal human being— read, Roxy Parker—would look positively geeky. But Luc, the artiste, managed to pull it off, and Roxy clamped her mouth shut before she started drooling.

"Luc's here under the patronage of a French benefactress,

putting together a portfolio," Abi was saying. "Still, he's more than happy to offer art classes to guests who feel that way inclined. Isn't that right, Maya?"

She turned their attention to the woman beside him who was equally as stunning, but in a younger, more sun-kissed Californian way.

As it turns out, Maya Thomas was British, not American, but her bronzed body had clearly left the soggy shores of Mother England some time ago. She was wearing a long, sexy silk number that was slit up one side and down low at the back with oversized beads dangling across a pancake-flat chest. Her sun-streaked, blonde hair was draped over her bony shoulders, fluttering up occasionally in the breeze, and she looked as though she wasn't wearing a shred of make-up. She had that just-out-of-bed look that Roxy had never even attempted to pull off, certain she would just come away looking sleep-deprived. Maya had it down pat. She, too, looked familiar to Roxy, but it was probably just her catwalk-caliber legs and *Vogue*-cover good looks. If a photographer had suddenly appeared with a strobe light in tow, shouting, "Work it, baby, work it!" Roxy would not have been surprised.

"This is one of our locals, Maya Thomas," Abi was saying while the young woman rolled her eyes playfully and exhaled a mouthful of smoke.

"Oh don't be silly, Abi, I'm hardly a local! I've been here five minutes."

Then, after a brief pause, added in her plummy English accent, "Thank God!"

She looked Roxy up and down—clearly a prerequisite to being on Dormay—then offered a small smile that revealed slightly crooked teeth. It cheered Roxy up enormously.

"Do you live on Dormay?" Roxy asked and Abi snorted.

"Might as well!"

"I do *not* live here, Abi! I just pop over on the weekends, and when I have art classes."

She glanced at Luc and Abi snorted again. Maya blew a

plume of smoke in her direction then turned her attention back to Roxy.

"So, you're a writer? How simply thrilling! I'd love to be a writer—imagine, creating all that mischief with words!"

"Well. I'm not sure it's all that mischievous. But, yes, it's a decent living."

"Is that why you're here? Are you going to write about all of us? How exciting!"

"Oh, well, I—"

"Okay, time to mingle," Abi said, dragging Roxy towards another section of the veranda where a stately looking couple were sitting on a plush cream lounge that had been positioned just out of the wind. They were sipping what looked like orange juice.

"Roxy, this is the Zimmermans, all the way from Switzerland would you believe? They arrived about a week ago, their second visit to Dormay. Ingrid and Bernard, meet Roxy Parker."

And then, as if to avert further questioning, she added, "Roxy's just here on a holiday."

"Of course! Are not we all?" snapped the muscular-looking woman who extended a firm hand to shake.

Her husband did likewise but said nothing, just stared up at her coolly. They were both handsome with the athletic build and tanned physique of people who clearly spend a lot of time outdoors. Probably into extreme sports, Roxy decided, hating them instantly. She noticed a stunning gold necklace around Ingrid's throat, with a shiny brown and gold pendant attached.

"I like your necklace. What is that?"

Ingrid reached one hand up to stroke it. "Tortoise shell," she said proudly and then, glancing at Abi, added, "it is imitation, of course."

"Better bloody be!" said the hotelier. "They won't let you out of the country with the real deal, love. It's endangered."

"Yes, Abigail, I am well aware of that." There was curtness in her tone.

She could be Helen's soul mate, Roxy thought but instead said, "So, no turtle soup on the menu here then?"

Abi looked at her blankly before doubling over with laughter. "Not bloody likely!" She straightened up. "But I can tell you, the locals love it. It's one habit I couldn't beat out of 'em, no matter how hard I tried."

"Seriously? They eat turtle meat?"

"Tastiest tucker you can find apparently. Not real PC but, well, it's their land isn't it? Their tradition. I turn a blind eye to the occasional turtle. That's the truth... just don't write about it." She winked.

At that moment the elderly waiter approached Abi but before he could say anything she announced, "Speaking of locals, it doesn't come much more local than Popeye. He helps out, mainly in the dining room, has been working here for decades."

He nodded his head politely then murmured something in Abi's ear. She sighed loudly.

"Apologies, people. Got a situation in the kitchen that needs sorting. Enjoy your cocktails, and I'll see you at dinner." She headed off.

Roxy turned back to the Zimmermans who were watching her closely.

"I think I spotted you guys earlier."

The woman looked momentarily put out. "What do you mean? Where was that?"

"You were just coming in from your dive, I think. Earlier this evening."

"Ah, yes, yes, just a dive."

Roxy could have sworn Ingrid's shoulders relaxed a good two inches.

"We love to explore the reef, don't we Bernard?"

Bernard nodded.

"So, you're here on a diving holiday then?"

"Of course, it is the best place for it, yes?"

"Well, I wouldn't know, I guess I'll find out."

"Best place this side of the Great Barrier Reef," came a

croaky voice behind her and Roxy swung around to find a man in his 70s with a neatly ironed safari suit and a freshly shaven face.

"Looks like I'm going to have to introduce myself since Abigail clearly considers me part of the furniture these days. Dr Fergus Spinks at your service."

"Hi Doctor Spinks, Roxy Parker. I'm just in from Sydney."

"Well, we can't blame you for that now can we? Come, let's freshen up that drink."

Roxy glanced down at her barely touched champagne glass but before she could protest he clasped one arm through hers and lead her away towards the small bar at the end of the veranda.

"Sorry about that, my dear, but I thought I'd better rescue you from the Swiss couple. Can't get an interesting word out of either of them—trust me, I know. I was stuck next to them at dinner last night. That's two hours of my life I'll never get back. However! I get the feeling you have a little more to say for yourself, what, what?"

Roxy laughed. "Well, I'll try and think of something vaguely interesting, although, to be honest I'm not sure I can compete with this crowd. They're an intriguing mob."

The doctor surveyed the room. "Phhf! Dull as dishwater the lot of them. All got their heads so far up their proverbials they can barely string a sentence together that doesn't start with 'I' and end in 'me'. So, you're a writer I hear?"

"Yes I am." Roxy caught herself and laughed. "Sorry, there's that 'I' word again."

He dismissed this with a wave. "And you're here to write Abi's life story, eh?"

Roxy was surprised. So the old guy knew. That was interesting. She nodded. "Have you known Abi long, Doctor Spinks?"

"It's Doc for short if you don't mind. Er, let's see, how long have I known Abi? Over 30 years I reckon. Is that long enough for you?"

Roxy beamed. "It's perfect! You could be a valuable font of knowledge! How do you guys know each other?"

"Oh let's just say it's a very long, and very scandalous story." He chuckled then placed a finger to his lips as if to silence himself.

"That's it?! You're going to use the word 'scandalous' to a writer and then leave it at that?"

The old man laughed again. "All in good time, my dear, all in good time."

Another waiter, much younger than Popeye, appeared to announce that dinner was being served in the dining room.

"Thank you, Maurice," Doc said, taking Roxy by the elbow again and steering her back across the veranda towards the lobby.

"Come along, young lady. I'll show you the way, and hopefully neither of us will get stuck with those blasted Snoozermans."

In the dining room, a large table had been laid with the finest of silverware and crystal wine and water glasses. Candles were burning at intervals and flowers strewn down the centre. Roxy was shown to a seat beside the doctor with Abigail at the head of the table on his other side. Next to Roxy was a spare seat and beside that, Maya, who was holding her wine glass out for Maurice to fill. Directly across from Maya sat Luc and beside him Ingrid and Bernard Zimmerman. The chair on Abi's other side was empty, as was the chair at the other end of the table. Yet all were laid out.

Joshua appeared looking surprisingly dapper in a black jacket over a blue striped cotton shirt and dark jeans and, after greeting them all warmly, took the seat next to Abi. Just moments later Helen strode in with a glass of water in her hand, glanced around the table with a quick smile, then sat down at the other end, facing her mother. She had changed into a simple black, sleeveless dress with a string of pearls around her neck and another string around one wrist.

"Wade's on his way," she said to no one in particular but Maya sat up straighter, nearly knocking her wine glass over in the process.

"Really? But... but he never comes over on a Monday."

Helen shrugged. "He rang about an hour ago. Said he needs to see me for some unknown reason. He won't be long."

"In the meantime, then, I'd like to propose a toast," said Abi, raising a replenished glass of gin and tonic.

"To our newest guest, Roxy Parker. May she enjoy her stay and leave more enlightened in spirit and darker in tan!"

She laughed heartily and they all raised their glasses to Roxy who, of course, was mortified. She felt like shrinking under the table or, at the very least rushing out and finding the first bottle of fake tan she could get her pasty paws on. She hid her face behind her champagne glass.

"I like your creamy skin," said Luc, reading her mind from across the table. "It makes you look, how you say, like an English rose?"

"Oh, huh-lo! I'm the only English rose here thank you very much!" said Maya, smirking.

"You will burn too quickly," announced Ingrid, waving the wine waiter away. Bernard, too, refused wine. "You must use the SPF 30, yes?"

"Um, yes, I have plenty of sunscreen with me," Roxy said, pointing at the bottle of cabernet sauvignon that was being held out to her along with some semillon.

Neither drop was Roxy's favourite—she was notoriously hooked on merlot—but any old red would do tonight, and besides, both drops looked like top-shelf stuff. Maurice filled her glass with the lush liquid and moved on.

"Put it all over you tomorrow," Ingrid was saying. "Don't even forget your ears. Yes? This can burn, too."

"Oh no! We can't possibly have burnt ears!" Maya rolled her eyes playfully at Roxy.

Just then a booming voice could be heard coming from the lobby.

"God help us," said Helen, deadpan. "His Highness has arrived."

Roxy smelt Wade Thomas before she saw him, his spicy aftershave slinking into the room seconds before he did, barking orders as he came.

"Double scotch, on the rocks, Popeye—and go easy on the bloody rocks!"

He stopped and stared at the assorted diners.

"Good evening all! Sorry to crash your little soiree."

He slipped his cream linen jacket off to reveal a crinkled black shirt underneath that wasn't quite hiding his slight paunch. Wade Thomas was a large man, well into his 50s, with a receding grey hairline and slight stubble on his face.

"Hope I haven't kept you, I've been very bloody busy." He stared directly at Abi. "Just had an enlightening chat with the Lands Commissioner as it happens."

Abi frowned slightly then simply waved one hand at him.

"Oh come, sit down, Wade, and don't make such a fuss. Entrees are about to be served. Popeye, can we just get on with it, please."

Popeye, who'd returned with Wade's drink, handed it over and then dashed off again. Wade took his seat beside Maya and placed a burly arm around her slender shoulders.

"So, how is my beautiful bride this evening? Have a lovely day did we?"

Maya smiled briefly. "Yes, Wade."

"What was it today? No, don't tell me. Let me guess. Hmmm... I know! Art classes with Luc, right?"

He turned his steely grey eyes towards the artist and Luc simply held his gaze, unfazed.

"So, what exactly have you been teaching my wife, Monsieur Bermont? Soft brushstrokes, I hope?"

Luc swept his dark fringe from his face. "She eeze quite the talent, your wife."

"I'll bet she is," Wade said, then catching sight of Roxy on his other side, turned to her. "My, my, I'm being rude. Who have we got here then?"

Roxy leaned back a little, as intimidated by his burly presence as she was by his overpowering perfume. Abigail made the introductions.

"Roxy Parker, this is Wade Thomas, our esteemed local Governor. And conniving property developer to boot."

She roared with laughter at this, the red flower falling from her ear as she did so. Abi picked it up and shoved it back in while Wade shook his head at her.

"Not that I've had any luck with you, Abigail Lilton."

He turned his eyes back to Roxy. "Don't listen to a word the old lady says. This region'd be stuck in grass huts and breastfeeding pigs if it wasn't for me."

Helen groaned. "Honestly, Wade, we don't need another lecture about how you saved the savages from themselves."

"Hey, watch it, Hel', don't call my people savages," interjected Joshua.

Helen swivelled her head. "I'm sorry? You're people?"

She was staring at Joshua with a look of amusement on her face and Joshua was reddening under her gaze.

"That will do, children," Abi said sternly and they both looked away.

Wade, meanwhile, hadn't quite finished.

"If it wasn't for me," he went on, "you wouldn't have a proper bloody international airport to fly into. You know they used to have a crappy old thousand-metre, single runway grass strip at the mainland? The mainland! It was as bad as the sorry excuse for a strip that Abi's got here at Dormay."

"Hey watch it, bucko!" she said. "Don't knock grass airstrips, it's all part of the—"

"Adventure? Yeah, yeah, so you keep telling me. But they have to get to the mainland first, Abi, you know that. They didn't even have a proper terminal before I came along. Just a dodgy shed with a few portaloos. Until I invested in a decent-sized, paved runway, air-conditioned terminal, proper customs department, the works, no one could fly in anything bigger than a DC-3. Now...well, what did you come in on?"

He stared at Roxy.

"Er, I think it was an airbus." Aircraft sub-types weren't exactly Roxy's forte. It had an engine, a pilot and it got her from A to B, that's all she remembered.

"Exactly!" he was saying. "And the Zimmermans over there, they came on a Boeing seven-four-bloody-seven! If it wasn't for me and my 'conniving' developing ways we wouldn't get half the tourists we get today."

He directed that last comment to Abi.

"Roxy's a writer, you know?" said Maya, clearly trying to change the subject. She had no doubt heard this rant before. "Isn't that exciting?"

"Really?" He turned his whole body towards Roxy this time and she leaned back even further. "And what are you writing about?"

Before Roxy could answer Abi held one hand up to silence her.

"It's alright, Roxy, let me answer for you. I think it's time I got this over with." Abi paused with every eye upon her but waited until all the entrée plates had been delivered and the staff had left the room before saying, "I can see you're all very curious and you won't leave the poor love alone until the truth is out, so here it is. I've invited Roxy to the island to write my life story. I think it's time I got my book out, and it's our quiet season so it's as good a time as any."

Cutlery clinked loudly against china at the other end of the table and Helen sat back in her chair looking stunned.

"Book? What book?"

"My autobiography of course."

"Your what? But... but you can't write to save yourself."

"Yes, that's true, Helen, which is why Roxy's here to—what's your term for it, love?"

"Ghostwrite," said Roxy softly.

"That's it! Roxy will be ghostwriting for me. Ghosting I think you guys call it. Sounds spooky doesn't it? She'll write it, I'll get all the credit—nothing spooky about it!" She laughed heartily at this and one or two of the diners joined in but Helen was not amused.

"Are you serious, Mother?"

"Yes, 'course I am, love. Roxy will be with us for a few weeks, depending how it goes. I've simply told you so you'll answer any questions she might have and then leave her alone to get on with it. I'll also be very preoccupied with Roxy so I'm counting on you, Helen—and Joshua, of course—to run the ship for me."

"Yeah, absolutely, Abi, no problems, I'm your man," gushed Joshua and Helen threw him a withering look.

She turned back to her mother.

"Sorry, but I'm slightly confused. I... I don't understand. I've been begging you—imploring you—to do publicity for years now. Years, Mother. You always insist on your precious privacy, to the detriment of the hotel, I might add. Now, suddenly, you're going to write a tell-all?"

"Well, I don't think we'll call it a tell-all, Helen. No need for the melodrama. I'm simply putting my story down before it's too late."

"Too late for what?" asked Helen and Roxy swept her eyes back to the hotelier, keen to know the answer to that question, too.

"I've already told your mother, I think it's a good idea," interrupted Doc.

Helen's eyes widened. "You already knew?"

He nodded cautiously and she held her palms out, defeated.

"Well isn't that grand. I suppose Maurice and Popeye are also in the loop?"

"Come now, Hel'," said Joshua.

"Don't tell me you knew?"

He shook his head emphatically.

"Well I didn't know, if it makes you feel any better," purred Maya, once again trying to keep the mood light, "but I must say, I think it's a fabulous idea!"

She raised her glass of wine high in the air, managing to spill a few drops across the tablecloth.

"Goodness, think of all the delicious stories you can tell, Abi! You've had so many famous guests here. Mick Jagger, Hugh Grant, Madonna!"

"I hardly think that will do the hotel any good, gossiping about our clients," said Helen, clearly trying to keep her tone civil but not quite pulling it off. "It's not very 'Dormay'."

"Now, now, Helen," chided the doctor but Abi touched his hand briefly and shook her head.

"There'll be no gossip," she said firmly. "It won't be that kind of book."

She glanced anxiously at Roxy. "It won't be that kind of book, will it Roxy?"

They all stared at the writer who stammered, "No, not if you don't want it to be. Not at all."

"Hell, I reckon it's not a bad idea, Helen," said Wade, finally weighing in. "Any publicity is good publicity after all."

Helen still looked doubtful and Abi turned their attention to the prawn dish that had been placed in front of them.

"Now, please, everyone, enough about me. We're here to have fun! How are those marinated prawns going down, Ingrid?"

The Swiss woman, who'd watched the conversation with clear disinterest, swallowed her mouthful and nodded her head slowly giving it considerable thought.

"It is good, yes, very good. Where did you get your prawns?"

As a long conversation ensued about the state of prawns in the region, Roxy stole a few glances at Helen. She couldn't help feeling sorry for the hotelier's daughter, despite her cold demeanour. She was right to be upset. Autobiographies were incredibly personal affairs and could strike fear into the heart of even the most distant family and friends. Abi should have passed it by her daughter long before now, and in a much more private setting. Not only was Abi's oversight insensitive, it would do them no favours. Already she had Helen off side and this would be no help to anyone, least of all the ghostwriter.

Why, then, did she do it, Roxy wondered? Was there an ulterior motive to bringing it up so matter-of-factly in front of a bunch of hotel guests?

As she polished off her entrée and glanced around the table, Roxy realised that, apart from the Zimmermans, none of these people were strictly 'guests'. At least, not the typical tourist type. For starters, the doctor was an old friend of Abi's and, as far as she could tell, had been living on the island for some time. Wade and Maya—what an unlikely couple, she thought, there must be 30 years between them— were expatriate locals from the mainland who clearly spent their downtime at Dormay. And Luc was practically staff.

"Don't let them put you off, my dear," the doctor murmured beside her. "Their barks are usually bigger than their bites. And Helen will come round."

"Glad to hear it," whispered Roxy. "But Abi's right, it doesn't have to be that kind of book if she doesn't want it to be."

"I'll keep my scandalous stories to myself then," he said, chuckling.

Second course was a grilled snapper over rice with Asian greens on the side and it was delicious, but Roxy noticed that Helen barely touched hers. Abi noticed, too.

"Not hungry tonight, Helen?" she asked from the other end of the table.

Helen took a large swig of her water glass. "Not really, thanks Mother."

Then she glanced at the Zimmermans. "But, please, I'm sure it's lovely. I'm just not feeling myself, that's all. Popeye, how about some more iced water, hey?"

The waiter returned with a jug of water and the rest of the meal was relatively subdued with the conversation turning to safer ground—the state of the local currency (something that had Wade in quite a frenzy) and the best place to buy decent skin-care products (duty free on the way out, slurred Maya with disgust).

Roxy was relieved when the final course, a mango sorbet that shut them all up, was eventually taken away and they were ushered back to the main veranda for coffee. The Zimmermans refused, keen to get an early night, and Maya, who'd managed to drink more than she'd eaten, stumbled off, hopefully to bed.

This time Helen locked arms with the writer and pulled her towards the edge of the balcony where the sea could be witnessed in all its moonlit glory. The wind had died right down and the waves sounded less like a crashing drum kit now and more like the tinkling of a distant piano. Helen had cheered up considerably since her earlier outburst and seemed almost upbeat.

"Now, let's see if we can spot you a flying fish before the night is out," she said, scanning the horizon. "They say it's good luck to spot one on your first night."

"Who says?" said Joshua joining them.

"Local folklore."

"Local folk-lies," he scoffed back. "Just to reel the tourists in."

"Don't take any notice of him, Roxy," Helen said, giving the hotel manager a Cheshire Cat-like smile. "He might look like he knows what he's talking about but believe me he's as 'fish out of water' as you are. Isn't that right, *Beela*?"

Joshua clenched his jaw tightly.

"Jesus, Helen, you just can't let it go, can you?"

He turned on his heel and left. Unperturbed, Helen kept scanning the view.

"Ah-ha! There's one! Did you see it?"

Roxy stared hard but shook her head. "No, I'm afraid I missed it."

"Never mind." Helen's green eyes gleamed in the moonlight. "You'll start seeing things more clearly the longer you spend with us."

Roxy wondered if that was a promise or a warning of some sort, but before she could ask what she meant, Wade strode up, two cups of coffee in hand. Helen brushed him off.

"I'm going to bed," she told them. "I feel drained."

Wade dropped the cups on a side table and took hold of one of Helen's arms.

"I need to see you," he growled.

She shook her arm free. "Not tonight, Wade. I'm really not in the mood."

"It's the only bloody reason I came out here, Helen."

She sighed impatiently. "You know where to find me."

Helen turned back to Roxy who was pretending to be preoccupied with the view. "Good night, Roxy, enjoy your sleep."

"Thanks," Roxy called after her.

Wade looked immensely relieved, scooped the cups back up and handed one to Roxy.

"Here you go, this'll put hairs on your chest."

Then he took the opportunity to have a good, long stare at the aforementioned chest. Roxy hoped she had disappointed him sufficiently; although, compared to his waif-like wife, she was practically Dolly Parton.

"Okay then, tell us about this book. You'll be needing to talk to me, naturally."

"You?"

"Of course, me! I'm in charge of the bloody region, I reckon I deserve a mention. Besides, I've been coming to Dormay since Helen was a pimply teenager. I can give you any history you need about the area, assist with publicity stills that sort of thing. I'm in thick with the chief tourist officer, you know?"

"Very impressive," she replied wryly. "But you'll need to talk to Abi about all that. I'm yet to find out exactly how she wants to work it. Not sure if it's about her exactly, or about Dormay more generally. It's really early days. Can I get back to you on that?"

Before he could answer, she placed her coffee cup back down on the table. "It's been a long day, I think I'll turn in. Will you be around tomorrow?"

"Christ no, I've got important business back at the mainland. Just come over when her Ladyship calls and when I feel like seeing my wife—who appears to have forgotten she has a real home."

"How do you get over here from the mainland?"

"Whichever way I like. I've got the speedboat this evening—takes about 20 minutes max. Sometimes I give the Cessna a run, occasionally the yacht if I've got all day, which I usually haven't, despite what Maya thinks."

He looked away then, deep in thought and, noticing the doctor zeroing in, Roxy quickly said good night and returned to her room.

Half an hour later, as she peered up at the billowing mosquito net and listened to the humming ocean outside, Roxy couldn't help wondering what she'd got herself into. She knew this job wouldn't be conventional but she hadn't expected this. There was something in the air here, some deep undercurrent that seemed to have everyone on edge. She might not be an aficionado of luxury island resorts, but it didn't take an expert to know this was no ordinary resort. Instead of light-hearted fun and frivolity, all she sensed was suspicion, friction and something else, too. Something she couldn't quite place.

Was it fear, perhaps?

CHAPTER 4

The sun screamed into the room and Roxy groaned. She'd forgotten to close the shutters the night before. She groped for her glasses and glanced at her travel clock. It was 6.47am. She stretched like a cat in the luxuriously soft Egyptian cotton sheets and then, realising she wasn't about to fall back to sleep in a hurry, climbed out of bed and hit the shower. Twenty minutes later and dressed in a white sundress and blue and white wedges, she was back in the dining room helping herself to fresh pawpaw and yoghurt.

The place was empty except for the room maid Mary who looked almost relieved when Roxy ordered a latte, and quickly scuttled off to fetch it as though terrified Roxy would take that job from her, too. The local staff clearly wore many hats at this hotel and Roxy wondered how many people Abi had under her employ. She glanced around. Last night's tables had been stripped back and separated, and she chose one out on the deck so she could drink in that stunning view.

Already Roxy spotted the Zimmermans zooming off in what she now knew was a Zodiac, one of the local men by their side, and she envied them their energy. It might be early but it was already very hot and she was feeling suddenly lethargic as she peered up at the sky and out to the horizon. There was just a small gathering of harmless looking clouds. So far, so good.

"Good morning, Roxanne!" croaked Abi who had entered the dining room from the set of stairs on the cliff side.

She stopped to wash her sandy feet in a basin at the top of the steps, then hobbled over to Roxy's table and sat down, placing her cane to one side and a sprig of stiff, candy pink coral in front of her.

"That's beautiful," Roxy said, picking it up and turning it over.

"You're welcome to it, just be sure to enjoy it now because the colour fades fast. Just like us, I guess!"

Today Abi was as colourful as her coral, a magenta *lap lap* tied around her bronzed and wrinkled body, a fresh pink frangipani at her ear.

"I didn't pick you for an early morning person," she said. "Great stuff, we'll get lots of work done that way."

Roxy winced internally. If truth be known, she despised mornings, especially bright sunny ones, but put on a cheerful smile and raised her pineapple juice to the dazzling sun.

"What's not to love?" she lied. "Have you just come from the beach?"

"You betcha! I always take a stroll first thing... well, it's more like a wobble these days just to iron out the creaks and say g'day to the sea. Dip my old toes in and feel young again. Sun rises just after 6 around here, so might as well join her. You know, I've walked the beach every morning for the past 40 years? It's probably half the reason I'm still alive!"

She chuckled at this then turned quite serious again. "Listen, love, I'm sorry about last night. What a bloody debacle! I didn't handle that well at all. I should've realised Helen would chuck a hissy. Don't let her put you off, though. She'll come to the party, always does. Ah, here's your coffee. Good, good. I'll have my usual, thanks Mary."

The young waitress took off again and Abi turned back to

Roxy who was piling the sugar into her cup. This early in the morning, she needed all the help she could get. "So, how do you want to go about this?"

"Well, it's sort of up to you," said Roxy. "The more time you can give me up front, the faster I can get on with this and the sooner you can get back to your life."

"How does it work?"

"I have my recording gear with me and we just find a quiet spot where you tell me your story. I'll ask questions to prompt you along the way. I usually like to work chronologically—it just helps give it some structure, but you may find you want to start at the present and work your way back. We can sort that out once we start talking."

"How long does it normally take, love?"

"Well, it depends how lengthy you want this book to be and how much detail you're prepared to give. If we can talk over the next week or so, I can send the interviews straight to my transcriber in Sydney and she can turn the text around fairly fast. I'd want another couple of days to iron out a few things and then I guess I return home and knock it all into shape. We can then liaise via email. I'll have plenty more questions once I start making sense of it all. I'll also email you the rough chapter drafts as I write them so you can correct and approve. I notice you have internet connection here."

Abi took the espresso that Mary was now handing her and said, "Yes, Joshua's baby, that one. If it were up to me, we'd still be beating wooden drums! He managed to get us a mighty great satellite to beam us in with the mainland. It's all French to me, but he knows what he's doing. He majored in computer science at school. Clever boy."

She paused, a proud look sweeping across her face. "Joshy's been a Godsend to me, you know? He's the son I never had. The brother I wish I could have given Helen. And an A-class worker, to boot. That's his real strength. You know, he probably puts in more hours, more sheer hard work at Dormay than anybody else, myself included! You can't put a price on that. If only…"

Her voice cracked a little, she shook herself out of it. "Ahh, never mind about all that."

"About all what? What were you about to say?"

"Hmm? Oh no, not important now. Let's get back to business or we'll never get through it all. I get off the track a lot so you're gonna have to be firm with me."

Roxy did a mock salute and she cackled.

"Okay, so I guess I can give you a few solid hours in the mornings before things hot up, and maybe late afternoon, before cocktails. Will that do?"

"For now."

"Rightio, I'll leave you to enjoy your breakfast in peace."

Abi finished her coffee with one gulp, reached for her cane and stood up.

"Do try the coconut milk pancakes, they're one of our specialities. Shall we meet, say, in half an hour at the lobby?"

"Great, see you then."

As Abigail hobbled off, Roxy returned to the buffet table to give those pancakes closer inspection. She was surprised to find Helen and Wade now sitting at one of the tables inside, their heads locked together in conversation. They had coffee cups before them and Roxy glanced at her watch. It was now 7.30am. An early morning meeting perhaps? Helen looked up, spotted Roxy and said, "Roxy Parker! How did you sleep?"

Wade swung his head round and grunted at her.

"Very well, thank you, Helen. You?"

She glanced from Helen to Wade and she noticed the woman blush just slightly. Wade stood up abruptly.

"I gotta get out of here, I've got a region to run."

He tipped his head at both women, growled something about the bill to a terrified looking Mary and left.

"Not a morning person then?" Roxy said to Helen.

"A miserable bastard all round, really," she replied, finishing her coffee and also getting up to leave.

"Morning, ladies!" Doc called out cheerfully as he entered

the dining room.

He was wearing an old, black Greek fisherman's cap and tipped it at them as he spoke. Helen ignored him completely and walked away.

"Hello, Doc," Roxy said. "Everyone seems a bit surly this morning. Something in the air, perhaps?"

Doc shrugged. "Don't ask me, I just keep my head down and mind my own jolly business."

Roxy looked at him sideways. "Somehow I doubt that very much. Something tells me you know exactly what's going on around here."

He laughed. "Very perceptive. I knew you were a clever one."

He helped himself to a selection of pastries and breads then followed her back to the veranda.

"Mind if I join you, my dear?"

"Not at all."

"Tell me, what's on your schedule this morning? A spot of swimming? Some snorkelling perhaps?"

"Sadly, I'm not really here for fun and games, I'm going to get cracking on this book."

"And you said you weren't here for fun and games, tsk, tsk."

He paused to order some English Breakfast tea off Mary.

"The Zimmermans take off already I suppose?"

"Yes, ages ago, looking way too adventurous for me. It's exhausting just watching them. So, come on, level with me. What's the story with those two?"

Doc slathered inches of jam on a piece of fresh bread.

"They're an odd couple that's for sure. Own some kind of jewellery shop back in Geneva I believe. Have turned up twice in a row now, same time as last year with very little to say and far too much to do. Short of meal times, I haven't seen them sit still since they got here. Busy, busy, busy."

"They must be fanatical divers. Is the reef really that good around here?"

"It's better than that. Thanks to Abigail it hasn't been

overfished or razed with dynamite like half the reef in the area. It's as healthy today as the first day I saw it. But no, they don't always dive. They seem fixated with the other side of the island, have taken long hikes through the area right around the strip. Probably do the dash up to the look-out and back every afternoon for all I know—it's enough to give an old guy like me the shakes."

"Do they take the sail boat out, too?"

"No, much too impatient for that. They're into speed and efficiency by the look of them. Now, me, I'd much prefer to lounge about on a sundrenched deck, the wind slapping against the sail, the water breaking against the bow..."

"Sounds poetic. I'd much prefer sitting on firm ground with a glass of merlot and a good book," Roxy said with a laugh, and he laughed along.

"Speaking of terra firma, what's the look-out like? I noticed a map to it in my room. It's called Abi's Point, right? View must be amazing from up there."

"Best view on the island. I'm not sure you'll want to haul your bottle of merlot up there, though. Damn hard climb, but it's worth it. I used to gallop up it! Now, well, the heart's not what it used to be. But we showed 'em there for a while didn't we?"

He patted the left side of his checked shirt as though chatting to a dear friend.

"So how long have you been at Dormay, Doc?"

The doctor sat back in his chair and thought about this for a while.

"I guess I moved here about ten years back. I'm British-born, in case the old accent has you stumped, but I grew up in Melbourne. Had my own company there. A group of medical practices actually. Very profitable."

"Really? Why did you leave, then?"

"Oh my dear, the heart doesn't always keep up with the head. They said I'd drop dead within a year if I didn't slow down and take stock. Bloody doctors!"

He winked and took a bite of his bread, dribbling a little

jam onto his cleanly shaven chin.

"So you retired to Dormay?"

"Yes indeed. Gave it all away for the Robinson Crusoe lifestyle."

"Sounds fabulous. Abi must have been happy to have an old friend around."

"Well, it took a bit of convincing I have to tell you, but she came round eventually. Now I like to think she does enjoy my company. I wasn't always this useless, either. I used to oversee the boat trips, and the walks, although I'm not up for much of that now. And of course it helps to have a doctor about should a rich socialite suddenly come down with sunstroke. *Quelle horreur!*"

"I'd imagine it's been ideal for Abi," Roxy said and then, noticing the time, picked up her sprig of pink coral and added, "Speaking of which, I'd better be off. We have a meeting in five." She stopped, turned back. "Love your cap, by the way."

His craggy face broke into a wide smile and he tipped it at her again.

Roxy dashed back to her room, placing the coral carefully on the window ledge, then collected her recording gear, notepad and pen. When she returned to the lobby she found Abi deep in conversation with Joshua, and the hotelier did not look happy.

"Willie's up to something, Joshy, I can smell it. The man is trouble."

She spotted the writer and said, "Ahh, here you are, Roxy. Josh, love, we'll continue this later. Okay?"

He glanced at Roxy and nodded. "Of course Abi, no probs. I'll see you at lunch, hey?"

"Trouble in paradise?" Roxy asked.

"Nothing I can't sort out," she said, leading Roxy away from the main part of the hotel and out the northern end to the small patio with sweeping stone steps leading down the cliff to the beach.

There was a shady nook at one end and a table had

already been set up with iced water and fresh fruit. She indicated for Roxy to take a seat and then did so herself.

"We can have a bit of privacy here," Abi said, pouring them both a drink. "Now, where do we start?"

Within minutes, Roxy had the elderly lady waxing lyrical about her childhood in Cairns. For an infamously private person Abi was opening up very easily and Roxy doubted it had anything to do with her honed interviewing technique. Instead, she guessed there was some specific reason Abi had decided to 'tell all' now. The woman was elderly but couldn't have been much past 70. Was she sick, perhaps? Roxy studied her for signs of illness but came up short. She seemed positively glowing and, apart from the obvious hip problem, appeared to be in perfect health.

What then, she wondered?

"You are such a suspicious person, Roxanne!" she could hear her agent chiding her as he always did when her imagination ran wild, and she gave herself a little shake and refocused on the interview. Whatever Abi's reasons, she would no doubt reveal them in good time.

Two hours later, Abi reached for her cane and, after a slight wobble, stood up.

"Rightio, that'll have to do for now, love, I have some staff issues to sort out. I've arranged for Joshy to meet you back at the lobby. He'll give you a proper tour of the island and answer any questions you have about that."

"Of course, thanks Abi. Did you want to reconnect after lunch some time?"

"Yes, look, you do your own thing and I'll come and find you around 3ish. Alright?"

Roxy nodded and gathered her things, then followed Abi down the stone pathway and back into the hotel. There they ran into Maya who was just finishing breakfast.

"Afternoon, Maya," said Abi. "Hard at it as usual I see."

She didn't wait for a reply but headed off to the kitchen.

"Battle axe!" Maya hissed before turning to Roxy with a crooked smile.

She was wearing pleated cream shorts belted at the front and a low plunging halter top that only emphasised her flat chest.

"Getting on with your mysterious book then?"

"Something like that."

"Well, it looks like her Highness has given you a reprieve. Shall we hit the beach?"

"Sorry, no, I've got a date with Joshua."

"Really?!" Her blue eyes lit up.

"He's taking me for a tour of the island, Maya, we're not heading to a shed to make out."

Maya giggled like a schoolgirl. "You wouldn't have any luck anyway. You're not exactly Joshua's type."

"Oh? And what is Joshua's type?"

She placed one finger across her lips. "Let's just say, he goes for ice maidens."

"In that case, I'm absolutely his type," Roxy replied and Maya burst into peals of laughter again.

"So what are you still doing around here anyway? I thought your husband said you were heading back to the mainland today?"

Her smile dropped and she blew a stray strand of hair away from her face.

"He can do whatever he likes. I am staying here where it's much more my style. Have you been to the mainland?"

"Just to catch my flight."

"That's about the only place worth visiting—the airport! Urggh, the place is just awful. Hot, sticky, and boring as bat shit with all these awful vagrants following me around! No thank you, I'll stick with Dormay. It's a lot more fun. Speaking of which—have some!"

She blew Roxy a kiss and sashayed past her, up the stairs.

Roxy wondered if Maya had her own room on permanent reserve, then spotted Joshua waving to her from the front door and raced through the lobby to join him.

"Good to go?" he asked, leading her down the stairs and into his 4WD.

She jumped in and held on as he reversed the car and began hurtling back down the road they had arrived in on just the afternoon before.

"Thought I'd take you for a tour of the coastline first, then we can head for the look-out."

"Sounds good."

She relaxed back into her seat, enjoying the icy air-conditioning and Joshua's apparent inability to make small talk. They were heading in a south-easterly direction, back towards the airstrip, but hadn't gone much beyond the small jetty when he slowed down at a clearing in the mangroves. He turned the car down a side track and towards a large sand dune in front of a totally separate beach she had not noticed from the road. He parked the car.

"This is Taboo Beach, the surf beach," he said, leaping out and racing around to open the door for her. "This is about the only part of the island worth bringing the boards to."

"What a pity I left mine behind then," she joked, grappling through her handbag for her sunglasses and then following him along the sandy pathway and over the dunes. They stopped and both removed their shoes before stepping down onto the hot, white sand. The ocean was incredibly loud and the waves that rolled in were wild and erratic.

"Not a great day for learners!" he yelled and pointed out to sea.

Roxy spotted someone on a surfboard well out and she looked enquiringly back at Joshua.

"Luc!" he said, and she was surprised.

Gorgeous, artistic and athletic! What more could a woman want? Seconds later, she watched as a wave wiped him clean off his board and she heard Joshua laugh beside her.

"Dunce!" he said, turning back to the car.

They drove on, reaching the airstrip about 20 minutes later, but Joshua didn't stop there. He continued driving, past the airstrip and back in a northerly direction towards the coast on the other side of the island. The road here was clearly less travelled, and he ploughed over fallen branches and through hanging vines, passing what looked like an old, dilapidated shed right on the beach front along the way. Its roof was covered almost entirely in a thick, tangled vine and there were several very faded orange life buoys hanging from its walls. She spotted some broken poles leading out from the shed into the shallow water of the bay.

"What's that?" Roxy called out.

"Oh, just the old boatshed. We don't use it now. There used to be a jetty there, too. It's the one I was telling you about that got torn to shreds in Cyclone Yono."

"Why did you even have a jetty on this side of the island?"

"Oh it was quite handy to be honest. Used to service the village and the airstrip—boats could meet up with planes. Couple of the neighbouring islands didn't have their own strips so they used to use this one. 'Course most have their act together by now."

Joshua kept driving for a few more kilometres until they reached a fork in the road. He stopped and pointed to his left, back in the direction of the hill.

"That's the road to the look-out," he said, then cranked the car into gear and chose the right-hand road. They didn't drive for long before they came to a clearing where an assortment of grass huts were scattered.

"This is the village, where most of the staff live," he told her.

Roxy spotted the ocean on one side and thick forest on the other.

"How many staff are there?" she asked.

"'Bout ten all up. There's Maurice and his missus Mary, and Popeye and old Tara. They all work up at the hotel, well, except Tara these days—she's getting on a bit. So's Popeye of course but that doesn't stop him. Then, there's two groundsmen who also help out with the boats, driving guests to the strip, that kind of stuff. One's Abe—that's Popeye's son, named after Abi—and a fairly new bloke called Willie. He used to work for Wade."

"Isn't he the one Abi was griping about?"

Joshua glanced across to her. "Willie? Oh he's alright. Abi gets a bit neurotic sometimes. Anyway, you'll see them both about the place. Oh and there's also Patricia, that's Abe's missus. She's the chef, and a top one at that. We really lucked out there. We bring in guest chefs from time to time, but to tell you the truth, I reckon Patricia pisses all over the lot of them. She's a natural. There's also a couple of young women who come from the mainland, they help clean the rooms, do the washing up, general domestic stuff."

"What's with the name Popeye?" she asked.

"He's got a gammy eye, you didn't notice?"

She confessed she hadn't. "He's not offended by that nickname?"

Joshua laughed. "Hardly. These people get called a lot worse by some of our guests."

"Oh?"

He hesitated.

"It's okay, Joshua, I haven't got my tape recorder on now."

He smiled. "It's just that, you know, the rich and famous don't exactly waste time with their Ps and Qs, man. They don't have to be polite, do they? The world revolves around them, after all."

She'd clearly hit a raw nerve and waited for him to continue.

"These people—my people—they put up with a lot of crap from Westerners who come here thinking they own the place, that they can do what they want with it, that we're not good enough. But it's not theirs to play God with is it?"

He ran a hand brusquely through his hair.

"Shit, sorry, man, I get a bit carried away."

"Fair enough. It's the same story everywhere, Josh. Money talks."

"Blood oath it does."

He left it at that and steered the car slowly past the workers' houses, which had been built in a traditional grass hut style. She spotted several small children racing out from the shade to wave hello and Joshua laughed, waving back.

"They're Mary and Maurice's kids," he told her and then, spotting several more appearing from the beach, "and those are Abe's and Patricia's."

Roxy waved, too, and couldn't help laughing at their wide, delighted smiles.

"Can we stop and say hello?" she asked.

He looked surprised by this then glanced at his watch.

"Better not, I gotta get you back for lunch. Abi'll have my hide. But, you know, you can backtrack anytime you like to say hi. They'd love that. It's just a short walk from the hotel. You walk east along main beach, there's a clear pathway, you can't miss it."

"Thanks, Joshua, I might just do that one day."

"Really? Good."

He seemed genuinely pleased with this and she knew she'd struck a chord. Roxy wondered how many other guests had ever bothered to take the time to meet the locals. Judging from Joshua's animosity, she suspected the numbers were low. He was clearly a proud man, even prouder of his people, and Roxy wondered how far his loathing for the rich and famous guests extended. It must be hard to keep up the friendly façade when you have patronising and racist guests.

Within minutes they had swung back around and were heading towards the fork in the road. This time, Joshua took the road that cut straight across the island and up towards Abi's Point.

"I'm just gonna take you to the base of the look-out," he told her, cranking the car up a few gears to tackle the steep incline. "You can continue up to the look-out any time you like but, sorry, it's almost midday so..."

"No worries, Joshua."

The air grew rapidly cooler now that thick jungle was surrounding them and the road became muddy and slippery.

He slowed down a little and then parked by a signpost that had directions to the top. They jumped out of the car again and within seconds Roxy was surrounded by mosquitoes.

"They're buggers up here," he told her. "I'd get you some repellent but we're not stopping for long."

"They don't seem to be eating you alive," she said, slapping at her arms and legs, and he laughed.

"Yeah, sorry, man, something in my blood I reckon. They hate me. Always go for the juicy tourists though!"

"They clearly have good taste."

"Anyway, this is the first stop for the walk. You continue along this trail and it winds its way up to the top. Takes about half an hour, an hour if you're a lazy bastard, but it's worth it. Awesome view from there, mate, awesome. You can walk to this point easily enough from the hotel, an easy 20-minute trek, or just ask one of us for a ride. Just don't forget your water bottle—"

"Ow!" she screamed, feeling another sting.

"And some Rid repellent. You might need tropical-strength I'd say." He chuckled. "I'm glad I'm amusing you so much."

"Sorry. They really do like you, eh? Come on, let's get you back to the hotel."

She was never so relieved to hop back into Joshua's vehicle and speed away.

CHAPTER 5

"Oh my God, I just loathe mosquitoes!" squealed Maya over lunch soon after.

She wasn't actually eating anything, was simply slurping away at what looked like an iced frappe, but had joined the small gathering on the main veranda anyway. A buffet of fresh meats, seafood and breads had been placed where the bar was the evening before, and they were seated in wicker chairs looking out at the view.

"They made a right meal out of you," Maya added, staring, horrified at the red welts that were now appearing on Roxy's body.

"Yes, apparently I'm quite delicious."

"I hope you're on a dose of an anti-malarial medication," interjected the doctor who was sitting nearby. "I've got plenty of quinine if you need some. Wouldn't want to come down with anything nasty."

"Oh no, that would be dreadful," agreed Maya. "Wade's had Malaria a few times, totally dreary. He comes out all sweaty and listless. Can't seem to shake it."

"Dreary? It can be deadly," snapped Doc. "Wade's got it in his system. He'll struggle with it for life."

"Oh I'm not sure I can handle *that*. You should see how beastly he gets with it. No fun at all."

"Yes, deadly diseases can be boring like that," said Roxy, drolly. "In any case, I should be fine, thanks Doc. My GP put me on Chloroquine before I came."

"Smart man," he said, wiping what looked like mayonnaise from his chin.

"Smart woman, actually. So, what about the locals? How do they handle it?"

Doc shrugged. "They don't seem to get it. Certainly not in the 10 years I've been here. Of course, they're continually exposed to the malaria parasites so they may have built up a natural immunity."

"Lucky bastards," Maya said. Then, more irritably, "Where the hell is Luc? He promised me a lesson today." She noticed Doc's smirk and added, "We're supposed to be studying oils today thank you very much."

"Of course you are my dear."

"I saw him at the surf beach less than an hour ago," Roxy said.

Maya looked mortified. "He went to Taboo and didn't tell me? Huh!"

She stood up, grabbed her hat and glasses and stalked off.

The doctor chuckled. "They couldn't be less obvious about it if they tried," he said.

Roxy glanced around. The Zimmermans were at the buffet table, Joshua and Helen were just leaving and Popeye was busy clearing away plates.

"So they're um..." She didn't quite know how to put it.

"Checking out each other's etchings?" Doc suggested, a cheeky glint in his eye. "Yes, on a daily basis I believe. Have been ever since he arrived about two months ago. Back then, Maya came to Dormay every second week or so. Now we can't seem to get rid of the ghastly girl. Might as well move in. I don't know why Wade stands for it, frankly. But, well, he has other fish to fry..." He took another mouthful of salad.

"Oh?"

"Money trouble," he whispered, spitting shredded tuna towards her. "He's been at Abi for months."

"Abi? What's she got to do with it?"

At that moment the Zimmermans took their seats not far from Doc and he tapped one finger to his nose.

"Perhaps another time, eh?"

He turned towards the Swiss couple who were now clad in matching beige shorts and shirts.

"So, Ingrid and Bernard, productive morning was it?"

Ingrid nodded her head stiffly. "Very productive, yes, thank you doctor. Wasn't it, Bernard?"

Bernard, who didn't appear to have a voice box, simply nodded his own head and bit into a slice of quiche.

"What exactly are you looking for out there?" asked Roxy casually enough but Ingrid seemed put out by the question. Again.

"We just like the reef," she relied sternly. "And the fish."

"You know, I've never actually been diving."

"And you come from Australia!?" Ingrid looked scandalised. "Not even the Great Barrier Reef?!"

Roxy shook her head apologetically.

"You must try it when you are here. Did you know, they have some of the best coral in the world? Right here, at Dormay?"

"So I keep hearing. I guess you don't see anything like this in your part of the world?"

She scoffed. "No! Nothing like this."

"But we have excellent cheeses," Bernard said suddenly, surprising Roxy.

It was the first time she had heard him speak. He smiled stiffly and then said something in what sounded like German to his wife. A small argument ensued and Roxy glanced at Doc who was busily devouring a chicken leg. She took this as her queue to leave, returning to her room to change into some swimmers.

Roxy had been on the island almost 24 hours and hadn't

yet hit the beach. Some would call that a travesty. She wasn't fazed in the slightest but felt it might be time to get it over and done with. She pulled on a black and white one-piece swimming costume and lathered every inch of exposed skin with sunscreen including, yes, her ear lobes. Then slipped her sundress back on, pulled on an enormous sunhat and sunglasses, swapped her wedges for white thongs and made for the door. Just before she reached it, she heard garbled voices coming from the other side of the room, below the windows. Roxy stepped back curiously towards them. Through the half-closed shutters she could just spy the small patio below. From her angle, Roxy couldn't see who was doing the talking but she could hear traces of a male voice.

"What do you mean (inaudible)... get rid of (inaudible)...?"

"Shhh," came another voice, more feminine. "Just calm down (inaudible)... not in my plan."

"Plan? Who cares about—"

There was a loud knock on Roxy's door and her heart nearly leapt through her chest. The voices below stopped and she drew back against the wall, hoping they hadn't spotted her, and not only because she was clearly eavesdropping. There was something very secretive about their tones, something desperate, too. She took a deep breath and stepped softly away from the window and towards her door.

"Who is it?" she hissed as quietly as she could.

"It's Maya, sweetie, do let me in!"

Roxy swung the door open to find the young woman standing outside, nothing but a brown and white checked Burberry bikini, matching ballet flats, and dark Gucci sunglasses on. A small butterfly tattoo fluttered out from the back of her bikini bottom and her tall, lean body looked amazing. If Luc wasn't having his merry way with her, Roxy wondered why.

As if reading her mind, Maya said, "Well, Luc's missed his chance, so I'm going for a dip. Want to come with?"

"Sure. I was just on my way there."

"Fabulous. Let's do it!"

They made their way through the lobby and down the main stairs to a rickety set of wooden side steps that lead all the way to the main beach in front of the hotel. The sand was not as silky smooth as Roxy was expecting. Instead it was sharp in places, littered with all manner of broken shells and bleached out coral. Where the water crashed into the sand on shore it tinkled like broken china, and all about she spotted dozens of near-perfect shells including an enormous nautilus that had likely washed up the night before. The sand wasn't perfect white either, instead boasting a kaleidoscope of coloured grains, from brown and red to black and pink and white and grey—every shade of the reef from which it had come.

Several large umbrellas had been dug into the sand beside freshly varnished deck chairs, and fluffy blue and white striped beach towels placed, folded, on each one. Maya shook a towel out and draped it over her chair before slipping off her flats and dropping down to sunbake. Then, noticing she was in the shade, jumped back up and pushed her chair out into the scorching sunshine.

"That's better," she said.

Raising her sunglasses to catch Roxy's eyes, she added, "Don't even mention the letters SPF to me, please! I'm not a child and I really don't need to be told. Again."

Roxy held her hands up defensively.

"And I'm not your mother, so burn away."

She slipped her hat, sundress and thongs off, placing them onto the adjoining chair, then picked her way carefully down to the water's edge. The ocean here was far less rough than Taboo, protected no doubt by the surrounding reef. The water rippled gently into shore, and it really was a perfect temperature. Not quite warm but certainly not cold. She slid in easily, thrilled that she didn't have to make a spectacle of herself, inching in slowly as she normally did, her teeth clenched in agony. She stopped just below her shoulders to avoid wetting her hair but needn't have bothered. Maya came crashing in beside her, diving like a pro into the glistening water and splashing the writer in the process. She was still wearing her sunnies and came up beaming.

"Ah, that's better," she said.

"Oh what the hell," said Roxy, dropping her own head under.

It felt amazing, and its translucency had her mesmerised. So glassy water really did exist outside of tourist brochures, she thought. Who knew?

"You're quite the mermaid," she said to Maya who was now floating on her back, bobbing along with the tide.

"Well, I have to get my swims in somewhere."

"What's wrong with the mainland beaches?"

"Sandflies, for the most part. They plague this area. Well, everywhere except Dormay of course. It's almost the only island in the region without them. God knows why."

"Are sandflies as bad as mosquitoes?"

"Oh my god! They're much worse! You got a few mozzie bites today? Boo-hoo! Stand on any of the beaches at Beela at dusk, and your entire body is covered in less than a minute. They even follow you into the water, the little devils. The welts are larger, itchier too. It's the reason Wade's resort is such a disaster."

Roxy combed her hair back with her fingers. "You guys have a resort?"

"Well, Wade does, sweetie. He's had it for a few years now so he can't blame me for that one. We've only been married 18 months you know?"

"No, I didn't. So, tell me about the resort."

"Oh it's nice enough. More modern than Dormay, which isn't saying much. Don't get me wrong, I adore Dormay, but it's a tad retro for my liking. Anyway, Wade's place, Paradise Point—crappy name, I know—accommodates three times the guests, too. But we don't seem to get as much repeat business, which is what Dormay survives off, or at least that's what Wade says. He's fixated with it. And I'm telling you, it's because of the blasted sandflies. The beaches are riddled with them and they seem to get worse each year. Wade says they weren't nearly as bad five years ago. He keeps threatening to DDT the entire region, and quite frankly I think he would if he didn't keep getting voted down by the local bloody council. Savages. Still, it means I have plenty of excuses to come to Dormay."

"Oh?"

She stood up, repositioned her bikini and began striding back to shore.

"Well, I can't be expected to bake on sandfly infested beaches, can I?"

No, indeed, thought Roxy, that would be short of torture. She followed Maya back to their towels, scooping up the nautilus along the way.

"So, you guys are only newlyweds." She placed the large reddish-white shell to her ear. "How did you meet?"

Maya dropped back onto her towel and began wiping the water off her long legs. "Boring story, really. I came out on holiday two years ago and he swept me off my feet. I came back six months later to marry him, and the rest, as they say, is history."

Maya spoke the lines as though repeating a mantra, almost mechanically, with no obvious emotion, then promptly changed the subject.

"Are you married? I don't see a ring but that doesn't always mean anything."

Roxy laughed, putting the shell aside. "No, no, I'm not married, much to my mother's disappointment."

"A boyfriend, then? Anyone special?"

Her green eyes sparkled provocatively.

"Er, no to that, too. I am currently a free agent, but then again, I am almost always a free agent."

Maya sat up and stared at her.

"Really? I wonder why?" She flickered her eyes across Roxy's body. "You're attractive enough."

"Thanks. I think."

"Sorry, I didn't mean it like that."

"I guess I'm just married to my work, that's all. Maybe one day."

Maya sighed wistfully. "Oh, to have such an exciting career... honestly I envy you so."

"I'm not sure you'd envy me if you saw the tiny apartment I work out of and the state of my bank account. Still, I enjoy it most of the time."

"And why wouldn't you!? You get to hang out at places like this, poke about in everyone else's business and get paid for it! Sounds divine."

Roxy laughed again. "Well, since you put it like that..."

"I have to say, though, I'm with Helen on this one. I can not believe Abi has hired you. She's normally so private. You know, I had an *Elle* magazine shoot all lined up for the wedding? They were going to do a pictorial piece—Wade was thrilled, Helen, too. But Abi put a stop to it. Outright refused."

"So your wedding was held here? At Dormay?"

"God yes, could hardly have it at Wade's joint and be all red and welty in my strapless Vera Wang."

"And Abi wouldn't let the cameras in?"

"Not even one."

Maya held one long leg up and studied it approvingly.

"They're banned, normally, you know? You do know that?"

She dropped the leg down and swung around to face Roxy, shifting onto her stomach as she did so.

"You can't go around randomly taking shots of people here, can't use cell phones either—not that they work here, anyway. It's all to do with Abi's precious Privacy Policy. A load of bollocks! Still, you'd think she'd make this one exception. For Wade, if not for me. She also banned the *Elle* journalist. So *embarrassing*. It's not like I'm Gisele Bundchen you know? I was lucky to get that offer, and she went and ruined it. For all of us. Although I have to say, I think Helen was angrier than I was! She didn't speak to her mother for the entire wedding. Honestly, you'd think it was her special day!"

She peeled herself off the towel and stood up.

"Come on, all this sun is starting to drag me down, or maybe it's all the chatter about my dreary wedding. I need a drink and a cigarette. Desperately. Let's head up for cocktails."

"Is it that time, already?" Roxy sat up alarmed.

"Well, not strictly, sweetie, but we can rendezvous in my room if you like. My mini-fridge is bursting with delights!"

Roxy gathered her things, carefully placing the shell into her bag.

"Would love to, Maya, but Abi and I have another session about now. I'd better get ready."

"Oh well, your loss. I'll see you at crappy hour on the main veranda then."

They made their way back to the hotel and followed each other through the lobby and up the internal stairs to the first floor. Maya headed off for her room at the front, directly parallel to Roxy's, and the writer wondered how an over-staying local managed to score such a premier suite. That one would have a startling view of the ocean in front. Perhaps Wade insisted on it, she thought, or paid generously for the privilege. (Although, hadn't Doc mentioned something about money troubles?) Roxy looked around. She had not yet worked out where everyone was sleeping, but she could tell Doc had the back room in the opposite corner to hers, as he had stuck a sign on his door that read: 'Doctors Rooms'. A dead giveaway. She also guessed that the Zimmermans, the only paying guests, would have been given one of the two best rooms in front, beside Maya, and that Helen, Josh and Abi all resided up the next flight of stairs where a small sign had been posted with the words 'Private access only'. Even though Joshua was part local, she couldn't picture him heading back to those grass huts at night.

As for Luc? Roxy shrugged, unlocked her door and slipped back in. Pricking up her ears, she could hear nothing, so she crept over to the window and peeked out. All was now quiet except for Maurice who was carrying a pitcher of water over to the table, no doubt for her next session with Abi. Roxy pulled the fresh shell from her bag and placed it on the window ledge next to the coral. She was starting quite a nice collection.

Roxy glanced at the clock. It was 10 minutes before 3pm so she jumped into the shower then changed back into her sundress and wedges, ran a quick comb through her hair and some lip balm across her sun-kissed lips, grabbed her gear and returned to the patio.

Fortunately, Abi had yet to arrive so Roxy settled into a chair and got her equipment in place. She was determined to appear professional even if she was in holiday heaven.

"Sorry, sorry!" called Abi, taking her own seat beside her. "Pour us a glass will you, Roxy. It's stinkin' hot today. You seem to be handling the heat well, for a tourist."

"Yes, I'm very impressed with myself." She filled both glasses with the cool water. "But I did just have a lovely swim at main beach, so I was cheating a little."

"Ah, main beach. My favourite place in the world. Okay, then, we'd better get started, I don't have a lot of time this arvo suddenly. More dramas." She sighed heavily. "So, where were we?"

"We were discussing your childhood in Australia. You finished by saying—"

"Oh, never mind with that now. I'd like to talk about Dormay."

"Well, sure, but I have to say it's often better, certainly easier, to go chronologically, starting with your early days. Still, if you'd prefer?"

"I'd prefer."

There was no room for negotiation so Roxy clicked 'play/record' on her small device, positioned it right under Abi's ample chin, then sat back and waited for her to begin.

Abi took a long sip of her water again and then smiled dreamily.

"I fell in love with this place from the first moment I saw it."

"When was that?"

"Exactly 40 years ago last June. I was a patrol officer's wife. Did you know that?

"No, I didn't."

"His name was Jed Lilton, he worked for the Australian Government and was based at the mainland, working to set up hospitals, schools, roads that sort of thing. Good worker, crap husband. When he wasn't beating me to a pulp he was having his way with the local housegirls or *haus* girls I think they spell it. Started playing up on me in the first month."

"Oh Abi, I'm so sorry."

"Well don't be! It was the best thing that ever happened to me. I gave him the flick and went out on my own. I'd fallen in love with the area instantly, of course, how could you not? Didn't have a lot of dosh, though, so when an opportunity came up to manage the plantation on Dormay I jumped at it."

"So Dormay was a plantation first. What kind?"

"Copra, love. Coconuts. They had a good little business going but it was too much work for the old Kiwi guy who used to run it. He was exhausted and couldn't hand it over fast enough. I had no experience, of course, but that didn't seem to matter. The local workers here helped showed me the ropes. I bought the place a few years after that. For a song if truth be told. I soon realised there was more money in tourism than coconuts, so I did the old house up and opened the doors. Never looked back."

"Are any of the original locals still around?"

"No, but their kids are. Both Popeye and Maurice were born on Dormay. Popeye was in his 20s when I first arrived, been a Godsend from the start." She smiled. "Whatever you say about me, love, they're the true locals. Dormay might be in my heart but it's in their blood. That's the important thing. This book is for them, you know? I'll be dedicating it to them, their families and those that came before."

"Joshua will be happy," Roxy said although she couldn't help wondering how Helen would feel.

"Joshua?" She looked surprised. "I suppose so."

"So, you took over from the Kiwi guy. What was his name?"

"Geoff Mailer." She spelt it for Roxy. "Nice bloke, just tired is all. He'd had enough. You know it's not easy working in these parts. Things break down and it takes a million years to get someone out from the mainland to repair it, or ship parts in from Aus. The locals, bless 'em, can be hard work, too. Lots of politics when you deal with these people. Some of them are a bit shifty—I'm having trouble with a staffer right now in case you hadn't noticed. And, yes, they can even be a bit lazy. Look, I love Popeye, he knows that, but I have to keep the whip on him or he'd be snoozing out the back half the time. Helen's always going on about it but it doesn't matter, see? It's a holiday place. No one's in any hurry."

And, as if to prove the point, she leant back and yawned.

"So was Helen born here, too?"

Roxy was keen to find out who Helen's father was but knew from past experience to let the client come to it in their own good time. Abi didn't muck around.

"No, love, I'm not as brave as the local women. I went over to the mainland for the birth and even that's brave enough. They've got a decent enough hospital there but you wouldn't want to get sick in it!"

She roared with laughter, then took a long sip of her drink.

"Helen's dad had nicked off by then, of course. It wasn't Geoff but before you ask, no I don't want him named. I didn't ask his permission to do this book, so it wouldn't be right."

It's a pity she didn't have the same consideration for her daughter thought Roxy but she just nodded away.

Abi continued. "He was a visiting yachtie, out from

Australia. I fell for him hard, it didn't last long and I should've known better than to give my heart to a sailor. They're gypsies you know. You can't tie a good sailor down. Well, not while they can still hoist a sail..." She looked wistfully towards the sea. "So, not long after he discovered I was up the duff he'd pulled anchor and taken off."

She sighed again. "I haven't had a lot of luck in love, Roxy, at least not when it comes to the male of the species. But I've always got plenty of love from the ocean, from this island, and from these people, which is why it's so important that I do the right thing now, while I still can."

"The right thing? What do you mean?"

Abi looked around for her cane, found it to her right and used it to stand back up. "We'll get to all that, Roxy, I promise. But I learnt my lesson last night. I've got a few people to set straight before I tell you anymore."

She leaned down and squeezed the younger woman's hand.

"I can see you and I are going to get along just famously. You don't push me, I like that."

Roxy wasn't sure if it was a complement or a warning, but she smiled anyway and gathered her things.

"Sorry I'm cutting us short," Abi was saying. "But as I say, I've got some stuff to see to."

"That's fine, Abi. Will we talk again tomorrow morning? Say, 9am this time?"

"Oh, earlier than that, love. I can't do the afternoon session tomorrow. Sorry, I know we need to get cracking on this but I've got important business at the mainland, a big meeting I can't miss. But I promise you, love, I'll cut the nonsense and focus on the book after that. So, how about we meet after my morning walk, about 7am? We can talk over breakfast. You're up anyway, right?"

"Right," Roxy lied as she kissed her sleep-ins goodbye.

They walked quietly back to the hotel and, once again, Abi wandered off into the kitchen, leaving Roxy to ponder what she'd meant by wanting to 'do the right thing'. Who was she writing this book for? Herself? Helen? Or the people of Dormay?

"You right?" Joshua asked, appearing by Roxy's side.

Before she could answer he handed her a note.

"A call came through for you from Sydney."

He returned to the front desk as she read the message. It was from her agent: Please call. Keen to know how it's going. Olie.

Roxy walked over to the desk where Joshua was tapping away at a computer. He looked up.

"You want to make a long-distance call?"

"Actually, I'd prefer internet connection. Can I use the computer?"

"Sure, I was just in there myself." He paused, looking sheepish. "I like to play computer games on my breaks."

Roxy laughed. "I guess all the sun, sea and sand gets a bit blasé after a while?"

He laughed too. "Yeah, well, it's what I grew up with so it's nothing special to me. I've been trying to talk Abi into getting a PlayStation or a Wii set up, you know, for the cooler, younger guests, but she won't hear of it. Says they should be out swimming and snorkelling! I'll talk her around. Anyway, computer's in the library, you know where it is. The instructions are by the monitor; your password is just your room number. It's a cinch but yell out if you need a hand."

"Thanks, Josh. I'm sure I'll be fine. By the way, I noticed my mobile doesn't get a signal here."

"Nope. I could fix that too with the right infrastructure, but... you know?"

"Abi?"

"Abi."

She laughed and made her way to the partitioned corner near the dining room that was used as the library. Stepping inside she spotted Helen at the monitor, studying something on the screen in front of her. Helen looked up with a start.

"Oh, hello Roxy," she said then turned back and quickly shut down the page. The screen went blank. "You want to use this?"

"Yes, but there's no hurry, I can come back later."

At that moment a sudden crash made both women jump. Helen leapt up and looked around the corner to find Popeye down on his knees just outside the kitchen tentatively picking up what looked like broken glass. She groaned loudly.

"Unbelievable." She turned back to Roxy. "It's all yours, looks like I've got some cleaning to do."

She scooped up a thin manila folder that was on the desk beside her and hurried out.

Roxy sat down in front of the computer and attempted to log in, however, it was soon clear that Helen had forgotten to log out properly and the internet was already up and going. Pressing the return arrow in the hope that she'd find her way back to the Google search engine, Roxy instead found herself on a page titled Regional Land Rights and Policy. It was the same page Helen had just been reviewing. Roxy glanced around to make sure she was alone, then scrolled down to take a closer look. As far as she could tell, it was an official Australian government AusAid site offering advice about settling customary land disputes in the Pacific region. She wondered why Helen would need that kind of information. Were they having trouble with land claims by the locals?

Perhaps she should ask Abi about it tomorrow, she thought, shutting down the AusAid site and logging Helen out. She was just logging herself in when Helen reappeared at the door.

"Hello again," Helen said, smiling coolly. "It's just occurred to me that I might have forgotten to log out."

"No worries, I did it for you. I'm logging in with my password now."

"Oh. Um, good." The woman paused, about to say something, then changed her mind and disappeared again.

Roxy shrugged then quickly got to work, logging back onto the internet and into her email account from there.

There were a stack of messages in her inbox but she ignored them for now, noticing, too, that none were from Max, and pretending it didn't matter. She gave herself a little shake and began to compose two messages. The first was to her agent, giving him a quick appraisal of her first days on the island:

"Hey Olie: Just getting started but Abi is already showing signs of being very open and cooperative. Hooray. This place is beautiful, several intriguing characters lurking about, too. All good entertainment! There's a story here and I'm not sure it's all about Abi. I'll be back in touch when—if!—there's something to report. Mobile doesn't work, so don't bother. xo R."

Next, she jotted a note to her mother, knowing only too well that there'd be hell to pay if she didn't. This message was more detailed. She described her trip, the hotel, and the beaches but didn't mention anything about intriguing characters. Roxy didn't need Lorraine Jones getting too curious. She signed it off with hugs and kisses and hoped that would placate her mother for a while.

Then, checking her watch, she decided to wait a few minutes to see if Olie would reply. He would still be at his desk at this hour and he might want to get in touch. She shifted over to the lounge, grabbed the first book on the coffee table and began flicking through it.

Titled *Myths & Legends* it was all about the local folklore and superstitions and had Roxy intrigued from the very first page. The author, a man named Christopher Lane, had a way with words, elaborating on every spooky detail from this once-primitive region's past. She scanned across stories of missionary-devouring cannibals, curse-afflicting witchdoctors and watery ghosts who scared native fishermen to their deaths. And she wondered if the current locals still believed in all of this mumbo jumbo.

Noticing that some time had passed, Roxy put the book back and returned to the desk. She logged onto her email account again and spotted Oliver's reply. There was one from her mother, too. She clicked on Oliver's first.

"So the cannibals haven't got you yet? Phew! All fine here in the

real world. Intriguing characters sound er, intriguing. But just stick to the main story, okay? I need you back here eventually. Glossy *mag have called wondering where you are and I may have another book in the offing. Anyway, have fun, stay out of mischief. Oh, that's right, it's your middle name. Olie."*

She laughed, replied with a quick, *"Envy is so unattractive in a man ;-) R"* and then opened her mother's email. This was just as she'd expected.

"Hello darling, lovely of you to grace us with a message at last. Don't have telephones on the island then? Charlie says hello. Be sure to take some happy snaps for us and stay out of the sun. You know how red and splotchy it makes you. I hope they're paying you well for the inconvenience. Any eligible's? love Mum."

Roxy groaned and quickly typed: *"Yes Mum, so inconvenient to be dragged to a five-star resort to work. Really, I don't know why I stand for it! And, newsflash, I've been gone less than two days!!!"*

Then, taking a deep breath, she erased the paragraph and wrote simply: *"Will keep in touch. xo Roxy."*

Roxy and her mother had long endured the kind of relationship that TV talk shows were built on. They simply never saw eye to eye. On anything. Lorraine Jones, now happily ensconced in a posh suburb of Sydney with her small-time investment banker husband Charlie, was a classic snob. She was conservative, bigoted and determined to marry her 'spinster daughter' off. Naturally enough, the spinster daughter was outraged by the very thought. She didn't need marriage and she certainly didn't need her mother's closeted views about her life and loves. Roxy had had plenty of boyfriends in her time, thank you very much. She just didn't want to marry any of them, even the adorable Max. Lorraine suspected that Roxy was still pining for her first love, her dad, who had died unexpectedly when she was young, but it wasn't that. Roxy simply liked her life just the way it was. It was going to take a very special guy to muscle his way in.

Looking around, she had to agree that right now, her life was pretty damn perfect. Here she was on a luxury island resort and being paid for it. *Man, schman,* she thought then glanced at the clock on the computer. There was still an hour before cocktails—enough time to get a decent walk in.

Roxy dumped her stuff back in her room and then headed off through the dining room, down the side patio and towards the beach on the northerly end. It was the same direction that Abi had walked that morning and, if her navigation skills were correct, it was also the way to the local village.

She wandered along the crisp sand for several minutes until she noticed a grassy opening at one end, a good 100 metres from the hotel at the other side of main beach. She walked up and spotted the track instantly. It led from the beach, through the mangrove and into thick scrub. To one side of the track, just a metre from the beach, Roxy noticed two deep holes had been dug out of the dirty sand. Some planks of wood, shovels and a cement mixer were piled together under a tarpaulin nearby and she wondered what they were constructing. Thinking nothing more of it, she began walking down the track in the direction of the village.

Roxy was looking forward to meeting those smiling children again and asking them what they thought of sea ghosts and witchdoctors. Abigail might have been on Dormay for decades, but there was another side to this place that was equally as intriguing, and she was keen to explore that, too. In fact, Roxy was so preoccupied with her mission that she barely registered the voices ahead of her. A man's gruff laugh suddenly stopped her in her tracks. She looked up. The sound was coming from around the next bend, just a few metres away. She couldn't see who it was—the thick scrub and tall grass proving an effective curtain—but this time she had no trouble determining its origins. That French accent was unmistakable.

"Ooh, *mon cher*, this is ridiculous, no? Everyone is happy here. We are all grown-ups, no?"

"No, actually, some of us are more juvenile than others,"

came a woman's voice. It wasn't Maya. "I am deadly serious, Luc. Mother knows everything."

Ahh, thought Roxy, it's Helen.

"And I mean everything. She's threatening to call Marie-Simone. Tell her what you've been doing with all your precious time. I know Marie-Simone can probably overlook one little indiscretion, but... this? It might make her think twice about sending next month's instalment."

"Argh, come on! This is ridiculous. Outrageous!"

"I'm sorry, Luc. It's over. No more. Got it? Now, if you'll excuse me I've got a doctor to see."

Realising the conversation was at an end, Roxy retreated as swiftly as she could and made her way back to the beach, wondering all the while what Helen was talking about. It sounded like she was discussing Luc's affair with Maya but she couldn't be sure. Roxy found a shady spot beneath a breadfruit tree and sat down, trying to look inconspicuous. Within minutes, Helen appeared from the scrub and looked directly at Roxy, a little startled. She didn't say anything though, just ploughed on across the sand back to the hotel. Within minutes Luc also appeared and, spotting Roxy, broke into a wide smile and cut across to her.

"*Bonjour, Mademoiselle,*" he said, dropping down beside her.

He had dark baggy shorts and a paint-splattered T-shirt on, and his black, tousled hair flopped across one eye.

"I did not expect to see you 'ere."

"Just hanging out," she said, then, wanting to change the subject, pointed one hand towards the deep holes near the track just behind them. "So what's with the bear pits? Abi hoping to catch some prey?"

He looked around, then back. "What? Oh, eet is a new construction. Um, how do you say, par-goal-ah?"

"Pergola. Oh, right."

"For Abi's walks. She likes to take the leetle rests now. Like you."

Roxy laughed.

"So, are you having a good time?"

"Yes, thank you," she replied.

"Very beautiful, no?"

"Sure is." She glanced around at the coral-littered sand and the tinkling water beyond.

"I was not talking about the island."

His voice had grown a little husky and he took hold of one of her hands, placing it to his lips and peering up at her provocatively. She burst out laughing, then flung one hand to her mouth.

"Sorry, Luc." She released his grip. "I don't mean to be rude but your charms are wasted on me I'm afraid. Although I have to say you do it exceptionally well."

He looked genuinely taken aback. "You do not find me attractive? Why is this?"

She laughed again, as intrigued by his candour as she was by his genuine surprise at being knocked back.

"No offence. You're gorgeous. You know that. But I'm here to write a book not muck about."

"Pff! What eeze it with everyone 'ere?" He raised a hand to the sky. "In France we can do work and play. Both things at once. 'Ere, we must do one or the other. It eeze boring."

"It's also professional, Luc. I'm not sure Abi would be too thrilled if she knew I was off fraternizing with the resident artist."

"Abi! Why does everyone care so much about Abi? She is an old woman. She has had her fun and now no one else can have some?"

He spat into the sand then shrugged, giving her another of his dazzling smiles.

"Ah well, it eeze your loss, *mon amie.*"

I don't doubt it for one moment, she thought as she watched him striding back to the hotel.

CHAPTER 6

The veranda was almost empty when Roxy stepped out onto it for the cocktail hour. Despite Maya's promise, she was nowhere to be seen. Luc and the Zimmermans were also absent, and Helen was a no-show as expected. Even Abi did not materialise, which left just Roxy, Doc and Joshua.

"Where is everyone tonight?" the writer asked before taking a long sip of the thick banana daiquiri Josh had just handed her.

"The Zimmermans are having a sunset picnic at the other side of the island near the strip," he replied. "We won't see them again tonight. Helen's in a meeting with Abi—"

"They've been at it for hours," whispered Doc to Roxy and she raised an eyebrow inquisitively.

"And I think Maya's having a lie-down in her room," Joshua continued. "She'll join us for dinner."

"That explains where Luc is, then," said Doc and, again, Joshua ignored the comment, clearly not interested in island gossip.

"Hey I wanna suggest a toast!" Joshua announced suddenly. "To life!"

Roxy and Doc glanced at each other surprised, then raised

their glasses and repeated: "To life!"

They each took a sip of their drinks then Doc asked, "And what's got you so excited tonight, young man?"

"I'm a proud man tonight, Doc. Proud I tell you!"

"Oh Lord, here he goes, on about his people again."

"It goes deeper than that my man. Deep!"

Helen appeared at the doorway then, a tired look on her face.

"Joshua, can I have a word?"

"Not joining us for cocktails?" Doc called out and Helen gave him a brusque smile and left again.

Joshua excused himself and followed her back into the lobby.

"Well, it's just you, me and the sunset," said Doc to Roxy. "Looks like it's going to be a really relaxing evening after all."

Dinner, an hour later, however, did not prove relaxing at all. Maya showed up first, dressed in a very short, very spangly dress that showed off more than it concealed, and was followed soon after by Luc in a crushed linen suit. As they waited for Maurice to fill their wine glasses, they snuck guilty looks at each other, grinning like idiotic school children. It occurred to Roxy that if Luc really was having an affair with Maya, he hadn't broken it off as Helen appeared to suggest just hours earlier on the village track. In fact, if anything, it looked like he'd turned things up a notch.

Helen arrived next, followed several minutes later by Joshua, but there were no happy, conspiratorial glances for them. They both looked stressed, avoiding each other's eyes, and Joshua's good spirits were now clearly deflated. Roxy wondered what Helen had said to the hotel manager to bring about this change of mood.

Abi came in last, apologising for her tardiness, then waved the wine waiter away. She was clutching her trademark G&T in one hand.

"Get Popeye to bring the entrées out straight away will you?" she told Maurice before settling into her chair. "How was everyone's day?"

Her tone was cheerful enough and, as no one responded, Roxy spoke up.

"I've had a great day, thank you, Abi. I managed to hit the beach twice, which is something of a record for me."

"I see it 'as done your colouring some good," said Luc, appraising her naked arms in her off-the-shoulder '50s silk taffeta dress. She shot a glance at Maya.

Maya held her glass out again to be refilled, smirking at Luc now. She looked like she was about to say something when a loud crash could be heard behind her. Everyone turned to see Popeye staring, wide eyed with an empty tray and several plates of what looked like peppered squid strewn across the floor.

"Oh what a surprise," Helen said.

"Now, now, accidents happen," Abi added quickly. "Just clear it away, thanks Popeye and get the main meals out. I don't think anyone will complain if we skip entrée tonight?"

She glanced around the table and they all shook their heads. Maurice appeared to help clean the broken dishes away, and within minutes the main course—a fish curry with rice—was being served, slowly and carefully by the younger waiter.

"What is it with these people?" Helen was saying between clenched teeth. "Honestly Mother, you give them far too much credit. They'll be the ruin of this place, you'll see. You'll regret it, you really will."

"That'll do, Helen," Abi said firmly, indicating Maurice who was still in the room.

Helen rolled her eyes and let it go.

A long, uncomfortable silence fell upon the group and it soon turned to Abi and Roxy to keep the conversation flowing. Eventually even Abi held up the white flag.

"You know, I just feel really ordinary suddenly," she told them, her face dripping with sweat.

Doc, who'd been in a world of his own during the meal, looked concerned and leaned over to place a hand on her brow.

"Oh leave it alone, Doc. I'm fine, just a bit bloody hot tonight."

Abi reached for her drink and took another large mouthful. "Need a good night's sleep, is all."

"Great idea!" spat Helen. "Perhaps that might clear your head a little."

"I might be old and wonky, Helen, but there is absolutely nothing wrong with my head."

There was no trace of good humour left in Abi's voice now.

Helen stood up, hands clutching the table in front of her.

"You know what? I don't really care about your head, Mother, I don't care about your hotel. I don't care about any of this! It's finally occurred to me that I am over it, I've had enough!"

Her sudden, unexpected outburst took them all by surprise and no one quite knew what to say, least of all Abi who was looking flustered and dripping with sweat. After a moment, Joshua got to his feet and reached a hand out to Helen.

"Are you okay, Hel'? Can I get you something?"

She sneered at him. "No, Beela, I think you've done enough as it is."

Pausing, she took a deep breath, dropped her arms to her side and tried for a smile. She managed one but it was as icy as her tone.

"Roxy, apologies once again. I seem to be making quite a spectacle of myself these days. Perhaps it's time I took my leave."

"Where are you going, Helen?" Abi asked, also struggling to get to her feet.

"Just to bed, Mother, don't panic. And, by the looks of it, so should you."

Helen left the dining room and Abi fell back into her seat, fanning herself with the menu card.

"Oh dear, I do feel a bit queasy."

"Hey, Abi, I can take you up to your room if you like," said Joshua but she waved him off.

"No, Joshua, dear, you finish your dinner. Please. That's enough of all of this nonsense. Helen's right. It's all been a bit of a soap opera around here lately. It's not normally this dramatic. Hopefully things will settle down soon"

Then, looking about a little confused, she added, "Why did Maurice turn out the lights?"

They all stared at her.

Doc said softly, "The lights are still on, Abigail."

"Really?" She began rubbing her eyes irritably.

Doc got to his feet. "Come on, my dear, let's get you to bed."

"I can do it—" began Joshua but Doc stopped him.

"No, I'd better make sure she's okay."

This time, Abi allowed her old mate to help her up and apologised once again to the diners, looking about the room blankly. She looked as though she had lost all focus, staring around the room but not quite connecting with anyone's eyes.

Doc looked suddenly very worried and began tugging her away.

"Okay, okay, I'm going, I'm going," she muttered, letting him lead her out.

That left Roxy with Joshua, Maya and Luc who all appeared to have quickly forgotten the outburst and were now in a world of their own. Maya giggled from time to time at some unspoken joke, Luc sniggered into his wine glass, and Joshua was so preoccupied, he barely registered a word Roxy said. Eventually, she, too, excused herself and made her way back to her room, leaving the lovebirds to ogle each other in peace, and Joshua to sit in stony silence close by.

Once inside her bedroom Roxy peeled her dress off and changed into pyjamas. She wasn't feeling at all tired though and, noting that it was still early—just past 9.30pm—she reached for her journal and began scribbling away. There was clearly something going on under the surface at Dormay, and she wanted to air her concerns before they dissipated.

Dinner had been a most intriguing affair. What was all that about? Something was clearly going on between Helen and her mother, and she wondered whether it had anything to do with the 'autobiography'. She made a note to ask Abi about it in the morning. She wondered, too, why Helen was even on Dormay. Unlike her mother, who clearly revelled in the tropics, Helen seemed very ill suited to it. Roxy could imagine her in Melbourne, Sydney, even New York city. But a hot and primitive Pacific island? She shook her head. It didn't fit.

She thought then of the other residents. Doc. Maya. Luc. They were all odd-balls in their own special way. It was not surprising that the Zimmermans had opted for a quiet picnic at the furthest point from the dining room, and its histrionics, as they could get.

"Perhaps I'll join them tomorrow night," she said aloud, only half joking.

What the ghostwriter didn't realise then was that there would be no more moonlit picnics at Dormay for any of them.

CHAPTER 7

It was a creaking floorboard that woke her first, followed soon after by the clicking of a door, and then silence. Roxy peered across to the clock radio. It was not yet 6.30am. She hadn't set the alarm for another 15 minutes but the damage was now done and she slowly struggled out of bed and into a shower for her early morning breakfast meeting with Abi.

An hour later, with her poached eggs eaten and a second cup of coffee under her belt, Roxy was growing impatient. Abi had yet to surface and at first Roxy was feeling cheated. The old girl was enjoying the sleep-in Roxy so craved. By 7.40am her annoyance had turned to concern and she began to seriously worry. She hadn't known the hotelier long but she didn't take her for a slacker. Abi hadn't looked too good at dinner the night before. Perhaps she was sick in bed. Or perhaps she'd got waylaid on her morning walk.

Mary, the only other person in the dining room, was refilling a bowl of fruit when Roxy asked her if she had seen Abi about. The young woman shook her head, no. Her brow wrinkled a little.

"She take very long walk today," she said in her soft, sing-song way.

"Oh, so she's already been up and out walking today?" Roxy asked.

The local woman shrugged and Roxy was not sure what that meant, but decided to check the foyer.

At the front desk Joshua was sorting through some newspapers and looked up as she approached.

"Mornin', Roxy," he said. "Want a newspaper?"

"No, I was just wondering if you'd heard from Abi this morning."

"Abi? No. Why?"

"Well, it's probably nothing but she was meant to meet me for a breakfast interview this morning at 7 and hasn't shown yet. Can you call her room and see if she's still there?"

He grabbed the phone and placed the call. After some time, he dropped it back on the receiver.

"She's not there. Well, I mean, she didn't pick up. She could be asleep of course."

"Does she usually sleep through phone calls?"

He shook his head, suddenly looking worried.

"I'll go up and see if she's okay."

"Thanks, Josh. I might head for the beach, see if she's still on her walk."

He looked at her, surprised, then nodded his head. "Good idea. You do that. I'll see you back here, eh?"

They both went off in different directions, Roxy making her way back through the restaurant to the side steps. She dumped her recording gear there and continued down past the patio to the beach. It was an overcast morning, very different from the day before, but the humidity was stifling and she sweated a little as she trudged along the sand. Looking both ways, she could see nobody in sight, so made her way towards the village track.

Perhaps Abi had fallen over on her morning stroll, or, better yet, got caught up chatting to the locals.

Roxy was just metres from the grassy track when something caught her eye. She stopped and squinted, not quite sure what it was she was staring at. It looked vaguely like a hairy old coconut someone had perched upright in the sand. She continued to walk, then stopped and squinted again.

It couldn't be.

She stepped forward, more slowly this time, a sudden chill rushing down her body.

Oh my god, it looks like...

She wouldn't let the thought form, she shrugged it off impatiently.

Don't be ridiculous, Roxy, you're seeing things.

Yet suddenly her legs felt like logs, her blood turned cold. She wanted to stop, to turn back and run. But she knew she had no choice. She knew she had to keep walking. To find out for sure.

Within seconds Roxy was close enough to know exactly what it was that had caught her eye on the edge of the sand. The husky coconut was not a coconut at all. It was a woman's head, drained of all colour, the grey hair sticking out in every direction. The eyes were clamped shut but the mouth had drooped open in what looked like a silent scream, the same scream that was now coming from Roxy's mouth.

She was running before she even knew it, her feet tripping over the sand as she fled that horrific sight. Everything around her was whirling, sound had ceased to exist, the ocean was nowhere to be seen.

Suddenly someone grabbed her by one arm and she lashed out, trying to escape.

"Whoa! Easy, easy! Roxy, it's Joshua! Are you okay?"

Roxy stopped, stared at his worried features and gasped as the ocean roared back into her ears.

"Oh, Jesus, Josh. It's...it's..."

She couldn't bring herself to say the hotelier's name, but pointed back in the direction of the track. He pushed her down to the sand.

"Stay here," he barked, then dashed up towards the grass.

Within seconds a loud, agonising moan could be heard.

Roxy dropped her head in her hands. It seemed like ages before he returned, his face ashen, his hands shaking.

"I've got to call... we need to get..."

He stumbled off again, back towards the hotel while Roxy remained perfectly still, sitting on that warm sandy spot, chilled to the bone. She couldn't move but it wasn't just the shock of it all. She didn't want to leave Abi alone. It seemed wrong, somehow, to walk away. So she stayed exactly where she was for the five minutes it took Joshua to return to the lobby and alert everyone.

Popeye came first, moving surprisingly swiftly for his age. He looked frantically at Roxy who pointed up towards the path. He dashed on. Next came Doc, being helped along by Maurice. When Doc reached her he gasped for breath.

"Please...tell me... No one has touched... anything."

She looked at him. "I never touched anything. But Joshua and Popeye..."

She let their names hang in the air. Doc swore under his breath and made his way towards the scene.

"Stay with Roxy," he told Maurice. "And stop anyone else from coming this way. Especially Helen!"

Maurice nodded and stood behind Roxy, as though on guard. His expression, like Popeye's before him, was distraught but he didn't say a thing. Just let the tears roll down his face, silently. Doc reappeared just a few minutes later with Popeye by his side.

"My poor, poor Abigail," Doc said softly, his voice almost lost in the ocean wind. "When did you find her?"

Roxy shook herself a little, tried to focus.

"Um, I guess about 10 minutes ago." She swallowed. "Where... where is her... body?"

She hated herself for asking but she needed to know. He shook his head, not answering and Popeye and Maurice exchanged a look that she could not comprehend.

"What is it?" she asked them but they both shook their heads, too. Whatever it was they weren't telling.

Suddenly, a hoarse cry could be heard from near the hotel

and they looked around to find Helen beating against Joshua who was trying to block her path. Doc sighed.

"I'd better see to this. Popeye, please stand guard over our dear Abigail. Do not let anyone near her. Do not touch a thing. We will have to get the police here. Roxy, come, you need a drink. We all do."

"But I don't want to leave her like that."

"It's too late for Abi now, my dear. There's absolutely nothing more we can do. Besides, she must remain as you found her until the police arrive. Whenever the hell that will be."

He held his hand out to her and she let him lead her back, towards the small crowd that was now gathering at the base of the patio, on the sand just below the hotel.

"I have to see her!" Helen was crying, her eyes wild with despair.

She still had her bed clothes on—a pink kimono-style dressing gown over silk pyjamas—and was clawing at Joshua who would not let go.

"Not now, Helen," Doc said sternly. "You can see her later. I promise you that." He placed one hand on her shoulder and she deflated then, dropping to her knees and sobbing into her hands. Behind her, Maya was crying, too, and Luc had her in a hug, his jaw clenching and unclenching, while Mary stood behind them all, looking terrified. The Zimmermans were still absent—no doubt off diving again—and Roxy was grateful for that. Abi would not want them around.

"Please, everyone, let's go back into the hotel," said Doc. "Maurice, see if you can find the Zimmermans and get them back here. Via the other side of the island if you can manage it. We don't need them running into her, too. Mary, fetch us some coffees, there's a good girl."

They returned to the dining room and took their seats, randomly around the veranda while Doc turned to Joshua.

"We need to call the mainland police. Do you have the number?"

Joshua nodded his head vigorously. "You can speak to my uncle, man, he's the Chief of Police. He's the best! He'll come."

He lead Doc away to the lobby while Roxy, spotting a box of tissues at the waiter's station, grabbed it and offered it to Helen and Maya. Meanwhile, Mary began pouring cups of coffee and tea, and brought over baskets of pastries that went untouched.

After several minutes of stunned silence, Joshua and Doc returned.

"The police chief is on his way," Doc announced. "He will be here within the hour. In the meantime, he has asked that we all remain calm and stay exactly where we are."

He took a seat beside Helen and patted her softly on the back. By this time, she had grown eerily despondent and simply sat looking out to sea, not saying anything.

Maya had no such qualms.

"I... I can't believe it!" she burst out. "Oh it's all so terribly tragic. Poor, poor Abi. How could this possibly have happened?"

She turned to Roxy who looked back blankly.

"I don't know, honestly I don't. She was late for our breakfast meeting so... so I went to find her. I never expected..."

"Of course you did not," said Luc. "It eeze a shock for us all, oui?"

They all nodded their heads and Maya burst into tears again.

"Oh God," said Helen so softly Roxy almost missed it. "I was so awful to her last night. I was angry... I lashed out."

"Don't punish yourself," Doc said. "I don't think anyone was themselves last night."

He pushed a cup of tea towards her and she ignored it. Then he produced a flask and offered her that. She waved him off so he held it out to Roxy.

"No, thanks Doc, I need a clear head," she said.

"I will 'ave some," said Luc, taking the flask and pouring a hefty dose of what looked like whisky into his coffee. He didn't have to offer it to Maya, she had already grabbed it from him and was doing the same. She also lit up a cigarette and dragged on it long and hard.

"Oh, shit!" Maya jumped up, stubbing her cigarette into her saucer. "I have to call Wade. He must know about this."

"You can do that later," Doc said but she ignored him and rushed off towards the lobby. Helen looked around then, as if seeing them all for the first time and strained her lips into a smile. She stood up and wrapped her arms around herself.

"I'm so sorry, I'm still in my pyjamas. I need to get dressed."

"There's no hurry—" Doc began but she cut him off.

"It won't take a moment."

Roxy said, "Can I help you, Helen?"

Helen turned to look blankly at Roxy for what seemed like minutes then smiled again.

"Yes, that would be perfect, thank you."

As Roxy collected the bag she had dumped by the side steps earlier, Doc came over to have a quiet word.

"She doesn't know," he whispered.

"Sorry?" Roxy whispered back.

"Helen knows her mother is dead, obviously, but Joshua didn't explain the details. She doesn't know about the head, about the way she... is. Please, do not utter a word about that. I'm just not sure she could cope. At this point."

"Of course not," Roxy said before running out to catch up with Helen who was half way to her room on the top floor, directly above Roxy's.

No sooner had they closed the door then Helen dashed for her bathroom and threw up in the toilet bowl. Roxy rushed to her side but she waved her off and began dabbing at her mouth with a towel.

"Should I fetch Doc?" Roxy asked.

"Don't fuss, please Roxy. I'm fine. It's just the shock of it all."

She flushed the toilet and splashed some water on her face.

"But Doc can—"

"No, no Doc." Her voice was clear, her gaze penetrating.

"Fine. But why don't you have a quick shower. You'll feel better."

Again Helen shook her head. "No, I need to get back to the guests. They'll be needing me."

"Everyone will survive for the moment, Helen. The Zimmermans are off diving and the rest of us can cope. Please, just look after yourself now."

Helen stared at Roxy with a look of incredulity and said, "But I have a hotel to run."

Then she stepped across to her wardrobe and selected an outfit. Roxy turned her back as Helen changed into a black pencil skirt and white blouse. She then applied a little foundation and lipstick, combed her hair down and slipped her feet into flat black pumps.

"That's better."

She sat on the bed and motioned for Roxy to join her.

"Now, tell me how you found her."

"I'm sorry?"

"I need to know, Roxy. How you found my mother. It couldn't have been suicide. Could it?"

Her eyes were frantic and imploring, and Roxy shook her head.

"Look, Helen, I'm no pathologist but it didn't look like suicide to me. I don't really want to say anymore than that. I—"

"Never mind," she stood up and swung her bedroom door open. "I'll find out soon enough."

Roxy followed her down one flight of stairs then took the opportunity to return to her own room, to dump her recording gear and straighten herself up. She stared at her reflection in the bathroom mirror.

Suddenly, without warning, her whole body began to shake and she dropped down onto the closed toilet seat and put her head in her hands. Finding Abigail like that had been such a tremendous shock, more than Roxy realised, and now she could not stop shaking. She also could not stem the tears that were flowing furiously down her face.

She had not known the hotelier very long, had not even had a chance to forge any real bond with her, but she had liked Abigail Lilton nonetheless. She seemed genuine. She seemed like a good person. She didn't deserve that.

Roxy breathed deeply, in, out, in, out, until the shaking slowly subsided. She grabbed a tissue and blew her nose, then pulled herself back up and stared at her reflection again. It was a sorry sight. She washed her face and applied some soft pink lipgloss hoping to add some colour to her drained features. She practised her smile but it only came out looking startled. She gave it up and returned downstairs. She guessed there wouldn't be too much smiling required today.

By the time Roxy reached the dining room, the police had arrived from the mainland, and Joshua had taken off to the small jetty to help them tie up. Doc was urging everyone to sit tight.

"They will be inspecting the body first, so please let's just wait here until they finish."

"The body? That's my mother you're talking about," Helen said, very calmly, very coolly. "And, I'm sorry, Doc, but who put you in charge all of a sudden?"

"Actually, excuse me, peoples, but I am now in charge," came a deep voice from the restaurant doorway and they all swung round to find a smartly dressed local man standing there, Joshua on one side, a uniformed police officer on the other.

"I am Chief Inspector David Davara. From mainland police."

He was short and stocky with a chiselled afro, crisply ironed, short-sleeved shirt and chinos.

"You are Helen Lilton?"

"Yes, I am," she replied.

"My sympathies for your loss. I knew your mother, Mrs Lilton, for many years. She was a good woman—very good to my family and to all the people around here. I had much respect for her."

"Thank you," Helen said.

"And, Doctor Spinks, I see you are still at Dormay?"

Doc stood up and shook the elderly policeman's hand.

"They can't get rid of me this easily! Good to see you again old chap."

"How long has it been?"

"Must be at least a year," he replied. "I believe we were both trapped at Wade's godawful hospital fundraiser. Boring affair."

Davara nodded his head. "Yes, yes. I remember. But, sometimes boring is good, hey?"

Doc nodded. "Sometimes indeed. It's a terrible business this."

"Yes. Yes. But we will get to the bottom of it."

He turned to address them all now. He had a quiet, assured manner and spoke each word as clearly and crisply as he could, as though addressing small children or, ironically, non-English speaking simpletons.

"Doctor Spinks is quite right. I will go and inspect the site now and be back soon to take your statements. Until then, *plis* (please) remain here with Inspector Sikani."

"Er, this way is faster, actually, Uncle Dave," Joshua said, stepping into the room to direct the Chief to the side steps that lead down to the patio.

Davara followed him out while his officer remained standing at the dining room entrance.

"Please come in, Inspector Sikani," Helen said wearily. "Have some tea, or something."

He held one hand up to indicate that he was fine.

Very soon another voice could be heard booming from the lobby and Helen groaned.

"Here we go," she said.

Maya sprung up and ran out, returning soon after

wrapped in Wade's arms.

"What the hell happened?" he demanded, first of Helen and, when she simply looked away, Doc.

"We're still trying to work that out, old chap."

"Still trying to work it out?! What's to work out?!"

"Don't get yourself in a bother," he said. "It won't do your heart any good."

"You worry about your own goddamn heart, Doc, I want to know what happened to Abi! I get this hysterical phone call from my wife telling me Abi's dead and then the blasted local cops try to stop me from landing. It's a travesty!"

He had worked himself into quite a state, his face red, his shirt pooled with sweat. Maya dropped back into her seat and Doc took Wade by one arm.

"Let's discuss this outside," he suggested but Wade pushed him away.

Roxy spoke up then.

"I found Abi near the workers' track this morning. It was no use. She was... gone," she said it as softly as she could. "The police are only just checking the scene now but I'm sure they'll have some answers soon."

Wade scoffed.

"You clearly don't know the first thing about our local police force then."

"In the meantime," Roxy continued, "we've been asked to stay calm and stay put."

This seemed to appease Wade who loosened his collar a little and pulled a chair out to sit down.

"Mary! Get us a scotch will you!" he called out and Maya glanced at her small gold watch.

"Wade, it's not even 9."

"I don't give a damn what time it is! Besides, if that's not the pot calling the kettle black I don't know what is."

He took a deep breath, then added less harshly, "Abi was a friend of mine, I'll drink to her if I like."

Maya sobbed again into her tissues while the rest of the group settled back into their seats and waited.

"I guess this means the end of your book, Roxy?" Maya said eventually, reaching for a spoon to check what damage all this crying had done in its reflection.

"Don't be ridiculous woman," Wade said. "Now we have to get the book out. To honour Abi's life."

They looked at Helen who had her back to them all again.

Doc helped himself to another coffee and said, "We will see."

This brought Helen back to life. She swung around to the doctor, delivering him an icy stare.

"We will see?" she repeated. Her tone was calm, much like it was before, but this time there was an icier edge and even Roxy braced herself for the onslaught.

"I'm sorry, Doc, but who are you to decide anything when it comes to my mother? You weren't married to her. You weren't even a very good friend to her. You ignored her for 25 years, then, when it suited you, turned up out of the blue and sponged off her for the next ten."

"I was a welcome guest here!" Doc croaked, his lower lip wobbling. "Your mother and I had a very special relationship and I will not have you speaking to me in that manner."

"He's right. Take it easy, Helen," Wade cut in. "You're distraught, we understand that but there's no need—"

"As for *you*, Governor Thomas," Helen continued, standing now and pointing a finger towards him. "You've been trying to steal Dormay from under my mother's nose for decades. You must be delighted by all of this."

"Oh Helen!" Maya looked aghast. "That's a scandalous thing to say! Take it back instantly!"

Helen swung now to her, forcing the younger woman to shrink a little behind her husband.

"Maya Thomas. Another bored, rich whitey using and abusing my mother's good will. Tell me... In fact, tell us all: How often have you paid for a room here? How big is your bar bill now?"

"I don't see how that's got anything to do with—"

Helen raised a hand to stop her. "She was my mother—

my mother. She was a good woman, she didn't deserve this."

She waved her outstretched hand around the room and then out, toward that deserted beach where Abigail had been found. Her voice cracked, her chin quivered.

"She didn't deserve... any of this..."

Everyone was silent, stunned, staring up at Helen waiting for the next onslaught. But the hotelier's daughter was spent. Her eyes had glazed over and her legs were now shaking. Doc stood up and helped her silently back to her seat. He ushered Mary over and asked for some chamomile tea.

Just then, Joshua returned to the veranda. He looked at Helen and then, worriedly at Doc who shook his head.

"What news have you got for us, Josh?" he asked.

"Err, I just wanted to let everyone know that my uncle, I mean Chief Davara, is on his way back. He'll talk to us in a minute."

"Thank you," Doc said and the younger man sat down, his eyes now firmly on Helen. He, too, looked extremely worried.

The Chief was soon back in the room having a quiet word with his second in command. Eventually he turned to the group, produced a small notepad and cleared his throat.

"Inspector Sikani will take each of your names and details, and then I will meet with you one by one on the main veranda, is it?"

He looked at Joshua who nodded.

"Good. Good."

"Just a second, Davara," said Wade, getting to his feet and Davara looked at him, surprised.

"Ahh, good morning, Governor Thomas, I see you have joined us. When did you get to the island?"

"What? Oh, um, not long after you. My wife called me. Very distressed. I have every right to be here."

"Of course. Of course."

"I hope you have alerted the Provincial Commander? He should be overseeing all of this."

"Commander Curraway has been informed of this incident and has put me in charge."

Wade didn't look too thrilled with this arrangement but let it pass.

"Look, I know you've got a job to do but I think you owe this mob a bit of an explanation. We're all bloody confused about exactly what's happened to Abi."

The Chief nodded. "Yes. Yes. It is very confusing."

He paused, then, addressing the congregation, said, "Our pathologist is on his way over to Dormay now and will tell us more when he can. But I can say that Mrs Lilton is indeed deceased and has been this way for some hours."

"No shit, Sherlock!" said Wade. "But what the hell happened?"

"We are still determining that," said the Chief clearly not flummoxed by the Governor's rudeness. He'd no doubt seen it all before. "There are certainly suspicious circumstances."

"Not a suicide then?"

This caught the Chief by surprise and his bushy eyebrows rose a little.

"No, Mr Thomas, this is not a suicide. This is why I need to speak with each of you. This is also why I must ask for nobody to leave the island, plis."

"What?!" said Wade.

The chief raised a hand to calm him.

"Except you, Mr Thomas, you have only just arrived, yes?"

"Yes I already told you that, dammit."

"Then you are free to come and go. But the rest of you, plis, I need your passports. You can give them to Inspector Sikani. And you must remain here until the investigation is complete."

Now it was Luc's turn to look outraged.

"But you are not saying eet eeze one of us, surely?"

"And who are you plis?" the Chief asked.

"I am Luc Bermont, resident artiste."

"Mr Bermont, I do not know who did this thing to Mrs

Lilton. I have only just arrived. So you must give me some time, yes? I must question everybody and get all the facts in one straight line. You understand?"

Luc looked like he didn't understand at all but let the matter drop.

"So we're prisoners at Dormay?" said Maya, sounding suddenly chipper.

"I am sorry but yes, Mrs Thomas. This is right. Of course," he indicated the beach and the ocean beyond, "it is not such a bad prison I think. Now, to business. I would like to start with the person who found the bod—" he stopped, correcting himself, "who found Mrs Lilton, plis."

Roxy stepped forward and he referred to his notebook.

"Roxanne Parker?" She nodded. "Come with me."

As he lead Roxy out and back towards the lobby she could hear Wade grunting, "Well that's a lot of bloody help!"

CHAPTER 8

A table had been set up on the main veranda with a pot of lemongrass tea, and Chief Davara pointed Roxy into a seat, then took one in front of her. He placed his notepad on the table and offered her a drink. She shook her head no. A third police officer appeared and silently took his post beside the door. Chief Davara clasped his hands together on the desk in front of them.

"Now, Miss Parker. Tell me first, plis, where are you from?"

"I'm from Sydney. I'm a writer."

She explained the purpose of her visit and how long she had been at Dormay. "This is only my third day," she said, thinking, but it feels like I've been here weeks.

"So you are here to write Mrs Lilton's biography?"

"Autobiography, actually. I'm what you call a ghostwriter. Well, I was here to do that. I don't know what happens now."

"Yes. Yes. And you have done interviews with Mrs Lilton?"

"Only a couple. We were due to talk again this morning when I... found her."

"Hmmm."

He mulled over this for a bit then jotted something down in his notepad.

"Okey dokey. Now, plis, tell me exactly when and how you found the deceased."

Roxy took a deep breath and launched in, explaining about the missed early morning appointment, about discussing her concerns with Joshua and then taking off to search the path.

"What time exactly did you find the deceased?"

"I guess it was about 7.50am. I left the dining room before a quarter to, had a quick word to Joshua and then headed for the beach."

"How did you know to go that way? To that part of the beach? This is a big island, no?"

Roxy shrugged. "I guess it's because Abi had come from that direction yesterday morning so I assumed that's the way she walked. To be honest I didn't really give it a lot of thought."

"So she walked this exact route every morning?"

"I really don't know. Helen would be better placed to answer that."

"Who else knew about this daily walk?"

Roxy shrugged again. "I assume everyone did. I don't think Abi kept it a secret. She told me she'd been walking the island every single morning for 40 years so..."

He nodded his head. "Good. Good. Okay, then what happened?"

Roxy continued with her story, explaining how she noticed no one on the beach at that hour but did spot what she thought was a stray coconut.

"I was so shocked to find it was Abi. I just can't register it."

"That is normal, Miss Parker. It will take you some time."

His voice was so soft, his eyes so empathetic that she found it hard to imagine him grilling a real murder suspect. Perhaps that was his modus operandi?

"So then what did you do?"

"When I spotted the head...when I saw Abi?"

"Yes."

"I didn't hang around if that's what you mean. I didn't touch anything, I just raced back to the beach and ran into Joshua."

"Joshua was there?" He scanned his notes. "I thought he was at the hotel."

"Yes, well, I guess he couldn't find Abi in her room so he came to help me search. Of course now that I think about it, it made more sense to check her room because she'd been a bit sick last night."

"Oh? What was wrong with her?"

"I don't know but she looked awful. Really pale and wobbly. She left dinner early. With Doc. He could tell you more. I'm surprised now that she hadn't cancelled our morning meeting. Or her early walk for that matter."

"It is a pity that she did not. Plis continue."

Roxy explained how she sat there for a few minutes before Popeye arrived followed soon after by Maurice and Doc, and of the small gathering by the hotel.

"Who else saw the body?"

"Just me, Josh, Doc and Popeye. But," she paused and he raised an eyebrow. "Well, I didn't really see a body per se. Just Abi's head, poking out of the sand. I don't mean to pry or anything but I'm having horrible flashbacks. Please tell me she hadn't been decapitated."

"No, no, I can assure you her whole body is there. The deceased has been buried, up to her neck."

Roxy sat back, shocked. "That's very strange, isn't it?"

"Perhaps, perhaps not. Can I ask, did you hear any boats about this morning?" She shook her head no.

"And you say you saw nobody else?"

"No, well, apart from Mary in the dining room and Joshua at the front desk. However..." she paused and both his eyebrows shot skyward this time. "It may be nothing but I did hear someone up and about very early this morning."

"At what time?"

"About 6.25ish."

Roxy recounted the story of the creaking floorboard and the shutting door that had woken her up that morning.

"Who do you think this was? Which room?"

She thought about it. "I couldn't say for sure, but certainly someone on my floor. I suppose it could have been Doc, or Maya, or—most likely now I think about it—the Zimmermans heading off on their early dive. It's probably nothing important."

The Chief didn't act like it was nothing important and took more notes. Eventually he said, "So, back to your book, plis. Did Mrs Lilton say anything in your interviews that made you suspicious? That indicated that her life was in danger, perhaps?"

Roxy slowly shook her head. "Not that I recall. But I have to say, without wanting to get anyone in trouble..."

"Yes?"

"Well there's been quite a bit of tension around here in just the few days I've been at Dormay."

"What kind of tension?"

"Oh I'm sure it's nothing, but, well, Helen wasn't exactly happy about the book I was writing, although I thought she was coming around. Then, last night, everything sort of blew up."

She tried to give as accurate a portrayal of the previous evening's antics as she could while Chief Davara scribbled away.

"Okey dokey," he said eventually. "Thank you, Miss Parker. That will do for now. When are you due to fly out?"

"I don't have a set booking if that's what you mean. We didn't know how long the interviews would take."

He nodded his head. "Good. Good. Plis, you must stay at Dormay for now. You understand?"

He turned to the other police officer and said something in his native tongue before turning back to Roxy.

"Officer Tokarara will take you back to the dining room.

97

You can go to your room if you like but plis don't go too far. I may have more questions."

"Of course," she said, following the young officer out.

Back in the dining room, Helen's name was called and she stood up stiffly and accompanied the policeman out. Roxy sat back in her chair and ordered another coffee.

"Extra strong, thanks Mary," she said.

Looking around the room she noticed that both Luc and Joshua had taken off.

"They've gone to hunt down the Zimmermans," Doc told her. "Maurice couldn't find them and, well, it's about time they were informed. Terrible business."

Maya finished her cigarette, stood up and stretched like a cat.

"I've had enough of all this waiting around, brooding. Tell that Chief guy I'll be down at the beach if he wants me."

"You're going swimming?" Wade asked, looking astounded.

"And why not?" she held out her arms, surveying her tan. "It certainly beats sitting around here getting all morose. Besides, I really can not take any more of Helen right now. The woman is out of control. I know her mother just died, but honestly!"

She walked out of the room and Wade took this as his cue, pulling his chair closer to Roxy.

"So, come on woman, what did Davara have to say?"

Roxy took a quick sip of her coffee, winced and then applied some sugar. "I did most of the talking. He just wanted to know when and how I found her."

"He's not alone! Look, now that Helen's not here, fill me in. Is it true the old girl's been beheaded?"

Doc interjected, outraged. "Absolutely not! Abigail's head is very much attached to her torso, I can assure you. I inspected the body myself and it appears she's been buried up to her neck."

"That's right," agreed Roxy. "The Chief confirmed it to

me just now."

Wade looked dumbfounded. "What kind of monster buries a woman leaving her head out for all to see? It's unheard of!"

"Indeed," said Doc. "All I can say is, thank goodness you found her Roxy, my dear. You seem a sensible kind of girl. Imagine if Maya had stumbled upon her or, heaven forbid, Helen."

Wade nodded his head vigorously. "But why bury her that way? With the head out for Christ's sake. Not exactly smart. It doesn't take Sherlock Holmes to know she'd be found fairly quickly."

Then, as if it had only just occurred to him, he added, "That's the way to the village isn't it?"

Both Doc and Roxy nodded.

"So maybe one of the villagers did this? A disgruntled worker, perhaps? That makes a bit of sense now. They can be vicious these people, bloody vicious."

Roxy glanced around to make sure Mary had not heard him. Fortunately, after providing Roxy with her coffee, she too had taken her leave.

"Look, the Chief wasn't giving too much away but I think I've worked out how the body got buried," she said.

They both stared at her, wide eyed.

"I don't know if you've walked that route lately but there were two pits dug into the ground for a new building, a pergola Luc tells me. I noticed them yesterday."

Doc leant back in his chair, clasping his hands together. "There was, too. Oh this makes more sense now." He tapped his fingers together.

"So you're saying the bastard, whoever it was, bumped her over the head and she fell into one of the holes by chance?"

"I don't know for sure, Wade, but whatever happened the killer must have gone to the trouble of filling the hole in, covering her body up. Because I certainly couldn't see any sign of it."

"Yet the head remained visible for all to see," Doc said. "Very interesting."

"Bumped her over the head you reckon?" said Wade to Doc and he nodded.

"Yes, as far as I can tell. She had some bruising near the right temporal lobe."

He indicated the side of his head.

"Did that kill her?"

"Probably, there was a bit of blood so she was most certainly alive when she was hit. Look, she was getting on, our Abi, and not in the best of health. It wouldn't have taken much brute strength to do her in."

"Hang on a minute," said Wade. "You're saying it could have been a woman then? Who cracked her over the head?"

Doc looked horrified. "I'm not saying anything of the sort! But, well, you recall, Roxy, she wasn't well at all last night. I gave her two paracetamol and told her to go straight to bed."

"So how did she end up out on the path?" asked Roxy. "And, just as importantly, how long had she been there?"

"Not too long from the looks of it, although I'm no expert. She wasn't yet stone cold, so an hour or two, I'd guess, at the most. But we'll learn soon enough when the pathologist arrives. I can tell you this, though, he'd better be up to scratch because he's got his job cut out for him."

Officer Tokarara appeared then and asked Doc to accompany him to see the Chief. The old man winked at Roxy and did as instructed. Roxy got to her feet, too.

"That's enough caffeine for me. I'm strung out enough as it is."

"Don't tell me you're heading to the beach, too?" asked Wade.

"No, not really in the mood. I think I'll just hit my room for a bit."

As she walked back up the stairs, a few things began niggling at Roxy. If Doc was right and Abi had only recently been killed, that means it probably happened on her morning walk. But why would Abi go for a walk if she was feeling so unwell? Perhaps she'd recovered by daybreak? Or perhaps she simply didn't want to break the habit of a lifetime.

"It's a pity," Roxy said to herself as she grabbed the book she'd been reading on her flight and lay down on the bed to finish it off, "because it was the last walk she ever took."

CHAPTER 9

The faint tap at Roxy's door surprised her and she opened it to find Helen standing on the other side, the hint of a smile on her lips.

"So sorry to disturb you, Roxy," she said. "May I come in?"

"Of course, Helen."

She closed the door behind them and Helen walked straight across to the window and looked out. Roxy returned to the bed and waited.

Eventually, Helen cleared her throat, took a seat at the small cane table and said, "I need your help."

"Of course, Helen. Anything you need, just ask."

"I need you to help me find my mother's killer."

Roxy's jaw dropped. "I'm sorry?"

"I've just had a conversation with that Davara fellow and quite frankly, I have no faith in him. Already he's talking about some random maniac coming onto the island and doing my mother in. It's ridiculous."

"Why would he think that?"

"Because, apparently, one of the village children says she heard a boat of some kind very early this morning, while it was still dark. Sounded like it was heading south, towards the airstrip."

"Then surely it's a possibility?"

"I don't see why. That's the other side of the island. Besides, people don't sail around to islands and start bumping old ladies off. It's absurd. It was probably an early morning fisherman or a tourist or something."

"Could it have been the Zimmermans, going diving?"

"Perhaps, although that's early, even for them."

"Okay then, but that means you think someone on the island—one of us— had to have done it?"

Helen nodded her head slowly, sadly. "Yes I do. And I intend to find out whom. With your help, of course."

Roxy stood up and walked over to where Helen was sitting. She sat down in the chair opposite her.

"And what makes you think it wasn't me?"

Helen laughed a small, wry laugh and shook her head. "Oh don't think it didn't cross my mind. You're the newcomer around here. But it doesn't make any sense either. Of everyone on this island you had the most to lose by my mother's death. You were set to score a tidy financial reward for her book; now she's gone, so is your paycheque. If you were going to bump her off, for whatever reason, I'd say it would be smarter to do so right at the end."

"That's very true. But I would have thought you had more to lose than me, surely?"

Helen flashed Roxy an impatient glance. "Well, of course, that goes without saying."

"Helen it's an interesting request, but I'm no investigator. I'm out of my league here. Surely you can take your fears to Davara?"

"I already did and he had nothing to say. Please, Roxy, I know you've done this kind of thing before."

Roxy raised an eyebrow and she shrugged.

"So, I looked you up on the internet yesterday. I... I was so upset with mother for not telling me about the book and I was worried. I wanted to make sure you were up for the task.

I just needed to check out your credentials."

"And were you satisfied?" Roxy was not at all offended. She would have done the same thing.

"Yes, as it happens. You have a pretty impressive resume of books and articles. But that's not the point. While I was searching I also noticed your name pop up in relation to several murder investigations. It seems you come in handy when there's murder about."

Roxy grimaced. "I can't seem to avoid it. I must have done something very nasty in a past life."

"Or perhaps not. You're still here, aren't you?" Helen paused. "Look, I'm happy to pay you a hefty retainer to stay and help me sort this all out. It's just that I can't trust anyone here anymore; no one, not even the staff."

'She wrapped her arms tightly around herself.

"You really think the staff had anything to do with this? And what about the Zimmermans? Surely they're not involved?"

"How do I know that? They're such a tediously odd couple. I have no idea what those two are up to most of the time, we've barely seen them the entire trip. No, sorry, as far as I'm concerned, they're just as guilty until proven innocent."

"Okay, fair enough. But I still don't think you can dismiss the random maniac idea. Yes, it sounds absurd, but stranger things have happened."

"It had to be someone from Dormay, Roxy, it had to be."

"Why? I just don't understand why you're so adamant."

Helen stood up and returned to the window. This time she picked up the nautilus shell and stared at it for some time. Eventually she placed it to her ear and listened.

"Hear anything profound?" Roxy asked and Helen shook her head.

"No, I never do. Joshua says I don't know how to listen, how to stop and really focus."

She placed the shell down and turned back to Roxy. "Well, I'm stopping now, I'm focusing, and I can tell you, there is something very suspicious about the way my mother died, the way she was buried."

"So you know?"

"Yes, I know. There was only so long they could keep that gruesome detail from me. But the way she was buried, don't you see, only a local could have known..."

She stopped, faltered.

"Known what?"

She took a deep breath, brushed her crinkly bob from her face. "The way my mother was buried in the sand like that, it's a local island tradition. Didn't Joshua or Davara explain that to you?"

"Explain what? Sorry, I'm a bit confused."

Helen sat down again and took a deep breath.

"According to traditional folklore, when a villager died in this area, the survivors placed the body vertically in the soft sand near the sea and left the head out for the crabs..."

She paused, swallowed, looking as pale as a ghost suddenly. "Once the skull was... cleaned, it was then removed and taken to a special burial site on the hillside. It was a Dormay ritual. And one that belonged to only a handful of islands in the region."

Roxy shuddered. "It sounds grotesque. So are you saying you really do believe a local did this?"

"Not necessarily. This... er, death ritual, it was written about in several books on the region including one down in the library."

"Ah, I think I know the one. Myths & Legends?"

"That's right. Anyone could have read about it in there or been told by a staff member. But it's not only the way my poor mother was buried, Roxy. It's the fact that someone knew that she would be walking that way at that exact hour. They knew that there was a mighty great hole already in the ground to throw her into. It's all too fortuitous for them. No, I'm sorry, but someone had to have planned this, to a T, and I need to find out who."

She brushed her hair back from her face, more irritably

this time.

"Look, my mother and I didn't have the best relationship in the world, everyone here knows that. But I stand by what I said in the dining room this morning. Oh I know I shouldn't have said it the way I said it, but the fact is there are several people on this island who have had a very good run thanks to my mother's generosity and heart. For her to die, like this, it's beyond cruel. It's wicked. And it's incredibly cynical. It's a travesty to her memory. I need to solve this, Roxy, I need to make sure it's done right, that whoever did this to my mother doesn't walk away, scot-free. And I'm terrified that with Davara in charge, they just might."

Roxy studied Helen's face and could see she was being sincere.

"Before I say yes, I have three questions." Helen looked at her eagerly. "Firstly, I still don't understand your dismissal of Chief Davara. He seems genuine, to me; he seems competent, too."

"He's a local, Roxy. I don't expect you to understand."

"Help me."

She leaned forward. "These people, they have this tradition, it's difficult for us detached white people to even grasp. It's to do with village and kin. They help each other out. And when I say 'help' I mean really help. If one can't have children, another will hand hers over. No questions asked. And if one is accused of a crime... well."

Roxy looked at her, incredulous. "You honestly believe that if Davara discovers it was Josh or even one of the local staffers, he's unlikely to press charges?"

"That's exactly what I believe. He might seem professional and Westernised to you, but there's a kinship amongst these people that runs deep. It's tribal, it scares the hell out of me sometimes and, quite frankly, it makes me lose all faith in our trusty Chief of Police."

"Okay, I see that, kind of. Question two, then: how do I know it wasn't you?"

Helen seemed genuinely taken aback. "Me?"

"I'm sorry, Helen, but I have to ask. How do I know you didn't do this? You said yourself, I'm only new here. I don't know any of you, not really. You also said you didn't have the best relationship with your mother." She tried a different tack. "Who stands to benefit by Abi's death?"

Helen's expression turned frosty. "If, by benefit, you mean, financially, then, yes, that would be me."

"You've seen the will?"

"Just now, in the hotel safe. I showed Davara. It hasn't changed in a decade. There's a generous provision for Joshua, of course, and most of the staff, two or three local charities, but for the most part Dormay is all mine."

Roxy stared at her, waiting and she said nothing.

"Helen, if I'm going to look into this then I'm going to look at it from every single angle. Unlike Davara, I don't have any allegiances. I just look at the facts and quite frankly, it's not looking too good for you." She began counting with her fingers. "One: I may have the least to gain, but you have the most. You get this place all to yourself, to do with as you like. That's motive, and a pretty strong one. Two: you knew about your mother's walk, you knew about the pergola pits, about the burial ritual."

"And three," Helen said, interrupting her, "I have absolutely no alibi."

"None at all?"

"I was in bed. Alone. I woke up to a terrible kerfuffle downstairs and came out to find Joshua and Maya distraught."

She placed a shaking hand at her throat. Swallowed hard.

"You're right. It doesn't look good for me at all and maybe that's why I need your help. Maybe I'm being as selfish as everyone else. I need to clear my name, it's true, but I didn't do it. You have to believe me. I couldn't... not like that!"

She looked up at Roxy, her emerald eyes darting across Roxy's face.

"Would I really be asking you to look into this if I did do

it? Right now Davara is pointing at some foreign being in a speedboat. He's not even looking at me."

"Yes, but he might. Eventually."

"Exactly, and we can't trust his motives. These people... They believe this island is theirs. They're not on my side. They weren't even on my mother's even though she deluded herself that they were. Davara would not hesitate to lock me up and take this island from under me, hand it back to the locals. You have to help me solve this thing."

Roxy felt quite exhausted and confused, not knowing who to trust, but she was also intrigued by this case, it was true. And here Helen was, offering her free license to poke about.

"Okay, Helen," she said eventually. "I'll do it. But I can't promise you I'll be successful. I can only try."

"That's all I ask. But you said you had three questions for me. What's your third question?"

"What? Oh, yes. I need to know that you're not hiding anything from me. Is there anything else you should be telling me?"

Helen glanced away, shook her head. "Of course not, I've told you everything."

Roxy doubted that very much but let it drop. For now.

"Well, you'll need to clear it with Chief Davara. If what you say is true, he won't be too happy with the idea of a foreigner poking her nose in."

"Leave Davara to me."

Helen stood up, the colour now returned to her face.

"Oh Roxy I am so grateful. I cannot tell you. But I have to ask something else of you, too."

Roxy raised her eyebrows again.

"I will tell Davara of your employment but I'd rather you didn't mention it to anyone else. They may just clamp up on you."

"Won't they be suspicious that I'm asking all kinds of nosy questions?"

Helen didn't think so. "You're a journalist aren't you? You can't help yourself."

Once again Roxy felt like she'd been smacked in the face by the smiling assassin, but as she was learning to do here, she let it drop. The two women shook hands and Helen let herself out.

Roxy sat quietly for a moment, reflecting on everything Helen had said. It was all starting to tangle up in her head, and there were loose threads fraying in every direction. She glanced outside then fetched her hiking boots and a small backpack. Now was as good a time as any to make the trek to Abi's Point, the highest place on the island. Roxy had already been assured the view was better up there. Perhaps, things would be clearer, too.

CHAPTER 10

Roxy pulled on some khaki trousers, a floppy cotton shirt, thick socks and the boots, then lathered her skin in Rid and sunscreen, filled up her water bottle, grabbed a cap, shades and sunscreen, pushed them all inside her backpack and made her way down to the lobby. As she grabbed a few bananas from the dining room she was surprised to find it empty, and relieved, too. Roxy needed a little space now, to think over what Helen had said and try and get some perspective. She didn't need giggling socialites and inquisitive doctors.

It was close to midday and Davara and his men had also deserted their post on the main veranda. The only human about was Mary, quietly setting up for lunch. Roxy admired her tenacity and wondered whether anyone would bother showing. At the front desk, Joshua was on the phone and she slipped past him and out the front of the hotel. A groundsman spotted her and indicated the 4WD but she shook her head. No, she'd rather walk. And so she set off, up the hill towards Abi's Point.

It took about half an hour to reach the base of the lookout and by the time she got there Roxy was already panting like a dog and soaked in sweat. She took a good long swig of water and, spotting the mosquitoes closing in, applied more Rid. Then she ploughed on, up through the forest towards the top. As she went she brushed past tangled vines, overhanging palms and spider webs, and resisted the urge to scream when something dropped down in front of her or rustled the undergrowth nearby. Butterflies and other insects busied themselves around her and birds called out to each other in song. There was constant noise and movement in the forest, and Roxy had trouble concentrating on the track as her eyes darted from left to right, to the branches above and back to her stomping feet.

She cursed herself a little as she went, suddenly pining for her small, clean apartment back in the relatively safe confines of Elizabeth Bay in inner-city Sydney. Her home was tiny, just a one-bedder with a neat little sunroom she had turned into her office, and now as she slipped and slapped her way up the hill, she longed to find the door to that cosy unit, step inside, and forget this whole mess.

Boy, Oliver was going to be proud of himself, she thought. He was right, she couldn't help attracting trouble, and yet again, she'd landed in the thick of it. Normally, though, the 'thick of it' involved inner-city streets or larrikin Aussie towns, not the wilds of the tropics. Here she felt well out of her depth. As she swiped at a mosquito buzzing around her nose, she wondered what was more dangerous, gun-wielding bad guys, or Malaria-infecting insects. She shrugged off her encroaching bad mood and continued on.

The muddy track was like walking on clay and she slipped several times, grasping at stray branches to break her fall, growling as she did so. It was steep, too, and she wondered how the fatter, less able tourists ever made it. Perhaps Maurice had to piggyback them up.

Vines grew like imitation plants here, perfect and fluorescent green as they wound their way up the rainforest trees, and if she wasn't so hot and bothered she might have admitted it was all incredibly beautiful.

Finally, suddenly, a welcome breeze broke through the growth. She stopped and lapped it up. The more she climbed, the cooler it got, thanks not only to the elevation but to those towering palms and ferns that acted as her umbrella. Eventually, a good 40 minutes later, she brushed aside some branches to step clear of the forest and out onto the side of the hill. A clearing had been etched into the edge of the cliff, and wooden railings placed around the exterior for safety. She doubled over slightly to get her breath back, then stood up and stared out.

What a view! It truly was spectacular, and instantly Roxy's foul mood evaporated, just like that, and she felt her spirits soar. Both Joshua and Doc had been right—it really was well worth the hike.

From here you could see out across the entire northern side of the island, from the churning white caps of Taboo to the shaggy brown rooftops of the local village. And directly below, the hotel, just a miniature white blob in front of that stunning azure sea. You could also catch a distant, hazy glimpse of the mainland, as well as several neighbouring islands; and between them all, smatterings of dark, shallow reef. There were various tiny white blobs heading between each one, boats no doubt taking supplies, locals or wide-eyed adventurers. She wondered if the Zimmermans were out there, somewhere, enjoying that serene reef, oblivious to the horror back on land.

Roxy leaned against a rock ledge and reached for her water bottle again, then slipped her cap off and wiped her brow. After several minutes, once her breathing had returned to something resembling normal, she reached back into her pack and located her journal and a pen.

It was true, Roxy had stumbled into several murder investigations in her time, mostly like this—in the middle of a writing assignment. And she knew that the best way to make sense of it all was to write it down, and fast. So she began to scribble the names of every single person present on Dormay at the time of Abi's death, adding the questions:

When exactly did she die? And how? She made a note to ask Davara.

Next she jotted down the word 'motive', and at first she was stumped. On this point, Helen was wrong. Roxy wasn't the only person who stood to lose by Abi's death. Just yesterday, Joshua had told her how he loved Abi like a mother. His devastation seemed sincere. Both Doc and Luc also seemed genuinely upset, and their positions on the island were now tenuous at best. Even Maya was less likely to treat the place like a second home now that Helen was in charge. It only took three days on Dormay for Roxy to know that Helen would run the place very differently from her mother. Roxy had a hunch the free ride was about to end for all of them.

But was it already over for Luc? Roxy circled his name several times and a motive began to materialise before her eyes. Of course! Hadn't she overheard Helen warning him that Abi was onto him, that she was going to spill the beans to his benefactress? Helen must have been referring to his affair with Maya, surely? In any case, no matter what it was, Luc had been infuriated. Could this spell the end of his cushy sojourn at a tropical resort? Would his benefactress be angry enough to cut him off completely? And was that motive enough to murder?

I guess it depends how much it's worth to him, Roxy thought. She wondered about his alibi. Did he have one?

Next she considered Wade. His alibi was obviously sound—he was at the mainland after all—yet he seemed to have motive stacked to the rafters. She'd already heard how Wade envied Abi's Retreat, how his own resort was failing. His wife had admitted as much. Perhaps Wade felt that with Abi out of the way, Helen, who was clearly less enamoured of the place than her mother, would be more likely to sell profitable Dormay to him and he could eventually recoup his losses. Roxy shook her head with agitation. But he couldn't have done it. He got to Dormay after Abi had been killed. They had all seen him arrive. She put a cross next to Wade's name. Sure, he had the motive, but no apparent means or opportunity.

Next, Roxy scribbled those words 'means' and 'opportunity', and several faces began bobbing in her mind, including the local staff, Popeye, Maurice and Mary, not to mention the chef, Patricia, the cleaning women and the groundsmen who also looked after the boats. Not only had Abi been killed on the track to their village, the way in which she had been killed certainly threw suspicion their way ('perhaps too much suspicion,' Roxy wrote). And while it was true that any of the guests could have read about the burial ritual from the book in the library—she made a note to look up the reference herself—Roxy had to agree that it didn't look good. She considered them for a moment.

She wasn't sure where Popeye and Maurice were that morning, but she knew that Mary was up and about. The only way Mary could have done it, however, was to run into Abi on the track before day break, bump her over the head, bury her and then make her way to the restaurant to calmly set up for breakfast. Roxy had seen the young waitress that very morning and she had appeared perfectly normal. It all seemed too unlikely.

She turned back to the word 'motive'. What possible motive, she wondered, could Mary or any of the staff have for that matter? As far as she could tell, they all adored Abi and she adored them right back. With the hotelier gone, their own positions must also be shaky. Helen had not hidden her disdain for them, for their apparent laziness and unprofessionalism. She particularly had it in for Popeye. Chances were, he at least would be packing his bags and moving off the island within the week. No, thought Roxy, it makes no sense at all.

Of course there was one staffer who wasn't exactly bosom buddies with Abi, or at least that's the impression she'd been given. Roxy wrote the name 'Willie' down and placed a question mark beside it. Abi had a problem with this particular staffer, of that she was certain. The question was: why?

Another thought suddenly entered Roxy's mind. She remembered that strange conversation she had overheard just the day before, below her bedroom window. It was two people anxiously discussing getting rid of something. She tried to recall exactly what they'd said, knew she hadn't quite got it right, but it went something like this: 'What do you mean you want to get rid of...?' 'Shut up and calm down, I've got a plan."

She studied the words, shook her head irritably. If only she knew who was speaking and about whom or what. For all she knew, they could have been discussing getting wine stains out of a tablecloth!

"Urrghh!" Roxy cried aloud, slamming the journal down on a rock face. The ropes were no less tangled than they had been at the start of this exhausting trek, and she didn't feel as though she was making any substantial progress.

Roxy reached into her backpack, pulled out one of the bananas and began eating it, staring out at the view, not really taking it in this time. She couldn't help wondering whether she was wasting her time. Was this all an elaborate set up; a ploy by Helen to throw suspicion from herself? She swallowed the last of the banana and dropped the peel back into her bag. Even if Helen was up to something, if she was guilty of doing her mother in, did it really make any difference? Roxy had just been given permission to investigate this case, and investigate she would. If that meant bringing the hotelier's daughter to justice, then so be it.

Eventually, with the sweat-stained journal secured away and nothing any clearer, Roxy pulled her pack back on and headed down the hill towards the hotel. The return journey, while tricky in the steeper patches, was certainly less gruelling, yet she still had to swallow an entire jug of water to replenish her body when she got back to the hotel. Her fringe was now matted to her forehead and her clothes stank of a heady mixture of insect repellent and body odour. Eau de phew! Yet she had one more thing she needed to do before she would allow herself a reprieve.

Roxy stepped into the library, glad to find it deserted again, and began looking about. The book that had caught her eye the day before, the one entitled *Myths & Legends* was nowhere to be found and eventually she gave up and settled on an Australian classic instead. Sure, she'd agreed to help Helen out, but perhaps, like everyone else, what she really needed right now was some quality time out. Maybe it would clear her head.

Back in her bedroom, Roxy tried to ignore the laptop that remained unopened by the side cupboard and instead prepared herself a cool bubble bath.

As the froth slithered around her weary limbs, Roxy shrugged back her guilt. She knew she should be out there, transcribing Abi's interviews in case they contained something of note—had she mentioned Willie? Had she indicated some kind of motive?—but she simply couldn't find the energy. Not yet.

After a good half hour soak she emptied the bath, wrapped herself in the fluffy dressing gown and lay down on her bed. It was time to take her mind off things for a bit, so she opened the book and lost herself in the adventures of Tim Winton's *Cloudstreet*.

CHAPTER 11

At exactly 6pm, Roxy stepped out of her room and into the hallway. She had not overdressed this evening, simply put on black three-quarter pants and a striped black and white top, and made her way down to the main veranda. Everyone had now materialised. The Zimmermans, looking quite shaken and unable to meet anyone's eyes were sitting on the lounge, juices in hand. Luc was standing alone, holding onto what looked like a whisky, leaning on the railing fixated by the view. Maya was sitting at a table with her husband, both stonily quiet with cocktails and a large box of tissues close by, and Helen and Doc were deep in conversation to the side. Roxy spotted Joshua at the bar next to Maurice and walked over.

"Hey, man, I've hardly seen you since..." He let the sentence dangle there for a moment. "So, what can I get you? Something strong?"

"Just a glass of merlot, if you've got one, thanks."

"Sure thing. How are you holding up? You okay?"

Roxy looked surprised. "I should be asking *you* that. I know you loved Abi deeply, I can only feel for you, for all of you."

Joshua clenched his jaw tightly and concentrated on opening the wine bottle.

"Let Maurice do that," Helen said appearing by Roxy's side. "I'd like to address all the guests, and you."

Joshua had already uncorked it and quickly poured Roxy a glass.

"It's done," he told her, then followed Roxy to some seats at the back.

The tension in the air that evening was palpable. Roxy wondered if everyone felt the way Helen did, that one of them was a killer. Roxy snuck a peek at each person in turn but all she saw was shock and grief. Helen asked Luc to take a seat and then stood before them all, one hand holding onto the railing. She tried for a warm smile. Failed miserably.

"Thank you, everyone, for making the effort to be here tonight. I know this has been a terrible, terrible day."

As Helen spoke Roxy couldn't help being amazed by the woman's transformation. In the three days Roxy had been at Dormay, Helen had gone from a cold professional and pouting daughter to a madwoman raving accusations at all and sundry, to this calm, vaguely human creature who appeared before them now. It was a positive transition, but surprising nonetheless. Roxy wondered how Helen had managed to turn up for cocktails herself, let alone apply her lipstick so precisely. If Helen had stood before them all with her hair in tufts and her pyjamas still on, no one would have blamed her. Still, no amount of grooming could hide Helen's obvious exhaustion. She might have sounded strong, but she looked as frail as a sparrow.

"This has been an absolutely traumatic day for all of us," Helen was saying, looking suddenly sheepish. "I really do appreciate the way everyone has handled this and I need to apologise for my... my outburst earlier today."

"Please, Helen, do not concern yourself with that," Doc said. "You've received an enormous shock. It's quite understandable."

He looked to Wade and Maya who both shifted their gaze as if they weren't quite ready to forgive Helen just yet.

"Thank you, Doc," Helen said. "Now, most of you are locals or employees of some sort so I really only address the Zimmermans when I say I am so dreadfully sorry for the way your vacation has turned out, and obviously I will graciously refund your fee."

"Yes, yes," snapped Ingrid, as if she expected as much, as if she wasn't talking to a woman in mourning. "But when can we go? We want to leave at once."

"That is not actually up to me, I'm afraid. Chief Davara is in charge now and has asked that we all remain on the island until he gives us the all-clear."

"The all-clear?" It was Wade now and he looked outraged again. "Listen, I'm a bit pissed off with all of this. The way Davara speaks you'd think one of us did it."

"Well, they could hardly suspect you, sweetie," Maya said, pulling out a packet of cigarettes, "you were at the mainland."

"Of course he doesn't suspect me, Maya, that's a ridiculous notion. But he can't possibly think you did it, either! Or any of you for that matter."

"Hey, man, he's just doing his job," said Joshua and Helen held up a hand.

"Joshua's right. Chief Davara would be a fool to let anyone leave until he's determined time of death, cause of death, alibis, that sort of thing."

Luc sat forward. "So, until 'ee solves this thing, the murderer eeze still out there?"

"Or in here," Doc muttered and Maya's eyes widened.

"Oooh it's just like an Agatha Christie novel!" she gushed, dragging on her cigarette. "You know: 12 people, stuck on a deserted island. Someone slips the dagger through someone's heart and that little French man has to work out *whodunit*!"

"He's Belgian, actually," said Roxy, "and there's nothing fictional about all of this, Maya. Helen's mother is dead and somebody really did do it."

"Oh, I know, I was just saying..."

Helen frowned. "Please, let's not go over all that again. I truly hope, and expect, that this will all get sorted quickly and that whoever did it—stranger or not—is apprehended and taken off this island pronto. In the meantime, we need to remain calm and get on with it as best we can. Which is why we will be continuing with business as usual, or close enough to it. And by that I mean, meals will continue to be provided as always, activities planned, drivers available should you need them."

Again, she was mostly addressing the Zimmermans now.

"We just want to be out of here," reiterated Ingrid and Helen nodded.

"I understand. But until that's permitted, I hope you understand we will do everything we can to make your stay as comfortable and normal as possible."

Ingrid sniffed and looked to her husband. He shook his head very slightly at her and said simply, "We understand."

"So that puts you off the hook and on holidays, then," Maya said to Roxy, blowing a circle of smoke. "No book to worry about."

"No, but I don't exactly feel in a holiday spirit, Maya."

"Of course you don't," said Helen, "but I hope you will at least try to relax. This will all get sorted out very soon. Now, please, everyone drink up. Dinner will be served in about half an hour."

Doc stood then and held his glass high.

"If I may, I would like to propose a toast to our dear Abigail." They all reached for their glasses. "To the finest woman who ever walked these shores. Who did more for these people than we will ever know. And who will be sorely missed."

They all chorused "Here! Here!" and drank.

Behind him the sky, which had been streaked with colour, blushed the deepest of reds and they all looked at the sunset with awe. It was a dazzling sight.

"Abi's come to say farewell," Doc said quietly and they all raised their glasses again, this time in a silent salute to the horizon.

Roxy's third dinner at the hotel was so very different from the two before. While Helen ate almost nothing as usual and Maya drank way too much, everyone was relatively subdued. There were no histrionics, no accusations, no fears verbalised, just common, idle chatter, the sort of conversation Roxy had originally expected of a luxury resort like this.

Surprising, she thought, that murder would make everything turn so lacklustre and normal. She wondered whether Abi would approve. Probably not. A gaping hole had clearly been formed by Abi's absence. Helen, now calmer and more controlled, was doing her best to smooth things over and keep things going, but Dormay's heart was no longer there. Roxy had only known Abi such a short time but already missed her uproarious laughter, her wobbly walk and her trademark gin and tonics.

Roxy was not alone and nobody had very much to say as they worked through their meal. She noticed that Maya and Luc were no longer eyeing each other off across the table. In fact they had been avoiding each other's eyes all evening, and she wondered whether it had anything to do with Wade's presence. Or had Luc finally broken it off with the young woman? Roxy dismissed this idea. After all, Abi was no longer around to threaten his position at Dormay.

Eventually Helen excused herself and went to bed, followed soon after by Doc. The rest of them made their way to the veranda where Roxy helped herself to a peppermint tea. Within minutes Wade was pulling her aside.

"Look, I've gotta get back to the mainland, lots to attend to. Maya needs to stay, she's caught up in all this... business."

He growled a little and Roxy was not sure if he was angry at Maya for being a suspect or Abi for putting her in that position in the first place. He took a sip of his espresso and got to the point.

"I'd like you to keep an eye on her for me. She seems to have taken a liking to you and, well, there's no baggage with you. Not like Helen." Roxy raised an eyebrow. "I'm not stupid, I know Helen has no time for Maya; thinks she's a giggling school girl."

He glanced across at his wife who was puffing away on another cigarette and laughing at some comment Joshua was making.

"In many ways she is very young, which is why I'm asking you to look out for her for me."

Well, she is half your age, what did you expect? Roxy wanted to scream at him but simply said, "Happy to, Wade. I'm just not sure what I'm looking for."

"Make sure she's okay, that's all. She can get hysterical, you must have worked that out by now. Now, if you'll excuse me, I need to have a word with Maurice."

He stepped over to the bar where the young waiter was filtering coffee. Roxy spotted the Zimmermans sipping teas on the lounge and took the opportunity to join them. She doubted very much that the Swiss couple had anything to do with 'this business' but she had a job to do and she might as well start crossing suspects off the list. She asked them how they were doing.

"We are fine," said Ingrid in that curt tone that suggested you were being impertinent for even asking.

"I guess it must have been a shock to you when you found out about Abi?" Roxy continued.

"Of course."

Bernard sat forward then and said, "I hear you were the one who found her. On the beach?"

"Yes," Roxy said. "Horrible sight. I'll never forget it, but it's probably just as well it was me and not Helen."

They nodded solemnly, so she swooped in.

"You're lucky you were at the other end of the island when it all happened."

"Mm," Ingrid agreed. "We were busy diving, we did not know about all of this."

"You guys are incredible," Roxy said, baiting the hook some more. "Up so early and making the most of every day. I admire that, I really do."

She leant forward conspiratorially, putting one hand up to shield her lips. "Considering some of us can't seem to drag ourselves out of bed until noon."

They all glanced across at Maya, and Ingrid tutted. "We believe in always using the day. We are not lazy."

"No, I can see that. So you must have been up and out pretty early this morning to miss all the action? I didn't spot you at breakfast."

"Yes, we went diving very early today. We return to Switzerland soon so wanted to get a long dive in."

"Did one of the staff take you out, or did you head off on your own?"

"Sometimes Willie helps us, sometimes we go alone. We are good with boats. We don't need help."

Roxy noticed she had not answered this question and was about to ask again—keen to know if they had an alibi—when Bernard coughed and stood up.

"It is late. We should get to bed."

Ingrid quickly nodded goodbye to Roxy and followed him out.

The writer took a sip of her tea and sat back to think. So, the Zimmermans were up early with nobody around to see them. She wondered if Mary could collaborate that. Spotting Maurice packing away the coffee, she got up and wandered over.

"Is Mary still at the hotel?" she asked.

"No, Miss. She is sleeping now."

He, too, spoke in the melodic way of the locals but his English, she noticed, was quite good. "She is always up very early for breakfast."

"Of course," Roxy said. "I might catch her then." She hesitated. "You don't work the breakfast shift do you?"

"No, Miss, I do lunch and dinner."

"That must be a relief—no early mornings for you."

He smiled widely revealing a set of perfect white teeth. No *betel nut* for him either, she thought.

"I get up early always, Miss. All the village gets up with the sun. We don't sleep in like guests." He chuckled a little. "Some mornings I do fishing for Abi..."

He stopped, looked stricken suddenly. She offered him a warm smile.

"This must be so hard for you, and the other staff?"

"Very hard, Miss. We are all sad. My children, they can not stop crying. Tara, Patricia, her kids. Miss Abigail was very good to my people."

"I know she was, Maurice." She sighed. "I'd better let you get on with it, get back to your family."

"Thank you, Miss."

On the way out, Roxy nearly collided with Doc who was on his way in, deep in thought. He looked up at her startled.

"Oh, hello! It's you, Roxy."

"Hi Doc, I thought you'd gone to bed. Are you okay? You look worried."

He brushed her off. "No, no, my dear. I'm perfectly fine. Just been checking up on Helen."

"Is she okay?"

"Oh, yes, I can assure you, she is in good health. She's stoic that one; a little too stoic if you ask me. You hitting the sack?"

"Mm, I'm not quite as stoic as some. I need serious Zzzs."

"That's the ticket! Will do you the world of good."

He stepped out onto the veranda and Roxy returned to her room.

Once inside, she reached for her journal and jotted down a few notes, starting with the Zimmerman's diving trip and ending with the fact that the entire village were up and about early in the morning. So why didn't anybody see anything, she wondered?

If only someone had walked down that track at just the right time.

Roxy sat back on her bed and thought about this. Helen was adamant that someone was up to no good, had planned this murder meticulously. But Roxy was not quite so sure. Both the timing and location were far too risqué. If these villagers were really up and about early—as indeed the Zimmermans were—then the murderer could not count on having the track all to himself at that hour. He certainly couldn't count on not being spotted entering or leaving the site. Roxy chewed on her pen, her brain cells ticking over. It seemed more likely that Abi's death was a random incident, a crime of passion, perhaps. She sat forward.

What if someone ran into Abi on the path this morning? What if they began to discuss something that lead to a fight, that lead to Abi's death?

Roxy threw the pen down and closed her journal. It was no good thinking about it anymore now. What she really needed was a good night's sleep because tomorrow she had a big job ahead of her. She needed to find out exactly what could make someone flare up so quickly, and with such devastating results.

CHAPTER 12

The sun tried to edge its way into the room through the slats in the shutters but wasn't having a lot of luck and Roxy smiled to herself as she glanced at the clock—7.05am—then turned over and went back to sleep. Sleep-ins were probably going to be the only silver lining of this terrible tragedy, but it was a silver lining nonetheless and she took the opportunity to stay snoring until 8.30.

Eventually, Roxy stepped into a shower and got ready for the day. Opening the shutters she discovered that whatever clouds were brewing had now blown away, so placed a swimsuit under a wide-belted skirt and top and went down to breakfast.

Mary was at her usual post, coffee pot in hand and Roxy waved her over as she took a seat out on the veranda.

"Some cooked breakfast for you today, Miss?" Mary asked hopefully and Roxy shook her head.

"No, I'll get a croissant in a moment. Can I ask you something?"

Mary looked surprised but nodded her head.

"Yesterday morning. What time did you start work?"

"Ah, six o'clock, Miss, I come and set up for breakfast."

"Of course, and did you happen to see the Zimmerman's about?"

"No. They usually come and get some fruit and bread and go again."

"But not yesterday?"

"No, Miss. Maybe they too busy!"

She laughed a little at this and Roxy smiled.

"So, did you see anyone else out and about early?"

Mary looked confused suddenly so Roxy said, "I guess I'm trying to piece it all together, in my head, you know? For Abi."

"Oh poor Miss Abi. Is very sad. All village very sad."

"Of course you all are. It's dreadful. So, anyone else beat me to breakfast?"

Mary didn't hesitate this time. "Yes, I tell police man yesterday, I see Joshua first—he come and get coffee and go again. Soon after I see Abi."

Roxy stared at her, stunned. "So you really did see Abi? When was that?"

"She walk through here, no look good, say she need fresh air. About quarter past six. I try to stop her, Miss. She look real bad. Tell me she been sick, ask me to clean her room. I tell her, no walk today, Missus! You go back to bed! But she no listen, she say she must walk today. Very important.".

"Did she say that, 'very important'?"

"Yes." Mary hissed. "She too stubborn Miss Abi. But I should stop her, I should not let her go."

Roxy squeezed the local woman's hand. "Hey, it wasn't your fault, you weren't to know."

At that moment Doc arrived and Mary hurried off to attend to him while Roxy's brain started whirring into motion. She didn't need the forensics report to know, now, that Abi must have been killed some time between 6.20am, just after Mary had seen her, and 7.50am when Roxy had discovered the body. It was a relatively small window of opportunity, but a window nonetheless. And as far as she could tell there were at least a few people up and about at that hour. Not only were the villagers up then, so were the Zimmermans, and so was Joshua. She wondered about him.

Doc arrived at her table and took the seat opposite her. He looked like he hadn't slept well. His eyes were puffy, and his face unshaven.

"This is a late morning for you, Doc," Roxy said.

"I could say the same about you, my dear," he replied.

"To be honest, I'm a fraud. Late mornings are much more my style. Abi was the only reason I was dragging myself up at the crack of dawn."

The mention of Abi's name brought a lull to the conversation and Doc concentrated on his grape fruit for a while. Roxy felt sorry for him, too. His best friend had been taken so savagely and yet he'd remained stoic throughout.

She waited a few moments before asking gently, "So what happens to you now?"

He placed his spoon down. "It's in the lap of the Gods I'm afraid. And Helen of course. But I'll be fine my dear, don't you worry about me. I would think you are in a mighty hurry to get away and back to your life now?"

"No, not really. I mean, yes, it's been a real shock, but there's worse places to ride the storm."

"Yes indeed. And something tells me you can hold yourself well in a storm."

"I guess so."

He took a tentative sip of his tea. "So, tell me your theories then?"

"Sorry?"

"Come now, my dear, a clever one like you. You must have a few theories."

Roxy chewed her bottom lip, wondering how far to trust him.

"To be honest, Doc, I'm still trying to get it all straight in my head. Have you got a theory?"

He placed his cup down. "Yes I do. I do indeed."

"Oh?"

"Did you know Wade was here yesterday?"

"Yes, we all saw him arrive."

"No, we saw him arrive for the second time."

He had that cat-got-the-canary look and Roxy frowned.

"What do you mean?"

"Only that our esteemed Governor came to Dormay much earlier yesterday morning. And completely neglected to mention it. To anyone."

Roxy's eyes widened. "Really? How do you know?"

Doc glanced around to make sure they wouldn't be overheard.

"Maurice came to see me last night, just after coffee. He was most distressed, poor lad. He had seen Wade's boat arrive at the jetty, just before sunrise—must have been about 5.45 yesterday morning. He didn't know whether to mention it to the authorities. Didn't want to stitch up Wade for some reason. God knows why, Wade's been pointing the finger at him and his lot from the start. Still, I told him he must speak with the police at his first opportunity."

"Hang on a minute, you say he saw Wade's boat at the jetty? Just near the hotel? You're sure he didn't mean near the airstrip?"

"No, no, he said he was out fishing at main beach, on the southern side, and saw it come in from the direction of the mainland, heading towards the jetty. Why?"

Roxy hesitated. "Because Helen told me that a local child had heard a boat out near the airstrip at about the same time."

"Couldn't be. That's the other side of the island. The child must have been mistaken."

"Hm, possibly, unless there were two boats, of course. And you say Maurice definitely saw Wade's boat?"

"That's what he tells me."

"But did he actually see Wade, or just his boat?"

Doc smiled and wagged his finger at her. "See! You're too smart for this lot. Indeed, Maurice says he did not actually see Wade, per se, just the boat. He couldn't see the jetty from where he was standing, plus it was very early. It seems

Maurice considered shooting across to the jetty to help him tie up but got a nibble on his line so kept fishing. He says he didn't think any more of it until he heard the boat taking off again, about 20 minutes later."

"That's a fleeting visit. And it was definitely Wade's boat?"

"As far as he could tell. I wouldn't put it past Wade, though." He leaned in again. "It seems pretty open and shut to me."

"Oh?"

"Wade must have snuck in early, skirted around main beach to the other side, then hidden in the bushes near the track, knowing too well that our Abi would be on her morning walk. He encountered her and did the deed."

"He'd have to be quick. It doesn't sound like he was here for long. Could he really have tied up a boat, bolted to the other side of the hotel, miraculously run into Abi, killed her, buried her, and bolted back again in such a short time? And all without being spotted?"

"What if he had planned to meet Abi? Had timed it to perfection?"

Roxy considered this for a few moments while they ate their breakfast in silence.

Eventually, wondering how much the doctor knew, she said, "Why do you think Wade would do such a thing?"

"A dozen reasons!" He lowered his voice again. "For starters, he's had his eye on this island ever since he got to the region."

"So I hear. When did he get here, exactly?"

"Oh, about 20 years back, I believe. Abi had already come, taken the pick of the islands and he was left with the dregs. This might be a lovely area but most of the place is infested with sandflies. For some unknown reason Dormay is quite immune."

"Yes, Abi was lucky wasn't she?"

"Luck had nought to do with it! Abi was smart, she knew a good investment when she saw one, and Wade has coveted

Dormay from the start. Constantly hassling her to sell up or let him come in as a partner. Said she was wasting the place. He was determined to turn this wonderful old hotel into some kind of trashy resort, complete with beach huts, pools, jacuzzis, the lot!"

"Sounds glamorous," said Roxy.

"Sounds obscene! Of course Abi was having none of it. 'Over my dead body,' she said."

He caught himself then and looked down. "Oh dear... oh dear."

Roxy placed one hand on his shoulder. "Well, if it was Wade, then he'll get found out soon enough. The police will be back today so Maurice needs to see them and let them know the minute they arrive."

In fact, the mainland police were already on the island and had established a new headquarters on the small veranda at the entrance to the hotel. No sooner had she finished breakfast, than she was being ushered into another interview with Chief Davara. As Roxy took her seat across from him, facing the ocean, that pang of guilt hit her again and she wondered whether Helen had managed to chat to him yet about her little PI job. If so, he was giving nothing away. He had his notepad and a pen before him.

"I have a few more questions for you, plis," he said and she nodded for him to continue. "I must ask you, did Mrs Lilton ever discuss the future of Dormay with you? In your interviews?"

This took Roxy by surprise. "How do you mean?"

"Did she say to you what she will be doing with the island when she has passed away?"

"No, not really. I mean, she obviously felt indebted to the locals, said she was going to dedicate the book to them, but I guess I always assumed it would go to Helen. Why? Helen is in the will isn't she?"

"Oh yes, yes, Miss Lilton is very much the main beneficiary of Dormay. That is true. I saw the will yesterday. But what I want to know is: did Mrs Lilton ever tell you that she had changed her mind about this? That she had other plans for the island?"

Roxy tried to think back. "Well, I do recall her saying something kind of related to that. I can pull the tapes out and go through them. But that could take a while."

"Try to think now, plis, if you can."

His deep brown eyes implored her, so she thought some more.

"Let's see...," she sat back and started whirring her brain cells into gear. "Okay, so, first she told me she loved the place, loved the people—really that goes without saying, it was so obvious to me from the start. Um, that's right... then she said something about needing to do the best thing by the island. No, not the best thing, the right thing. She needed to do the right thing. When I asked her what she meant by that she wouldn't elaborate, said she had to talk to someone first before she could explain it all to me. I'm pretty sure she meant Helen."

"Why do you think this?"

"Because, you see, Helen was still cranky at being left out of the loop about the autobiography. Abi had told Doc she was writing the book but didn't bother to inform her daughter."

"So Helen was angry?"

"Yes... but not viciously so. She was more disappointed than anything."

"Did Mrs Lilton talk to Helen? About 'doing the right thing'? Do you know?"

"I have no idea. Look, what is all this about? It would really help to know."

The Chief paused a moment, clearly puzzling over something.

Finally, he said, "I think you can be trusted. Certainly Miss Lilton thinks you can. She has mentioned her little job for you. She thinks you would make a good investigator."

Roxy blushed. "Look, I really don't want to tread on your toes—"

"It does not matter to me, Miss Parker, if you are playing detective. If this is what Miss Lilton wants, than so be it. But I have done some investigating of my own and it seems that Mrs Lilton had an appointment with her lawyer the afternoon of her death."

"Yes, Abi mentioned something like that," said Roxy. And then her eyes widened. "You think she was going to change her will! But why? And how?"

The police chief shrugged. "We can not know now for sure. But I do know that Mrs Lilton had earlier in the week met with the Lands Commissioner, the man who is responsible for the leases in this region, and she had made some enquiries about Dormay."

"What sort of enquiries?"

"She had discussed land rights in some detail. The Commissioner got the impression that Mrs Lilton was considering whether the local villagers were really the rightful owners of Dormay."

Roxy sat back with a thud. This had caught her completely off guard, and yet, somewhere in the back of her brain, a bell was ringing. Clanging, in fact. She just couldn't work out why.

So she asked, "Did the locals have a land rights request in?"

"No, no. The Commissioner tells me there were no submissions from the villagers. There has been, many decades ago, but nothing recent. No, it seems strange to me, but Mrs Lilton was doing the enquiring for them. This is most peculiar. Most expatriates, they want to hold onto their land, they do not want to give it back to the people."

Roxy studied his face then, looking for signs of the fanaticism that Helen spoke about, but the Chief was giving nothing away.

Eventually, she said, "Yes, well that does fit with what she was saying to me in the interview, about doing 'what's right'. Perhaps she really was going to sign it over to them. Still, I can't help thinking how disappointed Helen would have been."

Her eyes widened again. "Oh. You don't think Helen killed her mother to stop her changing the will?"

He held his hands up. "I do not know yet what I think, Miss Parker. Let us not get too carried away, too early. At this point, we do not even know if Miss Lilton knew of her mother's meeting with the Commissioner. She may have had no idea of the fact that Mrs Lilton was considering leaving Dormay to the locals. Indeed, we can not know for sure if that was what she was going to do."

Roxy's hands flew to her lips. The clanging bell had finally reached fever pitch. "Actually, Chief Davara, I think we do."

He looked at her puzzled.

"At the same time that Abi was giving me her last interview, Helen was looking up land rights online."

She took a deep breath and explained how she had happened upon Helen in the library, how Helen had hastily shut down the page and how Roxy had accidentally opened it to discover an Australian government website on traditional land leases. The Chief scribbled away.

"This is most interesting, most interesting," said the Chief. "Tell me, was Helen using the main computer in the hotel?"

"Yes, you can go and check the web browser's history, you'll find the page there. In any case, even if she was looking it up for some unrelated reason, and I can't think what, it's likely her mother did tell her about it. Helen and Abi had a meeting together that evening before she died. Doc told me, over cocktails, that they'd been at it for hours. I assumed it had something to do with the book. Now, well, I realise she had much bigger fish to fry."

The Chief looked at Roxy, confused. "She was frying fish that night?"

"No, sorry, that's just a figure of speech."

He let it drop. "So tell me, plis, did you see Miss Lilton after this 'meeting' with her mother? And how was she?"

Roxy hesitated. Despite Helen's frosty ways, she'd grown

on the writer and she wasn't yet willing to point the finger even more firmly in Helen's direction. But it needed to be said. The Chief was watching her, waiting patiently, his pen poised.

"When they joined us for dinner Helen wasn't happy, that's for sure. I remember one of the staffers, Popeye I think, ruined the entrees and she was pretty irate. Or not so much irate, more, um, unsurprised. She gave her mum a little lecture about how the staff would destroy the hotel in the end. I just thought she was being melodramatic. I mean, dropping a few plates isn't going to ruin a hotel. But of course if Abi was going to leave it to the locals, that would be a whole different story."

"Yes, yes, a whole different story."

Roxy felt her heart sinking. "I know it's not looking good for Helen but I honestly can't imagine her killing her mother, and leaving her body like that."

"It is too early to say but you must know, Miss Parker, that people do crazy things sometimes to the people they love. Love and hate, it is a very fine line."

And an overused cliché, she thought, letting it drop.

"You're right, I know that, but surely, if Helen knew about Abi's plans, others might have, too. I mean, Helen wouldn't be the only one to lose out if the island went back to the people."

"What do you mean?"

Again Roxy hesitated, and then told him of how Wade had mentioned meeting with the Lands Commissioner over dinner that first night, and of how he had wanted to speak with Helen urgently. Perhaps he had found out about Abi's plans and revealed all to her daughter.

"Look, I don't want to land anyone in it, but I heard there were a few boats about that morning—"

He cut her off. "I know about Mr Thomas's boat, Miss Parker. I am heading back to the mainland very soon to question the Governor."

"And the other boat? The one the village kid heard?"

He shrugged. "That one we are not so sure about." He smiled. "You have been busy with your investigating."

"Sorry, can't help myself. Just tell me you'll look into it further before you hoick Helen off in chains."

He smiled again. "No one is 'hoicking' anyone away yet Miss Parker. We still do not have the autopsy results."

"That's slow."

"That's our country. I am expecting them in a day or two. We haven't even established cause of death yet so, no, no, I will tread carefully for now. And, Miss Parker?"

"Yes?"

"You need to tread carefully, too. If you are doing the digging, as Helen tells me, then you must be careful. I can not stop you from asking people questions, but I need to warn you, plis. This is no game. This is real life and one person has been killed. There is nothing to stop the murderer from killing again."

She looked at him and shuddered. He was right of course. If there was one thing she'd learned in her time, it was that no matter who it was—Helen, Wade, even the charming Luc—once a murderer, always a murderer. If they thought Roxy was getting close, they would not hesitate to strike again.

CHAPTER 13

After chatting with the police chief Roxy considered heading to the beach when a better idea struck her. She grabbed a cool drink from the dining room and made a beeline for the hotel library. Once at the computer, she logged in to the web browser, looked around quickly, then took her cursor to the top of the page, to the word 'History' and scrolled down. She needed to double-check that Land Rights page, to make sure she hadn't conjured up the whole thing.

When she got to the day in question, Tuesday, the day before Abi died, Roxy quickly went through the various web pages that had been opened up that day. There was quite a collection, everything from airline websites to news pages, including a Swiss one called *Zurichsee-Zeitung*. There was a *Wikipedia* site on Indian Tonic Water and several health websites, including one on tropical diseases. And, yes, even a few on Roxy Parker herself. Helen wasn't kidding when she said she'd done her research. Eventually, Roxy located the one she'd used, twice, to email from, and took that as her guide. Just below it, in plain print was the AusAid site, the one on territorial land rights, the one that proved that Helen knew at least something of her mother's plans to give the island back to the locals.

She clicked on it and read down the entire page this time, but it didn't really offer up anything new. It was a paper written by an Australian land law consultant and provided a rather convoluted snapshot on settling customary land disputes in this and similar regions. There was plenty of historical and legal information, a rundown on the Settlement Act of 1971, and information on constraints regarding land disputes. It was heavily bogged down in legalese and Roxy's eyes were glazing over within minutes. She didn't know if Helen had found what she was after on this page, but she'd leave that to Davara and his men. She made a note of the website name and logged out.

At the main desk, Roxy found Joshua and asked after the police chief.

"He's gone back to the, er, crime scene," Joshua said. "Can I help you with something?"

She folded the paper over and handed it to him. "Can you give that to the Chief when you see him? It's very important."

"Sure thing, man. What's it about?"

"Oh, just something he might want to look at. I'll be up in my room if he needs me."

"Cool." He placed the paper to one side.

Roxy made her way back to her bedroom where she pulled her laptop out of its bag and set it up on the table by the window. She might not be good at legal speak but there was one area where she was a pro. She opened a new Word document page, then reached for her tape recorder, rewound it to the start and pressed 'Play'.

As Abi's voice came to life before her, Roxy ignored the heavy lump in her throat and began to type. There was no time for emotion, she was determined to transcribe the hotelier's interviews before the day was out, and with four hours logged up that would mean as much as eight hours getting it all down in print. She wanted to do the job properly, she didn't want to miss a word, an inflection, an emphasis of any kind, and so she began typing...

By lunch time, with half the work done and her stomach growling impatiently, Roxy leaned back in her chair and stretched. So far, there was nothing even remotely strange or suspicious about Abi's words. Roxy frowned. Had her death really come out of nowhere? Or was there something she hadn't yet told Roxy? Something she was hoping to get to? Something worth dying for?

"This crayfish salad is to die for!" announced Maya as Roxy began filling her plate at the buffet in the dining room a few hours later. She took the spoon Maya was offering and added some crayfish to the pile.

"What have you been doing all morning?" Roxy asked and Maya hitched her beaded skirt up to reveal her Burberry bikini underneath.

"What else is there to do on this Godforsaken place?"

"I thought you loved Dormay."

"I do, darling! But it's not quite so much fun when it's forced upon you. Besides, I normally only stay a few days. I just don't know what to do with myself."

"What about your art lessons with Luc?" She tried to say it without a wink, wink and a nudge, but the irony was lost on the young woman.

Maya sniffed. "No, thank you. I've had quite enough art to last me a while."

Luc appeared then and, spotting him, Maya picked up her half-empty plate and told Roxy, "If you'll excuse me, I'm heading back to my room. Alone."

That last word was directed at Luc and he shrugged, a half smile on his lips. Whatever was going on between those two was clearly affecting her more than him. He strode across to Roxy.

"And how are you this afternoon?"

"Fine, thanks, Luc. You?"

He shrugged. "I am frustrated. My work, it eese not coming along so well. I need inspiration."

He smiled provocatively, his black fringe flopping across one eye.

"Perhaps I can give you some art lessons, no?"

"No," she repeated firmly then left him at the buffet.

Josh, Doc and Helen were sitting together at a veranda table and spotting a spare seat next to them, she walked across. Helen was just getting to her feet.

"Here, take my chair, Roxy, you get a better view of the ocean."

"Oh I didn't mean to scare you away—"

"No, really, I'm done. Can't eat another thing."

Roxy glanced at her plate and it looked as though she hadn't even started on her meal. Helen turned to Joshua who was staring up at her worriedly.

"I'm going to head back to my room for a bit. Please, Joshua, if you could take over for the day. I don't wish to be disturbed."

He jumped up and began following her out.

"Are you okay, Hel'? What's going on?"

"I'm fine, stop fussing! You're like an old woman. Just, please, keep everyone away. I need some time out."

They both left and, sitting in Helen's seat, Roxy glanced across at Doc. He was shaking his head sadly.

"The poor chap," he said, stabbing at his pasta salad with a fork.

She raised her eyebrows.

"He's had a crush on Helen ever since they went to school together. You didn't notice?"

"Not really, no. That's a long time to have a crush. So, they went to school together?"

"Well, not exactly together. They wanted to go to the same school I believe but Abi wouldn't hear of it. She sent them to different boarding schools—Helen to a convent all-girls school and Joshua to St Pius Brothers College. Both in Brisbane. As far as I can tell, they're good friends, so long as no one is watching."

"What does that mean?"

"It means, my dear, that Helen is an incorrigible snob. She likes Joshua, they get along, hell, they're probably very well suited. But she has greater plans for herself than getting hooked up with a local lad."

"So they never..."

"Dated?"

"Yes."

He shrugged. "I may be sneaky Roxanne, but I'm not always successful at it. I couldn't tell you what they get up to in those long 'business meetings', but I do know if Joshua had his way, it'd be pretty amorous."

"But Helen isn't having any of it?"

"Not that I can tell, and it certainly didn't help that Abi was dead against it. She always saw them as siblings, I guess because they're so close in age. She once told me she'd be absolutely devastated if they got together. That it wouldn't be right."

"That's strong language. I thought she loved Josh."

"Yes, she did. But she was, well, wary..." He paused.

"Wary of what?"

"Oh, nothing, I've probably said too much as it is."

"You're going to leave me hanging like that?"

He chuckled. "Sorry, it's not really relevant, and certainly not my place to say." Doc scooped another mouthful of pasta up and managed to drop some back down onto his shirt.

"Dear, dear, I am so clumsy these days." He winked again at Roxy. "I need a nurse. Want the job?"

She laughed. "What is it with the blokes on this island?! All this sun and surf must be amping up your testosterone levels. No, thanks, Doc, I never was very into playing doctors and nurses."

He laughed too. "Well, you can't blame an old doc for trying."

As they ate, Roxy wondered, now knowing how close Josh and Helen were, whether Joshua also knew about Abi's plans to change the lease. And if he did, how he would feel about it. No matter how she looked at it, it could only be a plus for the young man. He was part-local after all. Surely, Joshua would be thrilled to actually own the place. If there was one person who seemed to love Dormay as much as Abi, it was Josh.

She scowled. Helen seemed to be looking guiltier by the day. If Abigail had lived, not only might Helen have lost the island, her inheritance and her means of support, the local lad she felt miles above may have ended up her boss. Could she allow that to happen?

"Penny for your thoughts," Doc said and Roxy shook herself out of it.

She stared at him and wondered what he, too, knew of Abi's discussions with the Lands Commissioner.

She decided to let it drop and, instead, said, "I was just wondering if Helen's okay. She didn't look too good just now."

"She'll be fine," Doc said firmly. "She came to see me a few days ago. She's just worn out, that's all. And now, of course, with her mother gone, and in such horrific circumstances... Do not worry yourself with Helen, she just needs to take better care of herself and get some sleep. I told her as much and I'm glad to see she's finally taking my advice. That'd be a first!"

At that moment, Chief Davara stepped into the room and they both looked at him surprised.

"I thought you were going back to the mainland," Roxy said.

"Ah yes, yes, I was just about to head back when I got a very interesting phone call from the pathologist." He glanced around the room. "Where is Miss Lilton, plis?"

"She's not well," Doc said. "She's in her room now and needs to rest. I really don't want you disturbing her right at the moment."

The Chief nodded his head. "If you say so, Doctor Spinks. In any case I need to speak with you, too, plis." He glanced at the plates before them. "When you have finished your lunch."

Doc stood up, tapping his belly. "Oh I'm done old chap. We can do it now, if you like."

Roxy stood up, too. "Is this about the autopsy results?"

"Yes, Miss Parker, we have some results back. Plis, Doctor, we go to the side veranda."

"Can I come?" Roxy had barely started on her salad but wasn't about to miss out on this.

The chief began to shake his head so she quickly added, "Whatever it is, Helen's going to tell me eventually anyway."

He considered this. "Okey dokey, you can come, too, Miss Parker but plis, bring your lunch, hey? I would hate to be responsible for wasting such good food."

She smiled and picked up her plate.

When they reached the side deck, the police chief asked them both to sit down then took his own seat at the table and pulled out his trusty notebook. He flipped through the pages until he got to the one he wanted.

"Okay, we have some very interesting results."

"Don't tell me," Doc interrupted. "She died from a blunt force trauma to the side of the skull."

The Chief nodded. "Yes, but that is not what is so interesting."

Both Roxy and Doc sat forward, intrigued.

"It would not have taken much blunt force, not because Mrs Lilton was elderly, but because she was sick, very sick indeed."

"Well, we knew that already."

"Yes, but did you know why she was so sick?"

He shrugged his shoulders. "She was weak, nauseas, had a splitting headache if I recall. I assumed she was coming down with a stomach bug. Wasn't she?"

"No, Doctor Spinks, this was no stomach bug."

The Chief was clearly enjoying himself now, teasing the information out and Roxy could see the Doctor was getting impatient.

"Well, out with it man!" he said at last.

"Mrs Lilton had high dosages of quinine in her system."

The Doc gasped and Roxy looked from him to the Chief puzzled.

"Quinine? The anti-Malarial drug? But what's so strange about that? She was obviously taking it to ward off the mozzies. I'm on something similar myself."

"No, she hadn't taken anti-malarials for decades," Doc said, his eyes now darting about the room, trying to think. "None of the old-timers do."

"Besides," added Davara. "She had far too much in her system. More than 10 grams. A daily dose is 2 grams at most. This is a toxic dose, Miss Parker. It could have killed her."

"Do you think she took it deliberately?"

"I can not be sure."

"Suicide?" said Doc. "Don't be ridiculous. Abigail had never been depressed a day in her life. Not after that philandering husband left her in the lurch in a foreign country, not after she discovered she was having Helen." He paused, choked up a little. "Oh no, Abi would most certainly not have tried to kill herself. It's absurd."

"So, then, she must have been deliberately poisoned," said Roxy.

The Chief nodded. "It is most likely since she was also hit over the head. The question now is—" he glanced from one to the other—"who would do this? Who would give so much quinine to Mrs Lilton and why?"

Roxy thought about this. "But I still don't get it. Did she die of quinine poisoning or the hit to the head?"

The Chief leaned back in his seat and put his hands together, prayer-like.

"She was certainly poisoned, Miss Parker, we know that. It is indisputable. But it did not kill her. No, no." He placed one hand at his temple. "The blow to the head is what killed Mrs Lilton. But she was not well. Even if she survived the quinine overdose, she would have been very weak."

"So it would have been easy for someone to follow her out that next morning to the track and strike her down. She couldn't have put up so much as a fight," Doc said. Again, the Chief nodded.

"What I want to know," said Roxy, "is why on earth Abi was up and about? If she really was so sick with quinine toxicity, why did she go on her morning walk as usual? She must have felt dreadful."

The doctor sighed heavily. "You didn't know Abigail as well as you thought, my dear. She adored the sea. It was her one great passion. It was the reason she struggled down there each morning, despite her hip troubles. She needed to get her fill. Perhaps... perhaps she felt it would clear her head, pep her up so to speak."

Roxy chewed her lower lip for a moment, deep in thought.

Eventually she said, "So how did it happen? How did all that quinine get into Abi's system?"

"This is a very good question, Miss Parker. Unfortunately we were not looking for poisons yesterday so we did not properly inspect her room."

The Chief shook his head angrily at himself. "We know she had been sick in the room, there was evidence of vomit, but that has all been cleaned up now. And we can not know now, for sure, how the quinine was administered to Mrs Lilton. It is a problem. But we did find plenty of gin in her stomach, too, so we think—"

"Oh yes," Doc interrupted him. "Of course! Her favourite tipple! G&T. She was drinking it that night, do you remember, Roxanne?"

"Yes, I do. With lots of lime."

The chief returned to his pad and began flicking back through the pages.

"Yes, yes," he was saying. "This is most interesting."

He stopped at an early page. "In Mrs Lilton's room that day we did find a glass with four slices of lime in it. This must have been her gin and tonic and we know, don't we Doctor Spinks, that gin and tonic is a great way to help the medicine go down?"

Roxy looked from one man to the next. "Huh?"

Doc explained: "The original Indian tonic water had a little bit of natural quinine in it and expatriates in these parts have been using it for centuries to fight Malaria."

Roxy's stomach tightened. Google websites began flashing through her head again.

"Indian Tonic Water?" she said.

"Oh yes," said Doc. "But, of course, it tastes so jolly awful. So they would add some gin and, yes, even some limes, to pep it up."

"This would be a good place to hide the extra quinine," the Chief said. "If only I had kept the glass from the bedroom. But, no matter. Listen, I must ask you, plis, both of you, do you know who prepared this gin and tonic. The one you saw Mrs Lilton drinking at dinner on Tuesday night?"

"Goodness, I couldn't say for sure," said Doc. "She usually makes them herself I believe. Or, gets Popeye or Maurice onto it. You don't think one of them—"

Davara held his hand up to stall him.

"Did she leave it alone at any point? Who else had access to her glass? Could someone else have put it in, when she wasn't looking, perhaps?"

Doc thought about this and the Chief turned to Roxy who had appeared to slip into a coma. In fact, her brain was working overtime and she kept thinking of the Google history page she had looked at earlier. She hadn't thought anything of it at the time but there was a *Wikipedia* page on Indian Tonic Water. She'd assumed it was for cocktail recipes, for the bar. Now, she was not so sure. There was also one on tropical diseases. She gulped hard. Malaria was a tropical disease. Those pages had all been searched around the same time as the one on land leases.

Oh Helen, thought Roxy. *What have you done?*

"Any ideas, Roxy?" he said again and she looked at him with a start.

She knew she should say something to Davara, that it was

only right to mention it, but couldn't bring herself to push that final nail into Helen's coffin.

Instead she said, "Sorry, can you repeat the question?"

When he did so she told him that the only other person who had access to Abi's drink that night was Joshua.

"He was sitting beside Abi at the dining table. He could have slipped the quinine in while everyone was talking."

Roxy studied the Chief's face wondering if he would rise to his nephew's defence but he simply looked at her expectantly so she continued.

"Or, better yet, when Popeye dropped the entrees. Do you remember, Doc, there was a big bang and we all looked around? Joshua could have done it then I suppose."

"And who was on her other side? At the dining table?" asked the Chief.

Roxy glanced at Doc and he shifted uneasily in his seat.

"Well, I was of course! But listen here, old man, you can't possibly think for one moment that I did this? What possible reason could I have for poisoning Abigail?"

The Chief held up a hand. "Plis, Doctor Spinks, do not concern yourself with what I think. I am just trying to get the facts together. To get a picture in my brain. You understand?"

This seemed to placate the doctor so he asked, "Who on Dormay would have a good stock of quinine?"

Once again Doc looked uncomfortable and he darted his eyes to Roxy and back to the Chief.

"Well, I do. Of course I do, dammit. I'm a doctor in the tropics. I always keep plenty on hand should a guest show up unprepared. We can't have them coming down with a deadly disease now can we?"

"How much do you have?"

"What? Oh, about six or seven packets. About 20, 25 doses I guess."

The Chief stood up and waved one hand towards the hotel. "Can you show me where your stock is, plis. I would like to check it is all there."

The doctor had paled considerably and glanced at Roxy again who tried to give him a reassuring smile. But she was suddenly very preoccupied. She needed to get back to the library and check out that *Wikipedia* page. As Doc was escorted up to his room, Roxy took the opportunity, stepping into the library and logging back in. She went straight to the web browser, clicked on 'History' and scrolled down.

There was nothing there.

She frowned then repeated the process, wondering if she'd done something wrong. But no, the entire History for the web for the past three days had disappeared.

"It's been wiped!" she said aloud, aghast.

Someone had beaten her to it. Helen, she wondered? Well I can outsmart you, she thought, typing the words 'Indian Tonic Water' into the browser. Almost the first page that appeared was the *Wikipedia* site she had spotted earlier.

"A-ha!" she said, clicking it open and beginning to read.

She might not have any proof that someone had been reading it on Tuesday, but at least she could find out what it was they were reading. Halfway down the page she noticed a link to the site on tropical diseases and clicked on that. It sprang open to reveal a variety of horrific sounding ailments including, yes, Malaria. Roxy scanned down the page, trying to take in as much as possible when loud voices could be heard coming from the staircase. She logged off and dashed out.

Chief Davara was returning to the lobby with Doc close behind, his face now bright red with what looked like rage and indignation.

"This is absolute nonsense!" he was saying. "I have no idea where my stock has got to. Damn it, man, anyone could have taken it."

At the bottom step, the Chief said, calmly, "But you told me just now that you keep your room locked up. I saw you use your key to enter. Who else could have your key?"

"Well, there has to be a spare at reception, surely. Ask

Joshua!"

They moved towards the main desk where Joshua was standing, looking confused.

"You guys right?"

"Yes, Joshua," his uncle said. "Can you tell me, plis, if there is a spare key for Dr Spinks' room? And if so, who had access to it?"

"Yeah, there's spare keys for all the rooms. Mary oversees the cleaning with a couple of the chicks from the village. Any of them can use it any time they like. But—"

The Chief held up his hand. "Is the key for Dr Spinks' room there now?"

Joshua turned and reached towards a group of keys at one side. He picked it out and handed it over.

"It is not missing," the Chief said.

"Of course it's not missing! They put it back!" wailed Doc.

"Who put it back?"

"Whoever took it, of course! Anyone could have taken it at any time. This joint isn't supervised around the clock. Is it, Joshua?"

He turned to the young man, his eyes imploring, and Joshua agreed.

"Fine, so tell me this, plis, who knew you had so much quinine in your room?"

"Well, everyone! I made no secret of it."

He turned to Roxy then, who was lurking in the shadows near the library.

"Roxanne, please, talk some sense into this man. You tell him how I offered some to you when you first arrived."

Roxy stepped out. "He's right, Chief Davara. He mentioned it during lunch, on Tuesday I believe. Maya was there, I'm pretty sure the Zimmermans were around, too. Any of them could have heard."

"The fact is, I mention it all the time. Every time a new guest arrives, I check to see if they're sufficiently covered. I offer it around. Anyone could have realised I had it, pinched the key when the main desk was unoccupied, and come in and pilfered the stock. Or—" His eyes lit up suddenly, "they could have spotted it while they were in to see me on some other pretext. Perhaps they'd come in for a cold or something and, when I wasn't looking, they could have jumped up and grabbed it out of my medicine cabinet and taken off with it. The cabinet's not locked, it would have been easy to find. I have people in and out of my room all the time. In fact, just the other afternoon I had—" he stopped, clamped his lips firmly shut.

The colour now drained completely from Doc's face and he reached towards a sofa chair that was placed against one wall, beside a wooden statue of a fierce looking warrior. He dropped into it. The police chief followed him over just as the Zimmermans walked in, hiking boots on and backpacks on their shoulders. They took one look at the assembled crowd, put their heads down and scurried off towards their room.

"You were saying, Doctor Spinks? What happened the other afternoon?"

"Huh? Oh, er, nothing. It's not important." He shook himself a little. "Look, Chief Davara, what I'm trying to say is, I have had many visitors over the past few weeks. It could have been stolen at any time by anyone. They could have rummaged through my cabinet and then put it aside until they were ready to use it."

The Chief didn't exactly look convinced but he wasn't stupid either. The doctor was right, it could easily have been taken by someone else.

He smiled brightly then, as though he hadn't just spent the past ten minutes accusing this man of poisoning and said, "Okey dokey, Doctor Spinks, I will need a full list of all the people who have been to your room to see you over the past few weeks. And a full list of the medicine you believe has been taken. But it seems very clear to me that this is certainly where the quinine has come from. I will also instruct my men to search the resort for any discarded packets. They have to be here somewhere."

He left the doctor sitting, drained on the sofa, and Joshua stepped out from behind his desk to join them.

"Oh dear, oh dear," Doc was saying. "It couldn't be. It's not possible..."

"Don't you panic just yet, Doc," Joshua said. "We all know you didn't do this, and my uncle's a fair man. He'll give you the benefit of the doubt. But I'm so confused. What's quinine got to do with any of this?"

Roxy pulled Joshua aside and filled him in. His jaw dropped.

"Crikey, they think Abi was poisoned to death?"

"Not to death, no. But it certainly didn't help."

She explained about the blow to the head. "My guess is, when the killer spotted her up and about the following morning, he, or she, realised their little plan hadn't worked. They probably hadn't given her quite enough. So, they followed her on her walk and, well, you know the rest."

Joshua leant against the wall, then dropped down to his bottom. He scraped one hand through his curly hair.

"This is all so insane and getting insaner by the minute." He turned to look up at Roxy. "I just don't get it, man. Who would do this? Why?"

He shrugged his head in Doc's direction and lowered his voice. "Surely, not?"

"Not necessarily," Roxy said. "We can't jump to conclusions yet."

She debated whether to say the next thing but decided that she'd had enough of secrets for now. "I have to tell you, Joshua, it's not looking great for you either."

He scowled. "Me?!"

"The Chief believes that whoever poisoned Abi probably put the quinine in her gin and tonic over dinner. It couldn't have been done too much earlier as the symptoms don't take long to show."

The Chief had not said as much, but she'd just gleaned this information from the web and realised for herself that

Abi's drink had to have been tampered with sometime between pre-dinner drinks and main course for the quinine to take effect. After all, Abi was showing clear signs of poisoning by the end of the mains.

"Do you remember how she was feeling suddenly ill over dinner? How she was sweating and feeling nauseas. How she excused herself?"

"Yeah, 'course. What's that got to do with me? I didn't pour her the G&T. Had to be one of the other staffers, surely?"

"Not necessarily." Roxy knelt down beside him. "It could have been placed in her drink after it was made. By someone sitting next to her at dinner, perhaps?"

She studied Joshua's face for signs of guilt. It dawned on her now that he knew very well that she'd been poking around on the internet—she'd given him the note for Davara after all—and could have snuck into the library at any time to erase the browser's History. He was a likely candidate.

But why? Perhaps he was in it with Helen. He was smitten with her, or at least that's what Doc claimed. Or perhaps he had his own reasons for doing the hotelier in. Whatever her suspicions, Joshua didn't look at all guilty or afraid. Instead, he just looked extremely hurt. A tear plopped out of one eye and trickled slowly down his face.

"I wouldn't do that, man, I wouldn't do that to Abi."

He put his head in his hands.

Roxy said, "I think we need to talk to Helen. She might be able to sort all of this out."

"No!" Doc was back on his feet. His colour had returned. "No one is to talk to Helen. She is not well. She does not need to hear of this. Not yet."

He steadied himself a little. Took a deep breath. "We will discuss it with her when she wakes up."

"When who wakes up?" asked Maya, appearing suddenly in her bikini, her dripping hair lank around her bony brown shoulders, a soggy towel draped across one shoulder, her beaded dress over the other.

"Never mind," said Doc sternly, giving both Roxy and Joshua a hard look. "This has nothing to do with you, Maya. I'll be in my room if anyone wants me."

He made his way slowly to the staircase while Joshua pulled himself back up and returned to the main desk.

Maya flashed Roxy a cheeky grin. "Oooh, isn't he tetchy all of a sudden? What have I missed? Wasn't that the police detective I saw leaving just now?"

She grabbed Roxy by the hand and dragged her to the main veranda. "Come on, woman, what's the goss?"

CHAPTER 14

Out on the deck, Maya glanced around. "Shall we grab a drink first? Where are the staff? Maurice! Popeye!"

Popeye appeared, as though by magic, and she ordered them both a glass of champagne.

"I'll have mine with plenty of orange juice," Roxy told him, glancing at her watch. It was just on 3pm. She turned to Maya. "What are we celebrating?"

"You tell me! Something's going down and I am clearly out of the loop. I *despise* being out of the loop. I can tell, however, Miss Nosey Parker, that you know all. You have that investigative reporter look about you. Come on, spill!"

Roxy hesitated, unsure how much she should divulge. She didn't really see any point telling Maya about the autopsy results or the native title lease for that matter. She knew how bad it all looked for Helen and didn't trust Maya to keep quiet. But at the same time, things didn't exactly look rosy for her husband either. They had all forgotten about Maurice's early morning sighting of Wade's boat. That still hadn't been explained properly.

Oh no, thought Roxy, there was a whole different angle she wanted to explore with Mrs Thomas and it had nothing to do with Helen or Doc.

"I tell you what, Maya, how about you spill the beans for me?"

Maya's perfectly plucked eyebrows shot up.

"Moi? What on earth have I got to do with any of this?"

Popeye showed up then to deliver the champagne and as he placed the glasses down, Roxy wondered just how much the younger woman knew of her husband's mysterious trip to Dormay early that fateful morning. Of course she could have been in co-hoots with Wade, but it didn't seem likely. They were hardly a united force. Roxy couldn't really picture the flighty blonde being involved in a murder plot. For starters she'd have trouble keeping it to herself.

But what about Luc? Just how serious was their apparent 'fling' anyway? If, indeed he had been forced to break up with Maya at Abi's request, would this really lead him to kill?

When Popeye had vacated the veranda, Roxy took a small sip of her drink and then said, very casually, "What I want to know, Maya, is why your husband lied about where he was the morning of Abi's death."

Maya had clearly not been expecting this and she almost tipped over her glass, rescuing it at the last moment. She darted her eyes around the veranda, then back at Roxy.

"What on earth do you mean? What are you saying?"

"I think you know exactly what I'm saying, Maya. Or, if you don't, you can probably guess."

She continued staring at Roxy blankly, so Roxy said, "Wade was over here very early yesterday morning, about the time Abi was killed. Then he went away and returned a second time after the police got here. I want to know why he made that first trip, so early?"

Maya feigned a laugh and grabbed her hair, tying into a messy knot behind her.

"This is all so silly. Are you saying, pray tell, that my husband sailed all the way over here yesterday morning to kill Abi, then sailed home again? I've never heard anything so ridiculous!"

She took a long gulp of her champagne.

"No, actually, I think Wade sailed all the way over here yesterday morning to spy on his wife."

Again, Maya was caught off guard, and she was speechless for a moment or two. She polished off her champagne with a second swallow and called out to Popeye for another.

Eventually, she turned back to Roxy and said as sweetly as she could, "Why would he need to spy on his wife? You really are full of wild accusations today."

If she'd started batting her eyelids innocently, Roxy would not have been surprised.

"Listen, Maya, I don't give a toss what you do with your private life. No interest whatsoever to me. But I do think you need to understand that at this point things are looking pretty bad for your husband. His boat was spotted docking at the hotel jetty just before sunrise yesterday. No one saw him, as such, they just saw the boat, so maybe it wasn't Wade. Maybe it was some interloper who'd nicked Wade's boat and taken off with it. But I doubt that very much. And I'm sure the police do, too."

Maya was more sullen now, not meeting Roxy's eyes so she ploughed on.

"Quite frankly, Wade's in thick. If you know why he was here... if he was here for some other reason, you need to speak up. Now."

Maya's rigid smile had disappeared, her youthful enthusiasm now completely evaporated. She wasn't having any fun anymore.

"Oh God," she groaned eventually. "I knew it was him, I just knew it!"

"Wade?"

"Yes, of course Wade. Luc and I woke up—" She paused, blushed a little and then scowled. "Oh don't give me that holier than thou look! We were just having a bit of fun!"

"I honestly don't care one way or the other. Just tell me about that morning. You saw Wade?"

"Yes! Well, not really."

"Maya, you either saw him or you didn't see him. Which is it?"

"I smelt him!" she blurted out.

"You what?"

"We were in Luc's pad."

"Pad?"

"Well, it's really his studio—he paints in one of the bungalows out on the lawn, between the hotel and the jetty? It has great light and, even better, lots of privacy. Anyway, we nick down there sometimes if we want to... be alone."

She had the decency to blush again. "I'd slipped in after dinner and, well, very early that next morning I woke up suddenly. I thought I heard an engine or something. Then, soon after, I got the feeling there was someone lurking about, nearby."

"Okay, but that could easily have been the Zimmermans, they were out diving as usual that morning."

Popeye returned again and she grabbed the glass from him and took another large mouthful.

When he left she said, "You don't get it. It *had* to be Wade. I could smell that toxic aftershave he uses. I'd pick it in a line-up." She rolled her eyes. "You can not imagine how many bottles of *Hugo Boss* and *Chanel for Men* I have given him, yet he still insists on wearing that God-awful scent. It's beastly!"

Roxy was growing impatient. "So, you smelt his aftershave? Outside your room?"

"Just the tiniest hint of it, but enough to freak me out I can tell you! I really got the impression he was spying on us. I jumped up, hid behind one of the drop sheets for a bit, then, when we thought the coast was clear, I dashed back to my room and Luc went off to see if he could spot Wade's boat. But he didn't. So we just assumed I'd got it wrong."

"What time was this, Maya?"

"Oh, God, I have no idea."

"Well try and think. Was the sun up?"

"Yes, just, but it was still early."

"So it could have been around 6.20am?"

Roxy knew that was about the time Abi was meeting her horrific fate. Maya shrugged.

"I couldn't really tell you. As I say, I just fled to my room at the first opportunity."

Roxy sat back with a start. "You were the door I heard, closing that morning! About 6.30am?"

"I guess that could have been me. I didn't really notice the time, I just slunk under the covers and hoped to God Wade hadn't busted us. If he had, I don't know what he would have done. When I next saw Wade, after the police had arrived, you remember, he was acting so, well, normal, as if everything was perfectly fine between us. He didn't seem angry with me in the slightest. So I naturally assumed I was just being paranoid. Oh God, I need a cigarette."

She looked at Roxy expectantly and Roxy shook her head.

"Oh Roxy, imagine if Wade really did see us! What if he's playing it cool? How mortifying! What am I going to do?"

"Maya, I don't think we need to panic just yet. But I think it might be time for you to have a serious conversation with your husband. You need to find out once and for all if he really did come to the island early that morning and, more importantly, why."

"But what if he didn't see us? What if he was here for some other reason?"

Her eyes looked hopeful and Roxy frowned.

"Somehow I think it would be better for everyone if your husband was quietly spying on you and Luc that morning, not knocking poor Abi over the head and burying her in a ditch."

"He wouldn't do that! He may be a dreadful bore but I honestly can not see him hurting Abi. I just don't see why he would."

Roxy stared hard at Maya. "Come on, you told me yourself he envied this place. I also know he had money troubles. Maybe he figured that Helen would be more likely to hand the island over to him with Abi out of the picture.

He could then turn it into the giant, money spinning resort he wants it to be."

Maya looked appalled. "That's insane! He didn't need Dormay. He told me, only yesterday afternoon, that he was about to come into some cash. There's no way..." She caught herself, stopped, considered this for a moment. "Oh shit."

"Exactly. Where was that cash coming from, suddenly?"

Maya frantically shook her head. "No, no, no! It was something to do with a business deal, back on the mainland. He would not kill an old woman for money. It's ridiculous."

She shivered a little and pulled her towel tightly around her body.

Roxy pushed her empty glass aside and stood up.

"Where are you going?" Maya asked, worried, and Roxy wondered whether the young woman was more concerned with hiding her adultery than she was with clearing Wade's name. Either way, there were tough times ahead. Wade was either a cold-blooded killer, or an embittered husband and she had a pretty good idea which one Maya would have preferred.

"Calm down, Maya. I'm just going to phone home."

She left Maya sitting out on the veranda, nibbling on her empty champagne glass.

In fact, Roxy returned to the library for what seemed like the 10th time that day and logged back on and into her email account. It was cheaper than a phone call. Easier too, especially when dealing with her mother. Surprisingly, and much to her relief, neither Lorraine Jones nor Oliver Horowitz had been in touch and she contemplated her next move. She decided not to say anything to her mother about the recent events but knew it was time to get her agent in the loop. She composed an email, giving as abridged a version of the past two days as she could, then clicked 'Send'.

While waiting for a reply, Roxy sat down on the small lounge chair. That's when she spotted the coffee table book on regional myths and legends. Someone must have put it back. Roxy's heart leapt. At last something was going her way! She picked it up carefully, as if it were made of glass, and turned straight to the index. Within seconds she was immersed in a macabre tale of severed heads and hungry crustaceans.

The traditional burial ritual on Dormay was first developed over a thousand years ago, when the islanders were headhunters and the region still practised cannibalism. It was a ritual that preceded the arrival of the Catholic missionaries and one that was so strong, so revered, that even white man's threats of hell and damnation could not shake the locals out of it.

At least four neighbouring islands also adhered to this strict, ceremonial burial process. Helen had described it well: when someone passed away by fate or foul deed, their loved ones smoked the body and then buried them standing vertically in a deep ditch right on the edge of the beach. This was vital. The body had to be close enough to earth, to ground the spirit, but near enough to the sand to encourage crabs to peck away at the protruding head's flesh. This was not seen as ghoulish at all, simply a practical way to clean off the skull before it was removed and taken to the main burial site (preferably on a hilly slope so it could look down on the land around it). The body was also eventually removed and reburied near the skull, but tradition dictated that the head had to go first, to oversee the mourning process and to prepare the body for rest. That's why it sat upright, protruding from the sand—because crabs could do a faster job than the natural decomposition process.

A tiny shiver ran down Roxy's spine and she sat back and thought about this. If truth be told, it wasn't a bad way to be put to rest after death: sitting out, watching the world from hence you came. She wondered whether the locals still adhered to this burial tradition, and who amongst them knew about it? Judging from the look Maurice and Popeye had shared that horrific morning on the beach, she had to conclude that they, at the very least, had some knowledge of this ritual.

But did it really matter? Helen was right, of course, anyone at the resort could easily have picked up this book in the library and got informed. Any one of them could have set Abi's body up to be discovered that way, to throw suspicion, perhaps, upon the locals.

Worse still, it might all have been a terrible fluke. After killing her, they may have thrown her into the nearest ditch, not realising it was not quite deep enough to bury her entire body, head and all. Perhaps the visible head was purely coincidental?

Roxy groaned. She was getting more and more confused by the minute.

"Something wrong my dear?" It was Doc, standing at the doorway with his fisherman's cap on. He looked much improved from his earlier outburst and she noticed he had changed his shirt and given himself a shave.

"No, nothing to worry yourself about."

"But I do worry, very much so."

He glanced behind him cautiously before stepping into the room and taking the seat by the computer. "May I have a word?"

"Of course."

She shut the book and set it aside as inconspicuously as she could.

"I know Helen has asked you to look into all of this, to do a little sleuthing."

"She told you?"

"Not in so many words, but unlike everyone else here, I'm not an imbecile. What I want to know is, my dear, whether you've come any closer to working out who it is? Who killed Abi that is."

Roxy shrugged. "Quite frankly, Doc, everyone's looking guilty to me."

"Really? Even the boring old Zimmermans?"

"Especially the boring old Zimmermans." He looked at her, puzzled. "Think about it: they've been hanging out quite a lot with that boat guy Willie and I know for a fact that Abi had a problem with Willie. She thought he was up to something, she told me so herself."

"What was he up to?"

"I don't know! Abi didn't quite say but those Zimmermans seem a bit on edge to me. I was thinking that was just their personality, being Swiss Germans and all that, but now I'm not so sure."

"And me?"

"Sorry?"

"You said, my dear, and I'm trying not to take it personally, that you suspected us all. So why do you suspect me?"

His expression was deadly serious and, remembering his earlier outburst, she wondered how candid she should be. She launched in.

"To put it bluntly, Doc, you of all people had the greatest means and opportunity."

"The quinine, right?"

"Yes. We don't know if your stash really got stolen from underneath your nose, or whether you used it on poor Abi. You certainly had opportunity—you were sitting next to her at dinner on Tuesday night, next to that glass of gin and tonic, and could easily have slipped the drugs in. You were also the last to see her alive, you took her back to her room, after all. Insisted on it, if I call recall."

He was nodding his head. "Yes, yes, means and opportunity certainly don't bode well for me. But, pray tell, what on earth would my motivation be? Why on earth would I want to kill my dear friend Abigail?"

"Well, I have to admit, your motive is pretty weak, but it is motive nonetheless."

"Go on."

She took a deep breath. "You knew about Abi's plans for the island, didn't you? About handing it back to the people."

He stared at her, clearly hesitating.

"I figured you're such old mates and if she told you about the book, she probably talked to you about this, too."

He slowly nodded his head. "Yes, Abigail did discuss it quietly with me on a few occasions. I tried to talk her out of it, if truth be told. I didn't think it would be very fair on Helen, but it was Abi's choice. Nought to do with me."

"Well, not necessarily. The way I see it, if you knew that Abi was about to hand the island to the people, perhaps you felt that they'd close down the resort, and you'd be out of a home. So you stopped Abi before she could sign away the lease."

He scooped his cap off, contemplating this.

"I'm sorry but I think it's all a tad tenuous," he said at last. "Being out of a home and, shock, horror, moving back to Melbourne is hardly worth killing for my dear. I have plenty of savings believe me. It's not like I'll be out on the streets. And there's another thing you're forgetting."

"Oh?"

"Even if I did kill Abi so Helen could keep Dormay, I couldn't be sure Helen would even let me stay on. Even Maya the moron can see we're not the best of friends. Half the time I suspect Helen can't stand the sight of me. I don't know why..."

He stopped, his eyes misting over. "So it's all a bit, well, unlikely, don't you think?"

"Yes, I do!" Roxy said, almost relieved.

She liked this old guy as much as she liked Helen and took no pleasure in accusing him of murder. "Which is why you're not actually top of my list."

He exhaled dramatically. "That's a relief."

He coughed, shifted in his seat. "So, what about Helen? What do you think about Helen?"

"I don't know what to think. She's coming out looking worst of all."

He scrunched his cap up in his hands and then unscrunched it again.

"I don't see why she should."

"Come on, Doc—means, motive, opportunity. She had them all, in spades."

"But you must know she wouldn't do this! Surely you can see that?"

His eyes searched hers, imploringly, and she held her hands up defensively.

"Hey, I'm trying to point the finger elsewhere, really I am, but even you've got to agree it doesn't look good for her."

He shook his head. "No, no I don't have to agree with that at all. Not when there's sneaky bastards like Wade and the Zimmermans about. That's where you should be looking. Believe you me!"

He stood up and she squished her lips a little to one side.

"What's going on, Doc? Is there something you're not telling me?"

He shook his head emphatically. "No, no, I just feel sorry for Helen, that's all. She has so much on her plate and then to have everyone think she did this, it's too much to bear." He pulled the cap back onto his head. "I'm going down to the jetty if anyone needs me."

Roxy watched him leave and wondered at his ferocity. He was the first to admit he didn't have the best relationship with Helen yet he seemed ready to go into battle for her. His loyalty to Abi clearly knew no bounds. Roxy sighed, trying to shake him off, then returned to the computer to find a message from Oliver in her inbox. She opened it with a smile.

"Well what a surprise!" he had written. "You continue to amaze me Roxanne Parker! You should get your own TV show—Murder She Ghostwrote—it'd be a huge hit. I hope you're keeping your nose well out of it but I know that's a physical impossibility for you so all I'll say is: TAKE CARE! I gather the book deal's now off? It's not your fault so you're within your rights to ask for a kill-fee. Damn, there's a pun if ever I heard one! Anyway, let me know how it all goes and when you're getting back. I can collect you from the airport. Olie."

Roxy jotted him a quick reply, explaining that at this point they were all still detainees at Dormay and she promised to get in touch when she had more news. She was just about to send it when something occurred to her. She sat back in her chair and tried to think. It was there, just out of reach, a distant memory right on the recesses of her brain.

Just as Abi had loved this island and the ocean surrounding it, Roxy Parker's passion, as morbid as it sounds, had always been true crime. From her early days at university she had got into the habit of cutting out news clippings of famous murders, kidnappings and other acts of violence that caught her eye, and pasted them in a series of scrap books she dubbed her Crime Catalogue. Oliver Horowitz preferred to label it The Book of Death and teased her mercilessly about the scrapbooks whenever he could. But they had served the writer well on several occasions, and today she had a feeling they would come through again. She vaguely recalled a news story about quinine from at least a decade ago that had her intrigued enough to snip it out and paste it in. She couldn't quite remember what it was about, but she had a feeling it might be important. If Oliver could find it amongst her collection at her home, she might just have the information she needed.

She pulled the keyboard closer and continued to type: *"Can you do me a HUGE favour? As fast as possible? Use the spare key I gave you and break into my apartment. I've got some scrapbooks I need you to look through..."*

CHAPTER 15

The word was out. That night in the dining room, everyone was buzzing with the news that Abigail had been poisoned with quinine. Wade, who'd returned to Dormay in time for dinner and with a very foul mood in tow, was telling the group he'd never heard anything so preposterous.

"It's all a bit bloody far-fetched if you ask me," he was thundering. "Abi was getting on a bit, not as bright as she used to be, she obviously just took more quinine than she meant to. Ten grams is hardly enough to start stressing about."

"It's enough to make you very sick, Wade," said the doctor.

"Lucky for the murderer, then, because she wasn't her usual sprightly self. Can't help thinking if she was, she'd have given him a right bollocking!"

Roxy had skipped cocktails, eager to finish off transcribing Abi's interviews and check her emails before dinner, and was running late so slipped into her seat beside Doc as discreetly as she could and waved the wine waiter away. She needed to give her liver a night off. She noticed that Helen had not yet materialised but everyone else was there, including the Zimmermans. Abi's chair at the head of the table sat empty again.

"We can't even be sure she had any quinine in her body," continued Wade and Doc looked outraged.

"Look, here, Wade," he said. "You can't dispute the pathologist's report—"

"Pathologist my arse! That means a half-literate local bloke in a shed out the back of the bloody hospital. You can't put any credence in what the 'pathologist' said. Nope, Davara's got it wrong. Again."

"Chief Davara knows what he's talking about," Joshua said, rising to his Uncle's defence. "He's not an idiot, man, he's good at what he does."

Wade appraised the young man and was about to renew his tirade when he thought better of it. He shrugged and let it go as Maurice and Popeye appeared with plates of steamed mussels.

They ate in silence for a while and Roxy darted a glance towards Luc and Maya. They were clearly avoiding each other's eyes again, Luc preoccupied with his meal, Maya with getting her glass filled and refilled. She was dressed more demurely tonight, her fitted black dress revealing little more than a black choker around her throat and tanned arms below cupped sleeves. Roxy wondered if she was playing the Good Wife now and whether if it was all too late.

Maya caught Roxy's eye and shook her head very slightly, as if warning her off. When Wade turned to look at her, she smiled sweetly and said, "So, Roxy, where were you at cocktails? You're usually up for a glass of vino before dinner."

"I was just doing a bit of work. I also needed to check my emails."

"Oh? Anything interesting?"

"No, I'm still waiting on something. But I did read some very interesting stuff on-line about quinine."

She paused to sip her water and Maya's eyes lit up.

"Oh yes, Miss Super Sleuth, what did you uncover?"

"Probably nothing you don't already know." She glanced at Doc then. "I was just looking up symptoms of quinine poisoning, that sort of thing."

"And?"

"And it's nasty stuff. In fact, I think it's pretty clear from the way Abi was acting that last night, that she really was suffering quinine toxicity."

This line she directed at Wade and he snorted, unimpressed.

"How do you mean?" asked Luc.

"According to my sources, quinine toxicity at the very least causes sweating and nausea."

"Abi was sweating like a pig that night! Do you remember?" Maya said.

"Everyone sweats here," retorted Wade. "It's the bloody tropics!"

Roxy ignored him and continued. "It can also cause severe vomiting, gastro problems, abdominal pain and even weird things like tinnitus—you know, hearing problems—and," she paused for effect, "it can also cause blindness."

"Blindness?" This was Doc now.

"Yes, according to the health website I looked up, you can temporarily lose your sight."

"Oh. My. God!" squealed Maya. "Do you remember? Abi said something weird about all the lights going out? I just thought she'd lost her marbles."

"Yes," said Roxy. "I remember that very well. She looked like she couldn't focus on any of us. Perhaps the quinine had blinded her."

Doc began shaking his head. "Oh dear, oh dear, I should have known. I should have done my research. She might be alive today."

"Don't you blame yourself, Doc!" said Maya. "You weren't to know. It's hardly your fault."

"It's nobody's blasted fault," barked Wade. "Davara will find that out soon enough. It was clearly some crazy man passing by the island. You mark my words, this will all get sorted out and we will go back to the business of living our lives."

"Well, except for Abi of course," said Maya, stroking her smooth black choker, and they all stopped and thought about this for a moment.

"So, what happens to Abi's Retreat now?" Ingrid asked eventually and for a few moments no one said a word.

Roxy wondered exactly who else knew of Abi's meeting with the Lands Commissioner. Had this also become general knowledge?

"I heard that Abi was going to give it back to the locals," Ingrid continued and at least one jaw dropped.

"The locals?!" said Maya, the only person around the table to look even remotely surprised. "How silly. As if!"

"How did you hear that?" asked Doc, ignoring her.

"The village people are all talking about it," Ingrid replied, glaring at him defiantly. "They say she was going to make the will change before she died."

"All gossip and innuendo, isn't that right Doc?" Wade said, frowning hard at the doctor, but he shook his head sadly.

"Sorry, Wade, I really see no point pretending anymore. It is true, yes. Abigail was seriously considering handing the place back to the people. She mentioned it to me on several occasions."

"No way!" squealed Maya, clearly delighting in this bit of gossip.

"That's right—mentioned—but she didn't actually do it, did she?" said Wade, also ignoring his wife. "So none of that matters a squat. The fact is Abi didn't change her will. The place belongs to Helen. It's Helen's decision."

"I'm sorry about Helen, I truly am," Doc continued, "but you also have to consider Abigail's wishes, what she wanted, before she died. Oh dear, it's all so confounding. What do you think, Joshua? You're a local."

They all looked at Joshua who had been surprisingly quiet throughout. He glanced up from his mussels and shrugged.

"I dunno. I mean, yeah, I guess it'd be the right thing to hand it back, but then you gotta feel for Helen, too, eh? This is her home, you know. And she does a good job of running this place. I'd hate to see—"

He stopped, shrugged again and continued eating.

Doc's eyes squinted. "You've changed your tune young man."

Joshua looked up again. "Huh?"

"I thought you'd be firmly in the locals' camp."

"Yeah but Joshua's not really a local, are you, Josh?" said Wade and the young man glared back at him.

"I'm more local than you'll ever be, *Governor*," he spat back.

Wade was unperturbed. "But you're not strictly from Dormay are you? Weren't you born on the mainland, at Beela?"

The penny dropped for Roxy then. "So that's why Helen calls you Beela? I've been wondering about that."

His jaw tightened. "My mum was originally from Beela but I came here as a baby. I've been brought up here and it's my home."

"Well, fair enough sweetie!" said Maya, one hand on her wine glass, the other still stroking her necklace. "Personally I have to be selfish and say that I desperately hope Abi's Retreat remains exactly as it is. No offence, Joshy, but I really can't see the locals running the place. Imagine it! Popeye holding court at the head of the table!"

She giggled at the thought and Doc coughed loudly as the man in question returned to fetch their plates. They all shifted uncomfortably and Joshua glared into his beer. Roxy decided that perhaps it was time to lighten the mood.

"That's an interesting necklace you're wearing, Maya," she said and they all looked towards the black choker around her neck.

"Oh, this?" she said, attempting to peer down at it. "Wade gave it to me, for my birthday last month. Not sure if it's quite *me* to be honest, but, well, Wadey tells me it's precious, so..."

"Precious? It's a bloody collector's item!" Wade retorted.

"It is black coral by the looks of it," said Ingrid. "I assume from this region, Wade?"

"You assume correctly. I got a local guy to knock it up into a necklace. Matching earrings, too."

Maya smiled stiffly. "Mm, very attractive as you can imagine."

"I think it eeze ugly," said Luc now and Wade's eyes darkened. "Why 'ave black coral when you can 'ave pink or purple or even gold? Black it eeze so ugly, non?"

Wade looked livid. "Because it's rare you dickhead."

"So? Eeet is rare. Pff! This does not make it beautiful."

"I think it is very beautiful," snapped Ingrid. "In my country this would fetch thousands of dollars."

"So?" pressed Luc. "Again I say, this does not make eet beautiful. Eet just makes eet expensive. And stupidly so."

Doc, clearly sensing more trouble to come, clapped his hands loudly and announced, "Okay, chappies, here are the mains. Let's eat up and enjoy!"

Once again, they all settled into another stony silence as crispy red emperor and salads were dished out.

As Maurice placed the last plate before him, Doc asked quietly, "Has Helen requested any food this evening?"

Maurice shook his head.

"She will need to eat something. I think fish will be a bit much but perhaps you could rustle up some soup and bread. Get it up to her as soon as possible."

Maurice nodded and returned to the kitchen.

As they ate their mains, Roxy yearned, suddenly, for a very large, very comforting glass of merlot, but held herself back. Instead, she studied the people around her. Unlike the previous evening, everyone was on tenterhooks tonight and it was not surprising. In the space of 24 hours, at least two people at this table had gone from grieving friend to chief suspects in that friend's horrific murder. Another two were wondering whether their illicit affair was about to be blown wide open and a marriage ripped apart, and two more were clearly over this island and its hysterical occupants. Roxy did not doubt for one moment that the Zimmermans would be clear of the place the minute they got the chance.

Only the local staff were getting on quietly with the business of life, performing their jobs more diligently than ever. Yet it seemed to Roxy that they had lost more than anyone else here tonight. Not only had they loved Abi, they had depended on her. Their lives were now up in the air, and yet their feet were still firmly on the ground, serving Abi's guests with dignity and grace. Roxy smiled warmly at Popeye as he refilled her water glass.

How much he must despise us self-centred white intruders, she thought sadly, and yet he offered her his wide, red smile anyway.

Just as they were finishing their mains, Maurice reappeared at the front of the restaurant, a tray of food in his hands.

"Excuse me, Doctor Spinks," he said, and they all turned around to stare at him.

"What is it, Maurice?" asked Doc, a little impatiently.

"Miss Helen, I can not wake her sir. The door... it is locked."

"She must be asleep."

"I bang hard sir. She no open door."

Doc and Joshua caught each other's eyes then and both men stood up abruptly.

"What in the blazes is going on?" demanded Wade but they were halfway out of the dining room by then.

Roxy's jaw dropped along with another penny. She jumped up and quickly followed the men out and through the lobby to the staircase. Joshua had passed Doc and was bounding up the stairs, three at a time, and within seconds had reached Helen's door. He was banging on it loudly.

"Helen! Helen! It's Joshua! Let me in!"

There was nothing but silence at the other end. Doc and Roxy had reached him by now and he turned back to Doc.

"You think she's in trouble, don't you?"

His eyes were frantic, his voice pleading.

Doc nodded solemnly. "We have to get in there."

"I'll get the spare key," Josh said but Doc held him back. "No time, just break it open." Joshua looked doubtful. "Now!"

The younger man stepped back and charged at the door. The lock broke easily and the door swung open to reveal nothing but darkness. Josh grappled for the light switch and Doc rushed to the bed.

Helen was lying face down in her silk pyjamas, the sheets strewn around her, one arm hanging lifelessly over the side. There was the putrid smell of fresh vomit and several large patches of it on the floor.

"Helen!" Doc was saying, patting her hand, then her face. "Can you hear me? Helen!"

She didn't wake up. He placed her in the recovery position on her side, reached for one arm and felt for a pulse. By now the rest of the group had joined Roxy at the door and they all held their breath.

Doc swung around to them. "Joshua, go to my room, get my medical bag."

He pulled a key out of his trouser pocket and threw it at him. "Quickly! Roxy, cold water, a wipe, something."

Roxy dashed into Helen's bathroom to locate a facecloth and flooded it with water. Spotting an empty ice bucket, she grabbed that too and brought them back to Doc. "Is she... alive?" she asked.

He looked at her stricken. "I can't get a pulse."

There were several gasps from the door and Roxy looked back to find wide eyes and pale faces. Next, she surveyed the room. There was a bottle of whisky by the side of Helen's bed and a glass. A small mouthful remained. Doc picked it up, smelt it and winced.

"What the hell's going on?!" yelled Wade from the door and Doc held a hand up to silence him.

"Somebody fetch Popeye's wife. She used to be a nurse."

"I'll do it," Ingrid said firmly, passing Joshua as he ran back in with the doctor's kit.

Doc reached for a hypodermic needle, a syringe and a small vile of clear liquid labelled MIN-I-JET. He filled the syringe with the adrenaline and injected it very slowly into one of her veins. They all held their breaths.

It seemed an interminably long time but of course it was less than a few minutes before Helen's eyes shot open and she gasped, her chest heaving upwards before collapsing again. Audible relief could be heard from behind them.

"Stay with me, Helen," Doc was saying loudly. "Come on, Helen, you can do it."

The woman was groaning now, slipping in and out of consciousness, waking occasionally to vomit into the ice bucket Roxy held for her, then drifting into blackness again. By now, Joshua had ushered the others out and all that remained were Doc, Roxy and the patient.

"Quinine?" Roxy said and Doc nodded.

"Looks like it."

"But who? Why?"

Before he could answer, Popeye's wife, Tara, appeared at the door, a steaming pot in her hands. She was a tiny woman, stooped over a little with tightly curled grey hair and a traditionally tattooed face. She went straight to Helen and began stroking the woman's cheek. She placed the pot to Helen's lips and let a little of the dirty smelling liquid drop into her mouth, before placing it to the side and stroking her cheek again.

Doc took Roxy's hand and lead her outside where the rest of them were now scattered, leaning against the wall or perched on various steps. Most of the staff were there, too, including Popeye, Maurice, Mary, Patricia and a few of the older local children looking alarmed. They all stared at Doc anxiously.

"We need to get Helen to the hospital, she needs some charcoal and fast," he told them all. "It's touch and go."

"We'll use my boat," Wade said and Doc nodded.

"I'll come, too," Joshua added.

"No! That won't help," Doc said firmly then softened his tone a little. "You need to stay here, with the guests. Wade, get your boat started. Maurice, help me carry Helen to the dock. We'll also need Tara for the trip. The rest of you, please, go back downstairs. We need you out of the way and Helen on the mainland as quickly as possible."

They all did as instructed and watched from the lobby as Helen was carried down the stairs, now quite conscious but wailing deliriously, Doc and Tara firmly by her side.

"Dark, so... dark..." she was moaning, her eyes rolling about, her mouth drooping open. They carried her gently out of the hotel and down towards the beach.

Less than 10 minutes later, the guests watched from the main veranda as Wade's boat charged away from Dormay and towards the mainland.

Maya was sobbing again, Luc now at her side, while the Zimmermans simply stood watching silently. Roxy sighed and, spotting Mary standing by the door, called her over.

"I know you're not on duty, but any chance of some coffee? I can help you make it."

"Yes, Miss, I can do it," she said, clearly keen to have a purpose and set about making a plunger full of coffee. Roxy reached behind the counter and pulled out some cups. Maurice soon returned from the dock and helped out while the small group took their seats.

"I do not understand any of this," Ingrid was saying. "Was Helen also poisoned?"

Roxy squished her lips to the side. "Looks like it."

"But why?!"

"Maybe she tried to kill herself," said Luc. "Maybe she was feeling 'ow you say—remorse."

"What for? You don't really think she killed her mother do you?" said Maya.

Joshua, who had been absent from the veranda, appeared at the door then. His face was stony, his eyes cold.

"She didn't try to kill herself," he said firmly. "No way.

Not Helen. It's not her... way." He turned and walked inside.

"But, but that means someone tried to kill her then," said Maya. "That means..." She stopped short, not wanting to say what was on everyone's minds.

Roxy took a cup of coffee from Mary and then followed Joshua into the lobby where he was now standing behind the front desk, staring at the phone. She offered him the coffee but he shook his head, no.

"Are you going to call your Uncle?" she asked.

He nodded this time but didn't move. Just stood staring at the phone.

"I believe you," Roxy said and he looked around at her.

"What?"

"I don't think Helen tried to kill herself either."

"But who would want to kill her? It's so insane. Everything's just gone mad. Mad."

Roxy reached over and squeezed his arm. "Call your uncle, then get to bed. There's nothing more you can do tonight. Maybe things will be a lot better in the morning."

He looked at her dumbfounded. "You're kidding, right?"

Roxy didn't know what more she could say to him. Yes, perhaps someone really did just try to take out Helen the way they tried to take out her mother. Perhaps it was just as well, then, that she was off Dormay and safe from further harm. But she couldn't say any of this to the distraught man standing, staring forlornly at the phone. As far as he was concerned his world had just come crashing down around him. There was no silver lining. Everything was bleak.

Roxy eventually left him and returned to the veranda but everyone had dispersed and all that remained were some dirty coffee cups and the glistening black of the ocean beyond. She stepped out towards it, holding onto the railing as the wind gusted up and whipped across her face. She scanned the horizon, desperate to spot a flying fish. Helen had promised it would bring her good luck. Right now, Roxy figured, they could all do with some.

CHAPTER 16

Chief Davara was not a happy man. His usually smiling eyes and soft demeanour had been replaced by a deep frown and clear exasperation, and while he was speaking in the local language, it wasn't hard to tell he was berating his nephew in no uncertain terms. Joshua was staring at the floor, not meeting his eyes. The young writer quietly slipped past them and into the dining room. The Zimmermans were just finishing off their breakfast.

"Come, join us," Ingrid said, leaving no room for refusal and Roxy did so, asking Mary for an iced latte at the same time.

It was stinking hot, the hottest day so far, and, despite her lethargy, she didn't think she could handle a hot beverage today. She glanced out at the beach and noticed that the sand looked scalding. The waves were barely ripples and there wasn't a breeze to be found. She longed for the promised rain. Hell, she'd even put up with a mini-cyclone, she thought. Anything to break the heat.

"You guys aren't diving again this morning," Roxy said.

"How can we dive at a time like this?" Ingrid replied, brushing a crumb from her perfectly ironed Polo shirt.

Despite the sporty clothes, the Zimmermans were both adorned with an array of gold jewellery including thick gold necklaces and bracelets. Roxy noticed Ingrid had what looked like a large ruby on one finger and was twisting this over and over as she studied Roxy's face. Bernard's watch, also glittering gold, looked very expensive, like a Rolex. He leant forward.

"What is going on out there?"

"Chief Davara is giving Joshua a bit of a spray," Roxy said. They stared at her blankly. "Basically, he's very angry."

Bernard looked alarmed. "But why is he so angry?"

"Dunno. Probably because he almost got himself another corpse last night. Speaking of which, does anyone know how Helen's doing?"

Ingrid was nodding. "Yes, she will be fine. Doctor Spinks called Joshua this morning and says he will be back with Wade later. This was a scary night, no?"

"Yes, very scary, especially for Helen."

"Tell us, what do you think is going on here?" said Bernard who was proving to be uncharacteristically chatty this morning. "Has this killer tried again?"

"I really don't know. I guess you should ask Chief Davara that."

Mary, looking worn out and worried, placed the iced coffee in front of Roxy and enquired about breakfast.

"I'll just grab myself some fruit, thanks, Mary."

The heat had stolen Roxy's normally healthy appetite and she wondered what Maya ate on days like these. Alfalfa sprouts?

"So, when this is all over will you be heading straight back home? It's Geneva isn't it?"

"Yes we will," said Ingrid, hooking into some ham and eggs. "We have a business to run. We were due to leave today so if we have to stay any longer things will get very difficult."

"You've got a shop, right? You sell jewellery?"

Ingrid's eyebrows rose sharply. "We design jewellery."

She dropped her fork and thrust her ring towards Roxy to admire. "It is much more than a shop."

"That's beautiful handiwork," Roxy agreed. "And it's a real ruby?"

Ingrid's eyebrows arched even higher. "Of course it is real. I only wear the best. There are several tests you can do to prove this."

"Oh? Can it scratch glass like diamond?"

The jeweller looked horrified. "We do not even do this silly test with diamonds. This can damage the jewel and lower its value. No, there are special tests for rubies, but most importantly—" she took the ring off and showed Roxy where it poked through at the back of the gold setting—"be careful of rubies that are placed in closed back settings. This often means they are glass. Also, glass rubies may have, how you say, bubbles? And scratches, that sort of thing. The ruby, the genuine ruby, will be perfect. Just the way I like it."

"You really know your stuff."

She noticed that Bernard was frowning. He had clearly had enough of this trivial conversation and was pushing his plate aside. He said something in German to his wife and they both stood up. They were good at doing things in unison. Like robots, thought Roxy.

"Time for us to go," he said and they nodded at Roxy and left the dining room, not by the main door, she noticed, but via the stairs leading down to the patio, bickering as they went.

After finishing breakfast, Roxy wandered through the lobby and out to the side veranda where Chief Davara was looking over some of his notes with Inspector Sikani. Davara glanced up when he saw Roxy and offered her a chair while Sikani left them to it.

"So now we have two quinine poisonings and still no suspect," the Chief said, his fingers placed together at his lips.

His brow was beaded with sweat but he appeared not to notice.

"Oh, so Helen hasn't been able to tell you what happened to her?" Roxy asked, surprised. "Is she still out of it?"

"No, no, she is quite lucid. But she is refusing to speak to me."

"Really? Why?"

He twiddled his fingers together and watched her for a moment.

"Perhaps you can tell me this, Miss Parker."

Roxy blinked several times. "Me? What have I got to do with it?"

"Miss Lilton will not talk to me, she will not talk to anyone but you."

"Me?" She repeated. "That's odd. Did she say why?"

"No, Miss Parker, she did not."

"So we still don't know if someone tried to kill her or if this was a suicide attempt?"

He shook his head. "My men found six discarded quinine packets on the terrace below Helen's window this morning. She either threw them out there herself last night, before she collapsed, or somebody else did. We will be testing them for fingerprints later. We have also taken the liquor out of her room and the glass for testing."

He was clearly on the ball this time but she knew as well as he did that the answers rested with Helen, and she was not speaking. At least not to him. Roxy wondered why. The Chief was also thinking along these lines.

"I am not stupid, Miss Parker. I know very well that Miss Lilton thinks I am not up to the job of investigating her mother's death. Perhaps she feels she can not trust me. But it is imperative that I am kept in the loop. This is a murder investigation. This is no time for fun and games. It looks very much to me like somebody on this island just tried to kill Miss Lilton the way they tried to kill her mother."

He took a handkerchief from his pocket and patted it against his forehead.

"I don't know who she is protecting or why, but I have had enough of the secrets and I have had enough of being patronised. It is my investigation. If somebody has tried to kill Miss Lilton, they may be the same person who killed her mother. I need to know."

"I understand that, Chief Davara. But I honestly don't know what happened to Helen and I would tell you if I did."

He stared at her again for a few minutes and then, seemingly placated, said, "When Miss Lilton does return to Dormay she will no doubt speak with you. I will expect a full report from you after that. Do you understand?"

"Yes, of course. When is she coming back?"

"I am not sure. Doctor Spinks does not want her to leave the hospital for a few days but I believe she is much better so..."

"Should I go over there, to the Beela hospital and speak with her?"

He considered this. "No, no, I would like you to stay here, plis, for now."

She nodded. "Listen, Chief Davara, I have no reason to doubt your credentials. I am only poking about because Helen is paying me to do so and, to be quite honest, it's better than sitting around twiddling my thumbs."

"Island resorts are not your thing, Miss Parker?"

There was a hint of his original good-humour sneaking through.

"No, not really. As you know, I thought I'd be working on Abi's book. It's not really my style to sit around on beaches and drink cocktails all day, although I notice some people manage it beautifully."

"Yes, they do. So tell me, plis, what have you been doing with your time? What have you uncovered?"

Roxy hesitated. It's not that she didn't want to work with the local police, it's just that she was hesitant to start pointing the finger every which way, especially after last night's incident.

The expression on his face indicated that he wasn't about to be put off easily, so she said, "Putting last night aside, for a moment, I've been thinking about Abi's death and wondering who had means, motive and opportunity. And, well, there are quite a few suspects."

"Such as?"

"For starters, there's that new groundsman, Willie, who also works the boats."

"What about him?"

"Not sure yet. All I know is Abi was suspicious of him. I overheard her tell Joshua that she thought he was up to no good. Perhaps you could ask Josh about him."

The Chief scratched his chin. "You think he had something to do with Mrs Lilton's death?"

"Maybe."

"That is where I think you are wrong. Willie Yamu has an alibi."

She groaned.

"Sorry to disappoint you, Miss Parker, but we know that Mrs Lilton was last seen by Mary at 6.15am so must have been killed some time between about 6.20 and about 7.15—according to the coroner's report. Well, I am sorry but Willie was diving with the Zimmermans at that exact time on Wednesday."

"Or so they tell you," she said and he looked at her quizzically.

"You have reason to believe the Zimmermans would lie to me?"

She thought about this. "Not really, I'm clutching at straws."

She couldn't help feeling disappointed. It would have been neat and tidy to pin this on the new worker, the same guy Abi clearly did not trust. She felt like she had landed back at square one. The Chief sensed her disappointment.

"I am afraid this is not as simple as we would like. Did you know, all the locals have an alibi for that morning, except Maurice who was fishing? The rest of them shared breakfast together at the main fireplace at the village. Of course Mary was at the hotel dining room, preparing breakfast then."

"So, she could have followed Abi down to the track and been back at her post any time between 6.15 and when I walked in at 7am. Or Maurice could have put his fishing line down and dashed across the length of main beach and done it."

"Yes, this is true."

He did not seem convinced and Roxy wasn't betting on it either. For starters, neither had a motive. In fact none of the locals did, it was in all their interest to keep Abi alive so she could sign Dormay over to them, not kill her before she had the chance.

"What I don't get is, why didn't anyone spot Abi's body at the beach before I did? Both Maurice and Popeye were at the hotel at the time, surely they must have passed her body to get there?"

"No, no I have checked this, too, you see. Maurice passed down the track earlier than Abi and was fishing when it happened. He went straight from the beach to the hotel kitchen with his catch. He did not return to the village in between. Popeye came to the hotel via the lookout track as he had stopped up there to check the pig traps. He does this twice a week. Unfortunately for Mrs Lilton, it seems no one used the village track between 6.20 and 7.15. The crucial time."

"Okay, so what about Joshua and Helen? What's their alibi?"

"I have their statements but they also have no substantial alibi. They were both alone during that crucial hour. Miss Lilton tells me she was asleep in bed, Joshua was doing some work around the hotel and managing the front desk."

"So we know for a fact that he was up and about." She took a deep breath. "Do you think your nephew could do such a thing?"

Davara shrugged. "I know this is why Helen is concerned. She thinks I will protect my kin. But to be honest, Miss Parker, I do not really know my nephew very well at all. His mother, Theresa, my sister, she was a good woman but very naïve. She got pregnant to a very bad man while she was working as a *haus girl*, and Abi heard of this and rescued her. Brought her out here to Dormay to work when Joshua was just a baby. I did not see much of Theresa or Joshua after that. He... he is mixed race, you know this?"

"Yes, it's pretty obvious."

"Well, what you may not know is that it is hard for these people because they do not really know where they belong. Some want to stay in the village, some want to live the life of a white man."

"Joshua wanted the white man's life?"

"Yes he did. This is his choice. I had no problem with this, but it would have been good to see more of him. We tried, my wife and I, to get him to come back to Beela, for traditional ceremonies, birthdays, this sort of thing. But he was not too keen. He always said he was too busy at Dormay."

Davara's eyes were cloaked in sadness and his voice was barely a whisper.

"This is his choice," he said again, as though trying to convince himself. "We must respect this."

Then, he shook himself out of it and tapped at his pad. "Okay, Inspector Morse, we still have not talked about Mr Bermont and Mrs Thomas."

He paused and Roxy saw this as her chance to redeem herself.

"I think I know what they were up to at that hour," she said.

"I, too, know about their overnight rendezvous, Miss Parker."

She stared at him surprised. "So the cat's out of the bag? If you know, does that mean Wade knows?"

"I have not spoken with Mr Thomas about his wife's affair. It is not my business to do this, unless of course it impacts the investigation."

"But you have spoken to him about his early visit to the jetty the morning Abi died?"

"He refutes the whole thing. Says it was not him, not his boat. He insists Maurice has got it wrong. In fact, he goes so far as to say that Maurice is framing him."

"Oh that's stretching it." She considered this for a moment. "So if Wade wasn't over here peeking on Maya and Luc—and I'm not saying I believe his story for one second—then Wade can't alibi them and they can't alibi him?"

"No, no. At this point, Maya and Luc have no substantial alibi. They tell me they were together overnight but they can not accurately account for their time between 6.20 and 7.15 on the morning in question."

Roxy thought about this. He was right of course. She had heard Maya return to her bedroom just before 6.30am but couldn't swear on a stack of Bibles that the woman had stayed there. After all, Maya could easily have snuck back out while Roxy was in the shower. As for Luc? According to Maya he'd taken off in search of Wade's boat, so he was up at that hour. As far as she could tell, this left them both open to suspicion.

What if Abi had taken a different route that morning and had spotted Maya leaving Luc's bungalow? What if she had chastised one or even both of them, and they had killed her in a rage? Then buried her body on the other side of the hotel, as far from Luc's bungalow as they could manage, to divert suspicion from themselves?

She shook her head a little irritably, releasing a trickle of sweat. It was such a stretch. The lovebirds already suspected Wade was lurking around. Would they really risk running into him—or anyone for that matter—with a corpse? Besides, everyone knew the staff and the Zimmermans were early risers. Only a madman or a fool would risk it. For all their foibles, Roxy doubted Maya or Luc fell into either of those categories. She suspected she was making it all a little more complicated than it needed to be. She brushed her arm across her brow and pushed her sweaty fringe away.

"So that leaves Doc. Don't tell me: he was also up and

about but no one saw him and no one can prove he didn't do it?"

The Chief smiled. "Close. He was awake but he was still in his room, getting ready for breakfast when Joshua came and banged on his door, telling him about Mrs Lilton. He then went straight to the beach to check for a pulse."

"That's when I saw him." She groaned. "So many suspects, so few alibis."

She could feel the sweat sneaking through her cotton dress now and stood up abruptly and walked across to the railing hoping to catch a passing breeze from there. It was dead still and the temperature felt like it was soaring by the minute. Just then she heard an engine in the distance and glanced across at Davara.

"That will be Doctor Spinks and Mr Thomas now," he said.

Less than ten minutes later, Wade came trudging up the front steps of the hotel, looking weary to the bone. His jacket was over one shoulder and his shirt was damp with sweat. He collapsed into a chair and reached for a refreshments menu, waving it at his face for a futile breeze.

Davara asked, "Is Doc with you?"

He waved one hand back towards the jetty. "Yeah, he's still down at the jetty, God knows why."

He turned to Roxy. "Everyone hunky dory back here? How's Maya?"

"We're all fine," she told him. "You look half dead."

He sighed, stroking the grey stubble on his cheeks. "Not as bad as poor Helen. She's had quite a night of it."

"And she'll be okay?"

"As far as we can tell. It was a bloody awful ride across, though. I don't think I'll ever get the stink of spew out of the galley. She threw up the whole way. It's probably what saved her."

"Did she tell you anything?" asked the Chief, sitting forward and Wade shook his head.

"Nope, she was still pretty out of it when I was with her

and Doc reckons she won't talk to him." He glanced at Roxy. "You're the only one she'll speak with. God knows why."

"So I hear. When is she returning?"

"Promised I'd fetch her later this arvo. She's keen to get home."

"That's quick."

"Too bloody quick but, well, she wants to get back to Dormay, to her guests. And to you."

Both men stared hard at Roxy as though she held all the answers and she felt an enormous burden pushing down on her now sunburned shoulders. She needed to get away.

"I might go and see how Doc's doing," Roxy said, turning back to the Chief. "If that's okay with you?"

He nodded. "Plis, I think he could do with a friend right now. Just remember what I told you, Miss Parker. No secrets, okay?"

She promised then stepped back inside the hotel to fetch some softdrinks before heading for the jetty.

A seagull heralded Roxy's arrival, screeching maniacally as she stepped out onto the dock. There was a very gentle breeze down here and she welcomed it as it slithered through her clothes and down her sweaty limbs. She stared at Wade's motor boat, a slick looking machine painted white with a thick red stripe down the side and the name *Gone Fishin'* scribbled across it.

How original, she thought, squinting into the sun, trying to see a sign of life. A slight movement caught her eye further along the peer and she looked to where the yacht, the *Helena*, was secured. Doc was leaning out across the stern, his fisherman's cap in place, his eyes peering out at the water, and she stopped and watched him for a moment. He seemed younger from this angle, and faster on his feet as he turned and started darting up and down the deck, checking the mainsail and the jib, and assembling ropes. He looked like he was about to release the lines and take her out for a sail. But hadn't he told her he was too old now for all that? Abi's words came flooding back to her:

'You can't tie a good sailor down. Well, not while they can still hoist a sail.'

That's when the blinkers finally came off and Roxy saw Doctor Spinks for who he really was. Fergus Spinks was not just any old friend of Abi's. He was the roguish sailor who stole her heart away. And she gasped at the revelation, and the fact that she had not seen it earlier.

Doc turned and spotted her, then waved one hand, indicating that she should join him, so she did, letting him assist her up across the railing and onto the deck. It was a small vessel, a 25-footer, with a secured cabin and plush cushioning for guests to enjoy leisurely sails. She handed him a bottle.

"Welcome aboard the *Helena*," Doc said, guiding her to the bow where they both sat, their legs dangling over the side, sipping their drinks.

"She's a beauty," Roxy said and he looked up at the mast and across the stern.

"Yes, a true gem. She might be small, but she handles like a pro. With the spinnaker up she really flies."

"She's yours isn't she?"

"Yes, I've had her for a good long while now."

"Are you taking her out?"

"Oh no, just checking everything's in shape. I just like to fossick about. It takes me back. To the good ole days."

Roxy took a sip of her drink and asked, "So how are you Doc, are you okay?"

He brushed the stubble that was now carpeting his face, and she noticed his shirt—the same shirt he'd been wearing since the previous dinner—was stained with the remains of the night.

"I'll be fine, my dear. Just weary is all."

She took a deep breath. "And how's your daughter? Helen?"

He was just taking a sip of his Coke when she said it and he nearly choked, coughing and spluttering so Roxy slapped him a few times on the back. Eventually, he put his bottle aside and stared across at her, shaking his head.

"Too clever by far," he said softly. "How long have you known?"

"I only just worked it out, to be honest."

"How?"

"I saw you standing there and it reminded me of something Abi had said about yachties and the one who stole her heart away. I know you've always liked sailing, Doc, so I finally put the timeline together. You've known Abi 30-plus years—about the age of Helen. I wondered exactly where you met. You never said. I figured it was unlikely you met in Australia—you're from Melbourne, she's from Cairns, it doesn't get much further apart than that. So why not Dormay? I also figured Abi would be unlikely to let any old bloke come live at the resort, take up a precious room for nothing. I figured you had to be more than an old mate. Then of course, there's the boat's name, the *Helena*. It's pretty obvious. You named her after your daughter."

He sighed and returned his eyes to the water that was lapping up against the hull. "Yes, you're right. I was more than an old mate to Abi. Much, much more. I was a bit of a lad back then, though. Had just started my medical practise, extremely stressful stuff, so I would spend my downtime sailing up and down the Australian coast. Then, one time, I made my first trip into international waters, sailed right around these parts and eventually anchored at Dormay. That's when I met Abigail. She was just setting the resort up, it was pretty basic back then I can tell you, but it was still beautiful and she... well, she was magnificent!" His eyes lit up. "Oh I wish you could have known Abigail in her heyday! She was quite the woman I can tell you. Gregarious, vivacious, breathtakingly beautiful. The fireworks were instant. For both of us." He smiled. "See, I told you my story was long and slightly scandalous."

"So why didn't you stay? Make an honest woman of Abi?"

"I was far too restless and too damn selfish for that I'm afraid. Abi understood—I mean, she wasn't happy, couldn't speak to me for years, and rightly so—but she understood, you see, that's the thing that saved us."

A gull flew across the stern and he turned to watch it for a few moments.

"We eventually got back in touch and then, after my heart diagnosis, I begged Abi to let me live out my final years here, closer to her and Helen. She wasn't having it at first but I talked her round."

He took another small, tentative sip of his Coke.

"You know, Roxanne, I didn't set out to be a bad father. It's not something you plan to be. I had made a few return voyages to see Helen over the years, but she never really took to me. More intuitive than her mother, that one."

"Does she know that you're her father?"

"No, that probably didn't help. Abi swore me to secrecy you see." He sighed again. "Too many blasted secrets on this island! It's what's got us all into trouble. It's the reason Abi's not with us today. It's probably the reason Helen nearly died last night."

"So how is Helen? Really?"

"Exhausted, drained, but she'll survive. In fact she's in pretty good shape considering what she's just been through."

"And what is that exactly?" asked Roxy. "It was definitely quinine, again?"

He nodded.

"Do you think she was poisoned or did she do this to herself?"

"I honestly can not say for sure. I suspect the latter mainly because she won't say a word. Just keeps shaking her head, won't meet my eyes. It's as though she's... embarrassed or something. It's truly tragic. She has nothing to be embarrassed about. If she was trying to forget, well..."

"Forget? Oh not you, too. You don't also think she was trying to kill herself out of guilt? That perhaps she was the one who killed Abi?"

He squinted back at Roxy. "I'd hate to think so, my dear, nothing would make me sadder, but who's to know what to think anymore? Helen, like her mother, has plenty of secrets, I know that, you probably suspect as much. Perhaps she was trying to end it all. Or perhaps she knows who did this to her and is protecting them."

"That's what the Chief suspects."

"He may very well be right. I just don't know. I can't help feeling that it's all my fault, though."

"Why? Because you didn't tell her you were her father?"

"No, no, nothing to do with that." He hesitated. "Well, I guess it is related to that in a way. I... I was trying to protect her, trying to keep her safe. It was foolish of me, I see that now."

"Protect? What do you mean?"

"I realised after the Chief searched my rooms that it was probably Helen who'd taken the quinine. She was the only one who'd come for a consultation recently, to see me about a different matter entirely, but I did leave her on her own for several minutes. Perhaps she spotted the quinine then and pinched it."

"To kill Abi?"

"Yes. No! I don't know. I wasn't sure, and I didn't want the Chief barging in on her, accusing her of that. So I kept it to myself. And now, well, what if she did steal the quinine? What if she used it to kill Abi and then to kill herself out of guilt?"

Roxy considered this. "Has she admitted any of this?"

"No she has not."

"Then maybe she didn't. You're just guessing, right? Maybe, just maybe, somebody else stole it, and tried to kill Helen just like they tried to kill Abi. We've got to find out, we've got to speak to Helen."

"Well it's over to you my dear. She won't speak to me. She seems to think you are the best person to solve this thing and is not interested in speaking with anyone else."

Roxy swallowed hard. "That's insane pressure."

"Perhaps not."

He turned to watch a school of fish dart to and fro under the glassy water.

"I could tell from the start that you're smart, smarter than anyone else around here, although I think we both agree that's not hard. Helen obviously agrees and feels that you're the only one she can trust. Says she hasn't been completely honest with you. Says she needs to set the record straight. Do you know what she means?"

He looked at Roxy keenly and she stared straight back.

"I have a bit of a hunch," she confessed, then raised her eyebrows. "What about you?"

He tapped one finger to the side of his nose. "I have doctor/patient confidentiality. But I will tell you this, Roxanne. I worry about bringing her back so soon. She keeps insisting she's not in any danger. But, as you say, we don't know what's happened..."

Roxy put her hand over his. "You know, Doc, I think we need to go with Helen on this. If she feels she can return to Dormay and she's safe, then I think we need to respect that."

Roxy struggled to her feet, scooping both empty bottles up along the way.

"What are you going to do now?"

"I'm going to check my email, Doc, because I'm waiting on something important, then I'm going to do what I've been wanting to do since I got here. I'm going to take a big walk, right around the island. I could really use some perspective."

"Splendid idea," he said. "It's a very hot day though, even for Dormay, so be sure to take plenty of water. And get Mary to organise a packed lunch for you."

He frowned suddenly. "Are you going to say anything? To Helen, I mean? About me?"

Roxy shook her head. "Not my place to do that. Although I think it'd be nice for you to do it, and soon."

"Really? You don't think it's a little too late for that?"

"Not at all. I think the timing's perfect. With Abi gone, it might help Helen to know she's not completely alone in the world."

He nodded, getting it.

"There is one other thing, though," she said and he looked at her curiously. "You do realise that this puts you firmly back on Abi's suspect list?"

He squinted again. "Oh? Why?"

"Well, I've got to ask myself, Doc: if Helen really is your daughter, how far would you go to protect her legacy?"

She jumped across the railing and back onto the jetty, leaving the old man to ponder this very question as she made the quick walk back to the hotel.

When Roxy logged back into her email account, she didn't know whether to laugh or cry. There was a message from Oliver, the one she'd been impatiently waiting for, a message from her old mate Max—*at last!*—and five from her mother. She cringed at the latter. The news about Abi's death must have finally filtered through to the Aussie press. She sighed heavily and opened Lorraine's first message.

"Oh my dear, we've just heard the most awful news. Am hoping I heard it wrong. Charlie says I must have. Isn't Abigail Linter (sic) the woman you're currently writing for? The 6 o'clock news tells me she's dead! Please tell me I heard it wrong, everything's okay. Love Mum."

The second email had been sent an hour later—no doubt after the 7 o'clock TV news had confirmed the death as suspicious—and Lorraine's tone had grown slightly more melodramatic. By the fourth note she was close to imploding: *"Oh Roxanne, we're so very worried! You must let me know you're okay! Is there a killer lurking about on that island of yours? Are you even alive?! Desperately wanting to hear from you."*

Reluctantly, and fortifying herself for the worst, Roxy clicked open the fifth message but relaxed considerably when she realised it had been written by her step-dad Charlie. He was characteristically calmer.

"Roxy, love, please get in touch with your mother. She's having a minor breakdown. Just wants to know you're okay. Love Charlie."

Roxy sighed again, glad her mother had not thought to track down the island contact number. Imagine the stream of irate phone messages poor Joshua would have to field.

Next, she clicked on Max's message, more curious than concerned.

"Hey, Rox. I hear through the grapevine that you're caught up in the chaos on Dormay. I know you too well to say be careful, so I'll just say I'm thinking of you and looking forward to catching up on your return. Love, always, Max. PS: Sandra dumped me. Surprise, surprise."

An enormous smile swept across Roxy's face and she felt her heart tingle. Perhaps there was a future for her and Max, after all?

"Oh no you don't," she scolded herself aloud. There was no time to think of Max now. She had bigger fish to fry. Roxy did what she hated others doing and sent them all a group reply: *"Hi guys, thanks for all your messages and please don't panic, I'm perfectly fine. The police have detained us here until the case is sorted. I'll give you a call when I get a chance. In the meantime know that I am safe and in good hands. xo Roxy"*

While both Max and Charlie would be cool, she didn't think for one moment that it would placate her mother, but she hoped, at the very least, it would stop the flow of hysterical emails.

Next, she turned her attention to Oliver's message and this one, despite its morbid content, kept her in good cheer.

"You were right," he wrote. *"According to that old article you've got, a 50-year-old woman took 48 x 5 gram tabs of quinine bisulphate back in the 1920s. That's 240 grams, Roxy. No wonder she didn't make it. It also mentioned other cases where the women survived: in 1955, a 31-year-old dissolved 15 grams of quinine in a glass of port. It says:* 'Within minutes her vision was blurred and there was a buzzing in her ears. Vomited repeatedly until she fell asleep.' *The next morning she couldn't see or hear, but pretty much back to normal within a few days. Also, according to the article there's been*

about a hundred quinine-related deaths and hundreds more serious quinine-related adverse medical events since 1969. Many of them, as you thought, by poor wretched women with no other choice. But tell me, what has this got to do with Abi? Isn't she in her 70s?!"

After reading it through twice, Roxy sat back, stunned. She had recalled reading something intriguing about quinine many years before. It had been intriguing enough to bother cutting it out and pasting it into her so-called Book of Death. Now, thanks to Oliver's good hunting skills, she knew why. And it left her both surprised and vindicated. Already she could feel several of the jigsaw pieces clicking into place, but there were still plenty of odd pieces lying about, not making any sense.

She sighed. *It's not over yet, Roxy Parker. Not by a long shot.*

CHAPTER 17

The sun was beating down hard when Roxy stepped out onto main beach and began walking up towards the village track and the place of Abi's demise. Despite the stifling heat and humidity, Roxy needed to return to the scene of the crime, and not just to search the area for more clues. She also needed to take this walk, today, to force herself past that spot if she was ever going to move beyond it metaphorically. When she got to the location, she noticed both pergola plots had been filled in and a bouquet of frangipani was turning brown where it had been placed nearby. She stopped, dropped her backpack to the ground, and bowed her head silently.

As the insects twittered around her, Roxy tried not to remember Abi as she had last seen her here, her head protruding so ghoulishly from the sand. Instead, she tried to recall her throaty laughter, her bright apparel, her larger-than-life smile. Sadly, she couldn't conjure them up. All that remained of Abi, for now, were slack eyes, wiry hair, a silently screaming mouth. She scowled, disappointed, and looked about. But there was nothing to see here anymore. The ground was now trampled—the police had obviously gone over it and over it—and all she could glean from the site was more bad memories. She picked up her backpack and continued on.

The track to the village meandered across sand and soil, with ragged grass, mangrove and coconut trees lining the way. Roxy stopped at one point to stare up at those trees and was mesmerised by the orange splatters that appeared like spilt paint down their sides. And at the top were those green swishing fronds, flying up from time to time, like a skirt let loose in the breeze. Most of the trees seemed to lean into the wind and some were so overloaded with coconuts it was a miracle they didn't topple onto her. She put her head back down and kept walking.

Within 10 minutes Roxy was at the village. She looked around, surprised to find the area devoid of life except for several chickens and a few mangy dogs that sidled up to her, their dull eyes staring, not daring to hope. She reached into her backpack and found her bread roll, pulled a few clumps off and tossed them in their direction. They bolted away, clearly expecting these to be painful missiles, not replenishing food. Slowly they returned to sniff and then gobble up the bread.

She saw a slight movement to the side and swung around to find a small boy sitting on the steps of a hut playing with a banana leaf he'd folded into a kind of boat. He peered at her with a shy smile. She wandered over to him being sure to keep a respectful distance.

"Hello," she said softly.

He smiled more widely, his teeth fluorescent white against thick black lips. She wondered at what age they began spoiling them with *betel nut*.

"Where is everybody?"

He looked confused. She didn't know Pidgin English, but she gave it a try. "Mama? Belong you?"

This seemed to work. He pointed back, inside the hut. Ah, thought Roxy, smart people. They were resting indoors during this hottest time of the hottest day. They were not striding about like mad Aussie women in the midday sun. She thanked him, waved goodbye and returned to the track.

The path lead off from the village inland towards the lookout but Roxy decided to continue walking along the coastline. This time, she found her way to the beach and stuck to sand and rocky edges as best she could. On several occasions, she had to backtrack into the bush when the coastline became too steep or impenetrable, but for the most part this island was beach-bound and within an hour she was at the old boatshed near the airstrip, the one that had suffered through a past cyclone.

She took a good long sip from her water bottle and stared at the old shed, intrigued. It was certainly derelict with an overgrown passionfruit vine almost pulling the structure down in parts, but there were several wooden cartons piled up to one side and hundreds of cigarette butts littering the ground.

Someone had been here recently.

She stepped closer and spotted what looked like a brand new padlock and chain wrapped securely around the front door. She tugged at it to no avail. Why was it locked up, she wondered? Was it to do with health and safety? Spotting a small, dingy window on one side, she dragged some of the cartons to the wall and climbed up to take a look. It was pitch black inside and she could see very little through the cobwebbed window. She could smell though, where it was slightly ajar, and it made her reel back in shock. The room smelt like old fish and hundred-year-old socks. There was something seriously dead inside.

"Can I help you, Missus?" came a deep voice behind her and Roxy swung around, nearly toppling off the cartons in the process.

There was a tall black man standing there, a woollen beanie on his head and a furrow chiselled deep into his brow. Roxy plucked a passionfruit from a nearby vine and climbed down, wiping her hands on her khaki trousers and attempting a harmless smile. But her heart was beating wildly all of a sudden and she could barely feel her legs.

"H-hello," she stammered. "You must be Willie. I'm Roxy, one of the guests. Just er, helping myself to some fruit."

She thrust the passionfruit towards him, her hand shaking. "And, you know, taking a look around."

His scowl deepened further. "There is nothing for you here," he said and she nodded her head vigorously.

"No, no of course not. Just hungry, that's all."

She glanced behind him to the track. "Okay then, I'd better be off."

She indicated the path but he didn't move, just stared at her strangely, and she tried to take deep, calming breaths while Abi's words kept ringing through her head.

'Willie's up to something, Joshy, I can smell it. The man is trouble.'

What if he was more than a rascal or a common thief? What if he was a cold-blooded murderer? And here she was, all alone with him, on the remotest part of a remote island.

With no one to help her.

Willie was very young, much younger than she realised, and had what looked like a safety pin crudely thrust through one ear. His curly black hair was hidden behind his beanie and he had a slight amount of stubble just above his lips—a teenager's attempt to grow a moustache. Where the sleeves had been torn off his cotton work shirt she saw thick, rippled biceps, glistening now with sweat. He moved suddenly, reaching into his pocket and brought something silver out. A switchblade.

She thought her heart would leap out of her chest. He flicked it open and held it up as Roxy's legs almost gave way beneath her. She darted anxious glances behind him, to the road and her escape.

He stepped closer to her. "I cut," he said.

She looked at him, startled. He indicated the passionfruit.

"Oh!" she exhaled loudly, the sweat dripping down her face. "Of course, right, the fruit. Yes, great, that would be...

great."

She handed it over and he stabbed into it and around it, slicing it into two. He handed it back and she tried to smile, sure she was looking more like a crazed nutter than anything.

"Okay, then, thank you," she said and he stepped aside to allow her back onto the path.

She tried not to run down it like a madwoman, tried to maintain a dignified pace, but every cell in her body was urging her to flee. Just in case. She glanced back, noticed that he was following slowly, at a distance, and she tried to take deep, calming breaths. She gradually picked up her pace, not daring to look back now, knowing that if he chose to continue following her, to catch up, hit her over the head and bury her in a ditch somewhere, there would be no one around to stop him.

No one to hear her scream.

The sweat was streaming from Roxy's body and she was panting loudly when she finally reached the open airstrip. A sudden, cool gust of air whipped against her like a splash of cold water and she sighed, thrilled by the cool change. Only then, out there in the open, did she dare to glance back. Willie was now nowhere to be seen. He had clearly stopped following her some time ago. She dropped the passionfruit she had been clinging to, gulped for air and kept walking.

At the small wooden terminal she looked back again. Still no one. She buckled over, breathing heavily, then reached for her water bottle and drank it eagerly, splashing water down her chin and top. Roxy didn't know where Willie had got to, but she wasn't about to stick around and find out. She continued on, back towards the hotel now, her pace slower, her breath calmer, her heartbeat steadier.

Half an hour later, Roxy found herself at the surf beach, Taboo, and she dropped down onto the sand under the fronds of a coconut tree that was leaning out, like a broken beach umbrella. She wasn't far from the hotel now and she was feeling much safer, more relaxed. She was also feeling a little foolish. Willie was probably a perfectly nice teenage boy, and he was probably scratching his head about now, wondering why the loony white woman had dashed off so fast.

She tugged her trousers off and peeled the wet shirt from her back to reveal her swimsuit underneath, then ran across the soft, sizzling sand to the water's edge and into the cooling waves. It wasn't as rough today but her weary limbs made easy flotsam for the tide, and eventually, exhausted but refreshed, she dragged herself out and back up the beach to her shady spot.

That's when she spotted the blue and white resort towel on the sand just a few metres away. She hadn't noticed it before and she looked across the beach then peered out to the horizon. At first she couldn't see a thing. Then she saw it, a tanned body rising up on its surfboard above a mighty wave and pummelling down the other end. Whoever this guy was, he certainly knew how to surf. She watched as he eventually dropped into the water, then climbed back on his board and paddled out to sea again. Roxy polished off the lunch Mary had made her—a cheese and salad roll—as she watched him make one more successful ride into shore. This time, he didn't turn back, simply waded towards the beach, shaking out his curly black hair as he came.

Once on firm sand, Joshua scooped the board up and threw it under one arm like it was a twig, then made his way to his towel. He noticed Roxy then and stopped, looking slightly startled before raising his spare arm to wave.

She waved back, watching him intently. Joshua was a very good-looking man, she hadn't really appreciated that until now. He was a handsome combination of dark, muscular islander and tall, lean expatriate, and she wondered, suddenly, into which world he really belonged. He dropped his board onto the sand, reached for his towel, padded his face with it, then strode across to Roxy and sat down beside her, puffing a little, his eyes blood shot.

"That was quite a ride," she said. "You should be giving

Luc lessons."

"Nah, he can stick to his art. It's more his style. You been here long?"

"Just long enough to see you ride a few tubes." She crinkled up her nose. "Did I get that horribly wrong?"

He laughed. "Yeah, pretty lame."

"Good to see you out from behind that front desk, though. You seem to work around the clock."

"Yeah, well, someone's gotta do it. It doesn't do itself. But, nah, I didn't get a good night's sleep. Needed to clear my head."

"Understandable. Your uncle not happy this morning?"

Joshua shrugged. "Oh he's alright. He'll get over it." He paused. "He thinks we're all hiding something from him. He thinks someone knows something and is not being honest."

"And do they?"

Joshua stared at her. "I dunno. I don't know anything. Do you?"

His eyes searched hers so intensely she was glad she was wearing her dark prescription sunglasses.

"I hear Helen's back this arvo," she said.

He looked away then, out to sea. "Yeah, well, whatever."

"You're not worried? For her safety? That the killer might try again."

He shrugged, shook his head, no.

"Yet you told me earlier that you don't think she tried to kill herself."

"No I don't."

"Then that only leaves one other option."

She was watching him closely but he remained expressionless, just staring out at the missed waves that were crashing into shore.

"Helen did take the quinine. Deliberately. But she wasn't trying to kill herself, was she?"

That caught his attention. Joshua snapped his face around to look at her. His jaw tightened. His eyes darted across hers.

"What do you mean?"

Roxy took a deep breath. She was feeling weary to the core now, from confronting Doc, from running into Willie, from circling the entire island. But she knew she was close to the end and it all needed to come out.

"I know Helen was pregnant, Joshua," she said finally. "I've known it for some time."

Joshua looked as though he'd been slapped across the face. His jaw dropped, his cheeks blushed, he couldn't quite meet her eyes.

She continued on. "It's not rocket science, Joshua. Helen's been nauseous since I got here. Barely touched her food. Tired all the time. At her age, it's always a bit of a giveaway. I also know that she'd gone to see Doc, probably to confirm the pregnancy. Was that what that brown package was all about?"

He looked at her strangely.

"The pharmacy package you got off the pilot when I first arrived? Was it something to do with the pregnancy? A testing kit perhaps?"

He slowly nodded his head but he still wasn't speaking, so she tried one final tack.

"It's yours, isn't it, Joshua? It's your baby."

The young man slumped suddenly, his head falling into his knees and he groaned so deeply he sounded half animal. But, still, he remained silent.

"That night at cocktails, when you were so happy, you said you were so proud," said Roxy. "You toasted life if I recall. You knew you were becoming a dad, didn't you? You were so thrilled."

He turned to look at her for what seemed like hours, clearly trying to decide whether he could trust her, and eventually, he nodded.

"Sure, why not? I don't see why this should be a secret anymore. Why it ever was to be honest. Yep, that's my baby. And I'm proud of it. It's mine. Was..." His eyes darkened. "She made a promise to me that day, man, she promised she'd keep it. But—" he stopped short, turned away again.

"But she broke her promise to you, didn't she? That's why she took the quinine? She dissolved it in some whisky last night when she knew we would all be preoccupied with dinner."

He sniffed, ran a hand through his wet locks. Said nothing again.

"I know all about quinine, Joshua. I've done my research and I know Helen did hers, too. Quinine is a little-known folk remedy for self-induced abortion. I read about it online and I've got clippings about it at home. For the past hundred years dozens of poor women have used it to abort their unwanted foetuses. Admittedly not with a lot of success, but still..." She took another deep breath. "You think she was trying to abort your baby, last night, don't you?"

"What do you think?!" His temper was now rising. "I don't bloody think she was trying to kill herself, she was too self-centred for that."

"You might be right. But what if you're not? What if someone really was trying to kill her. Like Abi?"

He shook his head, the wet curls splashing out around them.

"Nope, nope. Helen was doing exactly what Helen wanted to do. Miss Control Freak. She's always been like that. Can't possibly have an unplanned child. Oh, no, that's not in the rule book, see."

Ah, thought Roxy, one more loose end tied up. "So you were the guys I overheard talking below my window that day? She was telling you she didn't want to keep the baby? But why? Did she think a child would get in the way?"

"It's not a frickin' piece of furniture you can push aside," he hissed. "I thought I'd talked her round. She promised me she'd keep it. Shit, man, that was my baby! She had no right!"

"Hey, settle down Josh, it could all be okay. I didn't see any blood, so it may not have worked. The baby might be perfectly fine."

"After what she did to it? You saw her. Even if it is alive,

God knows what damage she's done. Shit!"

Tears began streaming down the man's face. His big brown eyes were brimming with misery.

"I love Helen, always have. More than she deserves. She rarely gives me the time of day. Just scraps, here and there, to keep me dangling. This is all I wanted from her. It's all I asked for. And she tried to kill that, too."

Roxy looked baffled. "What do you mean 'she tried to kill that too'?"

He looked at her stonily, his eyebrows arched.

"You're not saying Helen killed her mother, too, are you?"

She groaned. Was everyone on this island out to implicate Helen?

He shrugged. "Why not? I wouldn't put it past her. Abortion, murder, same thing."

His bitterness was so palpable, Roxy could almost taste it, and her heart ached for this young man. He needed some help and she knew where he could get it.

"Have you told your uncle any of this?" He shook his head. "Listen, Joshua, you need to speak with him about it. Whether Helen killed Abi or not, you need to tell him about the baby, the attempted abortion."

"It's none of his business."

"You don't know that. We're only assuming at this point that she tried to abort. Did she tell you that was what she was going to do?"

"No, but—"

"But we don't know for sure. Maybe the killer did try to strike twice. Chief Davara needs to look at all the avenues until we know the facts."

Joshua was still shaking his head.

"Not my place to tell him. Helen knows the truth, she can do the honours when she gets back."

He stood up and slung his towel around his neck.

"I've gotta get back. God knows the place will be falling apart by now."

He collected his surfboard and strode swiftly across the sand towards the road, leaving Roxy's head spinning behind him.

Roxy had taken a punt with Joshua. Had only guessed that Helen was pregnant, that she had ingested the quinine in a futile attempt to kill her baby, just as other desperate women had tried to do for almost a century; the same women Oliver had read about in her scrapbook. But her suspicions had all but been confirmed. She glanced at her watch. There was one other person who could tell her for sure, but she wouldn't be back for quite some time.

CHAPTER 18

Helen returned to Dormay sooner than anyone had anticipated. It was not yet 3pm when Roxy discovered her resting out by the patio, leaning back on a cushioned recliner chair. She had a cotton blanket around her body, and dark sunglasses on. Roxy was freshly showered after her gruelling walk, and had only come here to think, her own sunnies and journal in tow. She stared at Helen with surprise.

"When did you get back?"

"Oh, hello Roxy. Um, not long ago. Doc's steaming, of course. Said I should have stayed at the hospital another night." She shuddered. "No thank you. Discharged myself, Wade gave me a lift back."

"May I?"

Roxy indicated the wicker chair beside Helen and she nodded. They both watched the ocean for a few minutes, not speaking.

Eventually, Helen said, "I guess you've figured it all out?"

Roxy nodded. "Well, some of it at least. You're pregnant, right?" Helen nodded again. "So, how much quinine did you take?"

"Just 4 grams," she said.

"That's a lot, Helen. You're only supposed to take about an eighth of that at a time."

"Oh please don't lecture me, Roxy. I've had Doc in one ear, Josh in the other."

She held her hands up. "Okay, okay, no lectures. So, how's your eyesight?"

"Much better, surprisingly. 20/20 vision my doctor tells me." She sighed. "I didn't think I'd ever see again. Who knew four measly grams of quinine could rob you of your eyesight but not your baby?"

She choked back what sounded like a laugh, could easily have been a sob.

"You're very lucky you didn't lose both of them, for good. Not to mention kill yourself in the process. Joshua's devastated, you know, about the baby."

"Well he needn't be. It's still there, let me assure you all."

Her tone was bitter.

"I think he's more hurt that you would even attempt to take away his unborn child. And in such a dangerous way."

"Well it's his own fault, really."

"Joshua's? Why?"

She brushed an auburn strand of hair from her face. "Because I never would have got the idea if it wasn't for him."

"What do you mean?"

Helen turned to look at Roxy. "He didn't tell you?"

"Tell me what?"

"Joshua was the one looking up quinine, not me."

"Sorry? I'm confused."

"I just went to the library that day to investigate land rights. Wade had told me what my mother was up to, how she had been in to the Lands Commission—apparently the Commissioner's one of the many bureaucrats Wade's got firmly in his pocket. Anyway, he came here that first night you arrived, all pent up about it, insisting I stop her. I said he was being ridiculous, that mother wouldn't do that to me. But I have to admit, I was a little worried so, the next day, when you and my mother were doing that afternoon interview, I went to the library to do a bit of research. I just wanted to know what my rights were, that's all."

"That's when you stumbled on the Indian Tonic Water site?"

"Yes, well Joshua had just been on the computer... he had the page open before me. I thought, why is he looking this stuff up? Then I started reading and I noticed a strange link."

"The link to the abortion information?"

"That's right. Oh I know I was foolish, Roxy, I credit myself with more sense than that. But when I read that an extra couple of doses of quinine might induce abortion, I thought, great, get rid of the blasted thing."

"Why? Just because your mother didn't approve?"

"Oh she was fine with the pregnancy, just very worried it was Joshua's. She said it wasn't right."

"Why? That's what I don't get. What was Abi's problem with Joshua?"

She shrugged. "I'll never know. She just said he was 'a better worker than a man'. Whatever the hell that means. Odd, really, because I know she loved him."

That old bell of Roxy's began clanging again in the back of her head but she let it ring away for now. She had other, more pertinent questions to ask.

"Okay, back to the computer then. So you saw some info on how quinine can induce abortion?"

"Yes and to be honest I didn't really think much more of it. But after Josh had failed to get me a pregnancy kit I thought I'd better go and see Doc, confirm it once and for all. That's when I noticed Doc's supply of quinine. So I pinched some while he wasn't looking and, well, after he confirmed the pregnancy, I decided I needed to get rid of it, and fast."

"Whoa! Hang on a minute," Roxy said, holding up one hand. "Can we just go back a few steps. What do you mean Josh didn't get you a pregnancy kit? Didn't Davo, the pilot, fly one in on the day I arrived?"

"No. He was supposed to. The blasted man forgot to pick it up or something."

"But I saw Joshua get a brown parcel off the pilot. There was definitely something in it."

Helen shrugged. "Not my pregnancy kit." She laughed, a fake kind of gurgle. "Ironic really. If he had bought the kit, I might not have gone to see Doc and I might not have pinched the quinine..."

"But why do it that way? Why not go to the mainland hospital for an abortion?"

"In that roach-infested hovel? No thank you. I'd end up with septicemia."

"What about Australia? You could afford to fly to Cairns and see a good doctor there."

"How was I going to get away? When exactly? Davara has us all imprisoned here and there's so much to do now that mother has died. I just wanted this... *thing* out of me. I thought all it would take was a little extra quinine, I'd bleed through and be done with it. If I knew it was quinine that almost killed my mother of course I would have stayed clear of it. Oh, so stupid..." She beat one fist against her forehead. "If only I hadn't seen that blasted website."

Yes indeed, thought Roxy, it all comes back to that website. She had assumed from the start that Helen was the one who first looked up the Indian tonic water website that then linked into the site on quinine and its ability to induce abortion. Now, knowing that it was Joshua, everything was different. Joshua had admitted to using the computer that afternoon, during his break, but he'd said he was playing computer games. Roxy hadn't thought anything of it but, thinking back now, she didn't recall seeing any listings of computer games when she went through the web browser's history for Tuesday. Joshua had clearly been lying about what he was doing on the computer that day.

But why?

"I think we need to get Chief Davara back here and quickly," she said. "And we need to tell him everything."

Helen looked at her worried, but eventually nodded.

"Yes," she said wearily, "enough secrets for now. Let's finish it."

"Before we do, I just have one favour to ask you..."

Ten minutes later, Roxy was positioned behind the front desk of the hotel lobby, the phone at her ear, deep in conversation with Chief Davara. Thanks to Helen, Joshua had been sent on a fake errand to fetch her more of Tara's magical broth so Roxy could be left to have this conversation alone.

Davara had listened carefully to everything she had to say and promised to check a few things before he and his men made their return to the island.

"You have been very, very busy," he said and she could sense his smile from across the crackling line.

"Well, it's kind of like a jigsaw isn't it? The more pieces you get right, the clearer everything becomes. Of course, you'd know that."

"Yes, yes, I do indeed. Okey dokey, Miss Parker, I will check these things out and be back at Dormay before sunset."

"Great. Listen, there's just one final thing I need to ask you."

"Yes?"

"You mentioned yesterday that your sister, Theresa, was working as a *haus girl* when she fell pregnant with Joshua."

"That is correct."

"Can I ask: Do you know who the father was?"

He sighed. "No, not really. Theresa was very stubborn, she would not tell anybody, but of course, we had our suspicions..."

Abi must have had her suspicions, too, Roxy realised now, so she asked one more question of Chief Davara: Who was Theresa working for at the time she fell pregnant? When Chief Davara gave her the answer, the final piece of the jigsaw clicked into place.

CHAPTER 19

The sun was edging its way towards the horizon, taking some of its mighty heat along with it and leaving a flash of vivid orange and red in its wake. It was a startling sunset, even by Dormay standards, but nobody noticed it that night. They were all seated, stiffly, on the main veranda, drinks in hand, waiting for Chief Davara to speak.

It was just past 6pm and he had called an official meeting with all the hotel guests and expatriates. The local staff had been given the night off and several of Davara's men were posted at the door while his deputy Sikani was standing to attention near the bar.

Roxy, who had dressed carefully tonight, in a Thai silk jacket with a diamante broach, and a matching skirt, glanced around the veranda. Wade and Maya were sitting together on one lounge, both also dressed impeccably, but no part of their bodies were touching and Maya was sucking on a cigarette as if her life depended on it.

The Zimmermans were together on another lounge, Ingrid twirling her faux tortoiseshell necklace nervously, Bernard as still as a hawk. Luc and Doc were on stools at the bar, and Joshua was behind it, pouring drinks.

Helen, who was sitting in a plush armchair right at the front beside Roxy, gave Davara the nod and he stepped forward.

"Thank you, people, for all your patience and for coming here tonight," he said softly. "This has been a most intriguing case, it has tested us all, yes, yes?"

There were a few murmurs around the room but nobody was speaking up.

"Now, I have to tell you, I have spent the past hour in a meeting with Roxanne Parker and she has uncovered some very interesting things. I think it would be only right for her to explain. It was her hard work, so I will hand it over to her first."

Wade sat upright, looking confused. "Roxy? What's she got to do with any of this? She's just a blow-in!"

Davara held one hand up to silence him. "Ah yes, but a very smart blow-in, Mr Thomas. Plis, give her your full attention. Miss Parker?"

Roxy stood up and turned to face them. They all stared hard at her, every single one of them, and she felt suddenly nervous as their eyes bore into hers, some looking worried, some confused, some just sad. But she was determined to have it out, and so she began.

"I know it seems a bit weird me standing up here like Hercule Poirot." She flashed Maya a quick smile. "So I thought, first, I'd better explain. The day Abi was killed, Helen came to my room and asked me to help her investigate her mother's death—"

"So that's why you've been poking about!?" said Maya, looking suddenly offended.

"Yes, Maya, but I should add that I have had some experience back at home helping the police with murder enquiries, and I've done quite a bit of investigative reporting in my time."

Wade muttered something beneath his breath and Roxy tried to ignore him. "Anyway, as I was saying, Helen was determined to find out what happened to her mother and wanted as much help as possible."

She glanced across at the police Chief. "Chief Davara was kind enough to let me do a little 'poking' as you say, so I did. And, with a lot of help from the police department this afternoon, I believe we now know who killed Abi."

Luc sat forward then. "Really? So who would do this 'orrendous thing?!"

"Well, Luc, if truth be told, I suspected each of you at various points."

Bernard stood up looking outraged. "Each of us? This is nonsense! How could you suspect Ingrid and myself? We are just tourists, here, diving."

"Sit down Mr Zimmerman," said Davara firmly and he did as instructed, still glaring.

"Since you mention it, Bernard, I'll start with you." Roxy waved one hand out towards the ocean. "You're right, you and your wife have been very busy diving. A little too busy if you ask me. From the moment you got here, you've been out exploring that reef on the other side of the island and we all just assumed you were fanatical divers. What we didn't realise is that you're actually poachers."

There was a gasp from somewhere in the room and Bernard went to stand up again but inspector Sikani was now beside him, one hand pushing him back into his seat. The Chief indicated for Roxy to continue.

"I thought it was odd, that night, Ingrid, when you told me you were wearing fake tortoiseshell. I didn't think that was your style and you said as much a few days later when you showed off your enormous genuine ruby ring. That's when you told me you only wear the best. I started to think, why would you be wearing cheap plastic tortoise shell when the real deal is out there—" she waved her hand again—"for the taking? Same with the black coral which you couldn't help admiring that night on Maya. It got me thinking. What if you weren't just diving quietly on the reef, but helping yourself to its many treasures? I mean, you're a jeweller, how could you resist? Just a few turtles here, a bit of coral there.

It's such a secluded part of the island, there would be no one to see you do it. Plus, who could blame you? There's so much out there, so much for the taking."

"There is more than enough," agreed Ingrid but Bernard barked something in German and she gulped her lips shut. Roxy continued.

"So, you enlisted the help of one of the boatsmen, Willie, to catch the turtles. Abi had already mentioned that some of the crayfish spears were missing. Perhaps he was using them to spear the poor creatures? In any case, Willie was able to store the goods very easily in the old boat shed on the other side of the island, near the airstrip. Nobody ever goes near that anymore. He has it locked up. It's the perfect hiding place. That's probably the reason you went to that side for your picnic the night Abi died. You were working in the shed, preparing the goods for export."

"This is ridiculous!" Bernard tried again but Chief Davara spoke up this time.

"No, Mr Zimmerman, it is quite true. We have already searched the old boatshed, we have found the remains of some recently killed turtles, black coral fragments and a range of other protected species. Most of it, we now know, was taken away by Zodiac very early on the morning of Abi's murder."

"That's right," said Roxy. "Willie obviously loaded it into the Zodiac at the old boatshed which is why the village kid heard the engine out near the airstrip that morning. He then drove the dingy around the island to the main jetty to rendezvous with another boat—the one Maurice saw—to take the goods to the mainland."

Bernard looked ready to burst. "You can not prove we have anything to do with any of this!"

"Yes, yes, we can Mr Zimmerman," said Davara. "We have Willie in our custody now."

The Swiss man's look of indignation faltered and he sat back in his chair. Roxy stepped across to Ingrid.

"There is another way to prove what you've been doing,"

she said, taking her broach off. She stepped across to one of the side tables where a candle was burning, and waved the broach pin across the flame, then pointed it towards Ingrid's neck.

"May I?"

The woman looked appalled, clutched onto her necklace and shook her head no, so Roxy turned back to the wide-eyed congregation.

"Ingrid is wearing the same tortoiseshell necklace she was wearing that first night I arrived, the one she assured Abi was a fake. I'm not convinced, I think it's the real-deal, but there is one way to prove it. If it really is imitation, one made of celluloid, this hot pin should penetrate the plastic surface quite easily. Mind if I try?"

Ingrid continued shaking her head, refusing to let go of her necklace. Bernard was now steaming.

"Really! What has any of this to do with Abigail's murder? That is what I would like to know!"

"That's a very good question, Bernard," Roxy said, pinning her broach back onto her jacket and returning to her post.

"I knew that Abi was onto Willie and I suspect you did too. You were there that first evening when Abi mentioned the missing crayfish spears. She was determined to find out who took them. Perhaps you feared that once she spoke with Willie the game would be up, so you had to stop her."

"No!" yelled Ingrid now. "This is not true. Yes, yes, we take the shells and coral, and why not?!"

Bernard barked something at her but she ignored him this time. "What use is it under the water for a small handful of spoiled celebrities to see? We take it to turn it into masterpieces for people to enjoy. What we design at Zimmerman—these are classics that will last forever. I will admit to this, but we did not hurt Abigail! We are not murderers!"

Roxy nodded. "I agree with you, Ingrid, I don't think you killed anyone. Well, except for a few poor turtles of course."

She looked relieved but Bernard was fuming beside her, shaking his head in disbelief.

"Then who the hell did this?" demanded Wade impatiently. "Can we just forget about this silly poaching business and get to the important bit, please."

"Good idea," said Roxy, "which brings us to you."

His face flushed red and his eyes looked ready to pop. "Me?! What the blazes have I got to do with Abi's death?"

"Oh I don't think you had anything to do with Abi's death," said Roxy and he relaxed considerably. "But I do think you had something to do with the poaching."

It was his turn to stand in outrage and the Chief shot him a warning glare so he sat back down again. Maya looked at him aghast.

"What does she mean, Wade? Tell her she's being silly."

He looked away, crossed his legs, didn't say a thing, so Roxy continued.

"I couldn't work out how the Zimmermans got their stash of illegal goodies out of the country. Abi had already mentioned that first night at cocktails that customs were very strict in this country, so I started to think, who would have the clout to pass it through customs no questions asked?"

Everyone knew the answer to this question and they all turned to stare at Wade.

"I figured the man who approved and built the international airport, boasted about it constantly, has to have at least a little power when it comes to the customs department."

Chief Davara said, "We have also detained your man at Customs, Mr Thomas. He will open up like one of your precious clams. They always do. He will tell us how much you pay him to look the other way. We have already learned that the Swiss customs are less concerned about such matters, especially when they have a signed letter from the regional Governor approving the export."

"Maya also told me you were coming into some money soon," added Roxy. "I wondered if that had anything to do with Abi's death. But no, it was probably your juicy payment from Bernard and Ingrid. Am I right?"

Wade looked defeated then, didn't even bother to dispute the issue and Maya stared at him anxiously.

"Sweetie, tell them they're just being horrid! That it's all complete nonsense!"

"We know it was your boat, Mr Thomas," said Davara. "It was your boat that rendezvoused with the Zodiac at the main jetty the morning Abi died—to take a shipment of coral and shells over to the mainland for export to Switzerland."

"No, no, see, that's where you're wrong," squealed Maya. "Wade was here to spy on me. I could smell him outside my window."

At some point over the past 24 hours she had clearly decided that confessing to adultery was better than having her husband accused of murder.

"No, Maya," said Roxy, "that was just Wade waiting on the jetty for the Zodiac to arrive. The exchange was very quick, from one boat to the next, and he was off. You probably woke up to hear him leaving. What Wade didn't realise was that his strong aftershave would leave a lingering reminder of his presence."

Maya wasn't having any of it. She turned back to her husband.

"This is all so nonsensical. You tell them, darling, it had nothing to do with that. It was all about me!"

He looked at her pitifully. "No my lovely. It had nothing to do with you. Nothing at all." An edge came into his voice. "You really think I would waste my time and sneak over on my boat to catch you and that French bastard in the act? What for? Every man and his bloody dog knows what you two have been up to. Couldn'ta been more obvious if you tried." He snorted. "Frankly, sweetheart, I couldn't give a shit what you and that ponce got up to."

"Excuse me!" began Luc but Wade roared at him.

"Shut it Frenchy!" He turned to Maya. "Actually, I should

thank you, Maya. You gave me plenty of good cause to come over here as often as I liked. Thanks to you, I didn't have to be sneaky about it. I could meet with the Zimmermans at Dormay whenever it pleased me because you never left the bloody place."

She looked at him horrified and then away, tears streaming down her face. She picked up her drink and buried her face into it.

"Yet you were very sneaky the morning of Abi's death, Wade," said Roxy, "and that's what roused my suspicions. I agree, you aren't the kind of man who'd lower himself to spy on his wife. But if you weren't here spying, why come over in the cover of darkness? And then deny it? I figured you were up to something. It didn't take long for Chief Davara to confirm my suspicions." She shrugged at him. "You know, it would have been better if you had pretended to be spying on Maya. I might not have gone down that path."

He growled and looked away again.

Helen coughed. "I'm sorry, Roxy, but I'm still very confused. You've obviously uncovered a nasty racket going on here right underneath my nose, and I have to say I am so grateful to you for that. I know my mother would be, too. But what has any of this to do with her? You don't think they killed her to shut her up?"

"No," said Roxy. "I honestly don't think your mum had quite worked it out yet. She probably would have eventually, but I don't think it was the reason she was killed."

"What then?" asked Doc. "My dear this is all so confounding."

"Well, as I've told you before, Doc, I did suspect you for some time, too."

"Yes, yes, all because of the blasted quinine."

He didn't have the same look of outrage as the others, simply a touch of sadness and a touch of fear, too, and she knew why. She chose her words carefully, not wanting to give too much away.

"I wasn't sure whether your stash really got stolen from

underneath your nose, or whether you used it on poor Abi. You certainly had opportunity—you were sitting next to her at dinner, next to that glass of gin and tonic. And you were the last to see her alive that night. Josh wanted to help her back to her room but you were quite insistent that you go."

Maya was nodding her head furiously, wiping away her tears.

"That's right! He was, too, all very determined to accompany Abi to her room. He could have drugged her in there."

"And you had no alibi for the morning, Doc."

He was shaking his head sadly. "Can I just say, in my defence, that if I was going to drug poor Abigail I'd do it properly. I'm a doctor, after all. I wouldn't fudge it up so badly that I had to follow her to the track and hit her over the head the following morning. Honestly, that's very amateur. Cruel, too. I would have done it properly."

He sniffed, wiped a tear from one eye. "But, yes, you're right as always, Roxanne. I did have the means and opportunity."

"But why?" asked Helen, unconvinced. "Of everyone on this island Doc was my mother's best friend. Why would he do such a thing, Roxy?"

Doc shot Roxy a look of such trepidation that she couldn't answer for a few moments.

Eventually, not wanting to spill old family secrets here tonight, she said simply, "You're right, Helen. No real motive that I can speak of. Which brings us to Maya and Luc."

Luc stood up indignantly and Maya looked scandalised.

"Me!?" she said. "What have I got to do with any of this?! I haven't done anything wrong!"

Wade snorted beside her. "Except cheat on your bloody husband, of course."

"We've discussed that, Wade," she hissed through crooked teeth. "I told you it won't happen again. It was a mistake."

"A few months worth of mistakes by the sound of it," he said, then glared at Roxy. "But she's right. What's Abi's death got to do with Maya for God's sake?"

Roxy leaned against the veranda railing and took a quick sip of her wine.

"A few days ago I overheard a conversation between Helen and Luc in which she warned him that Abi was not happy with his philandering, that she was about to have stern words with his benefactress. It got me thinking. Would Luc or even Maya kill Abi to stop her from revealing their affair?"

"Ridiculous!" cried Luc, and Roxy nodded.

"Yes, that's what I thought, especially when I began to think about it like a French woman might. I just couldn't imagine an elderly French widow being disturbed in the slightest by a younger, good-looking man's affairs in a foreign land. She must, surely, expect that. I mean, I hate to play stereotypes, but, really."

"Exactly!" said Luc, looking pretty pleased with himself. "I told Helen this. I told her, eet will make no difference 'ow many lovers I 'ave."

"Ah yes," said Roxy, not quite letting him off the hook yet, "but it would make a difference if you had a child to one of those lovers. That might make her angry. Supporting a stray lover is one thing, supporting his progeny, quite another."

Wade looked horrified at his wife and she sat forward with a start.

"But... but, I'm not pregnant!" Maya blurted.

"No," said Helen, quietly. "But I am."

For a moment it was as though time stood still and even the crashing waves seemed suddenly subdued. Every eye had turned to stare first at Helen, and then, more tentatively, at Luc. It was Maya who finally broke the spell.

"Luc?! Surely not... You? And Helen?" She looked disgusted by the thought and he shrugged slightly.

"Oui," he said eventually, and no sooner had he said it when a bottle smashed to the ground behind them. Roxy already knew who had dropped that bottle, she had been watching Joshua carefully through this exchange, waiting for the inevitable distress. Helen, too, had been watching and struggled to her feet, trying to get to him but he was holding one arm out, stiffly, like a stop sign.

"Don't you dare!" he said. "Don't you fucking dare come near me."

"Oh Joshua, I'm sorry. I didn't mean to hurt you. I really don't know whose baby it is. Luc and I... we were just a fling. Hell, you and I were just a fling."

"We were more than that!"

"No, Joshua, you wanted more than that. I—"

"You never knew what you wanted!" he spat. "You just did exactly what your mother told you to do and fuck the rest of us. But I knew. I knew that with your mother out of the way you would finally see clearly. For the first time in your life, you would see me for who I am and we, we would have been a couple at last. Dormay would have been ours."

Helen didn't appear to be listening now. She had stopped walking towards him, had wobbled a little and then dropped back down onto her chair. She was shaking her head with a look of horror on her face and he turned pale then, realising what he had done. She glared at him, aghast.

"You?! You... killed... my mother?"

There were more gasps around the room as the group slowly cottoned on. Joshua, too, realised what he had said. He was shaking his head fervently, but no one believed him anymore.

"For what?" Helen was screaming at him. "For me?! For the baby?!"

He pushed his hands through his hair, he looked suddenly sheepish.

"I did it for us!"

Helen had paled too. "But... but you loved Abi so much... How... how could you do that to her?"

"I loved Abi more than she deserved," he spat back, a red glow creeping into his cheeks. "Abi never thought I was good enough, for you, for Dormay. She just worked me to the bone, made me clean up after those bloody lazy local bastards, and then to thank me, was going to hand the place over to them. No questions asked. Dormay, the hotel, the whole lot! Are you serious?"

"But I thought you loved the locals," said Maya now, her blue eyes wide with shock.

He scowled at her. "What's to love? They're fuckin' slackers. They never worked a hard day in their life. I've covered for them since I was a child. My mum before me. She told me, these people don't deserve this place. All they do is put their hand out to Abi and she keeps giving them more and more. Then, as a final stab in my back, she was going to hand them Dormay. Just like that! Not give it to me, not to Helen, but to the people whose ancestors were born here and never did a fuckin' thing with the place. If it had been up to them it would still be a few grass huts and some coconuts. As for me? I helped turn it into what it is today, into a world-class resort. But do I get any thanks for that? No I don't. I'm from Beela, right? So I'm not strictly 'a local'."

He did the quotation marks with his fingers and Roxy wanted to walk across and swipe him one, but she let him continue on.

"I don't get a thing—well, apart from a pathetic payout that doesn't come close to covering it. Guilt money, that's all it was."

He had stepped out from behind the bar and his whole body was shaking. He wasn't really addressing anyone now, just throwing his voice around, his eyes darting desperately from left to right.

"You know what Abi said to me? 'You can go back to your home now' like she was handing me a gift. What home? I haven't been on the mainland since I was one! Dormay is my home. *My* home."

"Ah, Joshua," said Davara softly from the side.

His eyes were laced with sadness and Roxy felt for him more than anyone at this point. The Chief had been incredibly strong throughout this exchange but it must have been hard watching his nephew hang himself. She wondered if he wanted to caution him, to shut him up, and she admired his restraint.

"Dormay would not have been yours anyway," he said. "With Abi dead, Dormay still belongs to Helen. You are not the beneficiary."

Joshua stopped then, turned away, finally looking ashamed. So Roxy spoke up again.

"But you thought Helen was pregnant with your child, didn't you? You thought, finally, you had a legitimate claim to the island. Then, to find out Abi was going to give Dormay to the locals anyway. Deny not just the woman you loved but your unborn child. It was too much for you, wasn't it? Of course, you must have suspected what Abi was up to for some time because you'd already got the pilot, Davo, to bring you a supply of quinine, just in case. I watched him hand the package over. I thought later that he must have given you a pregnancy kit for Helen, but she says he'd forgotten it. So what was in that parcel? Boxes of quinine, right?"

He didn't answer her so she continued on. "You'd obviously been considering doing it for some time, but then, just before dinner on Abi's final night, Helen confirmed your worst nightmare. She told you Abi was meeting with her lawyer the next day to sign the land over to the locals, to the true locals of Dormay. That's when you attacked. You must have run back to your room, grabbed some quinine and dropped a little of it into her G&T during dinner that night. Probably during the kerfuffle over the entrees."

"I hardly gave her any!" he said at last. "The tiniest amount."

"That's because you didn't get the chance to," scoffed Roxy. "Before you could pour the rest in, Doc was whisking her off to bed. That's why you offered to take her up, you wanted to finish the job. When that didn't work, and you spotted her up and about the following morning, you followed her to the track and killed her."

His jaw clenched and unclenched. "It wasn't like that. I tried to talk some sense into her. I gave her plenty of chances. But she insisted she had to do the right thing. *The right thing?!* And then, worse, she laughed at me. She fuckin' laughed when I told her I loved Helen, that Helen was having my baby. She said... she said the baby wasn't even mine. I... didn't believe her. I thought she was just trying one more way to break us up. But this... this fuckin' French dick? Jesus, Helen, how could you?!"

He threw his body across the bar, hid his head in his hands and began to weep, big gulping sobs.

Doc stood up and stepped back from the bar, as though repulsed by the sight of the man. He looked like he had aged 10 years in 10 minutes, and he was shaking his head furiously at Joshua. When he spoke, he could barely get his words out.

"So... so... you not only... resent the woman who took you in, under her wing, gave you wealth, education, a life!? But you poison her? And when that doesn't work, you hit that beautiful, elderly, sick woman over the head and shove her into a dirty hole to die?!"

He was spitting now and Joshua was just shaking his head, not looking up.

"You buried her like that, with that lack of dignity. With her poor head out for the crabs to feast on!" He choked back a sob.

"I thought it would make the locals look guilty," Joshua whispered hoarsely.

"You really hated them all that much? The locals, Abi, even Helen?"

"Not Helen!" he said, looking up, his face streaked with tears. "I have always loved Helen. Too much."

"No!" growled Doc. "You don't love anyone but yourself. How could you possibly love Helen and do that to her mother? To her unborn child? Oh no, young man, deep down you are filled with hate. You think you are entitled to this."

He waved one hand around the place, indicating the resort, the island, the moonlit ocean beyond.

"Why? Because you worked here for a few years? Abi paid you well didn't she? She paid you fair and square? You were entitled to *nothing*. It wasn't yours to take!"

"What about you old man!" he spat back. "You're one to talk. You've lived off Abi for years. Helen's right about all of you—Wade, his bimbo fuckin' wife over there— you've all used and abused Abi for decades."

Maya muttered some outrage to Wade but Doc simply shook his head sadly and returned to his stool.

"Ah, Joshua, you might be right but at least we all loved her. Without question. That's the difference. And we didn't kill her and leave her to die in a ditch. All alone."

Chief Davara nodded at Inspector Sikani then and the young officer moved towards the bar and took Joshua by the arm. He didn't put up a fight, didn't say anymore, he simply bowed his head and let them lead him away while Helen sobbed quietly into her shaking hands.

Two more police officers entered the veranda then and approached the Zimmermans who both looked stony faced, their heads held high as they were escorted out of the hotel and to the waiting police vessel. By now Maya was at the bar, pouring herself a very large wine, so Chief Davara sat down beside Wade. The Governor looked at him, almost matter-of-factly, as though he'd sat down for a chat.

"It's your turn next," Davara told him and Wade nodded mutely. "We will not hold you overnight but I expect you to report to my office tomorrow by lunch time. Do you understand?"

He nodded again then sighed heavily as he stood up and followed Davara out. On the way both men looked back at Roxy. Davara offered her a small triumphant smile while

Wade simply shook his head irritably at her, wishing perhaps, that the ghostwriter had never set foot on Dormay.

Within the hour, Joshua, the Zimmermans and Wade had all been escorted off the island and the remaining residents—Roxy, Helen, Maya, Luc and Doc—were seated at an unset table in the dining room. Roxy and Doc had managed to find bread and meats in the kitchen fridge and they made a small platter for those who felt hungry. Very little was eaten and even less was said. It had been an exhausting evening, draining them all, so eventually they drifted off to bed, each one heavy hearted and alone.

As Roxy drifted off to sleep underneath the billowing mosquito net with the ocean roaring away in the distance, images of Abi began to float in front of her eyes. But this time there was no silent scream or glassy-eyed horror. This time, the elderly hotelier was smiling warmly, a bright hibiscus flower wedged into her frizzy grey hair, her bejewelled fingers waving Roxy goodnight.

CHAPTER 20

The rain came at last on Roxy's final day and she welcomed the torrential downpour as she flung open her wooden shutters and drank in the cool air. It had been a dramatic evening but she had slept well last night, the best sleep of the entire week. The pieces were now all in place and she felt an enormous burden lift as the rain shuddered down. She spotted the nautilus shell she had souvenired after that first time at main beach and the sprig of coral Abi had given her, and was about to place them both in her half-packed suitcase when a gentle knock interrupted her. She placed them down and padded over to the door to open it.

Helen was standing outside, a little colour had returned to her cheeks. She was clutching a cheque.

"I thought I'd better repay you... it's the only way I know how."

"Please, come in," said Roxy, returning to her packing. Helen closed the door and took a seat on the bed, placing the cheque beside Roxy's bag.

"I love the rain," Helen said. "It always cools the place down. It's quieter in the rainy season, too. Or, at least, it used to be. I don't think this year was a good example."

"No, it certainly wasn't quiet. So, what are you going to do now?"

Helen shrugged. "I'm going to do what my mother wanted. I'm handing Dormay back to the people."

Roxy looked up at her, wide-eyed. "Really?"

"Absolutely. She's right, this isn't our land, it never was. It got stolen from their ancestors many moons ago and it's time to give it back. Besides, my heart was never in the place. She knew that. In many ways, I realise that if my mother had disinherited me from Dormay it would have been a gift. A way out."

Roxy nodded. "Where will you go? What will you do?"

She patted her lower belly and smiled. It was the warmest smile Roxy had ever seen cross her face.

"Who knows? But I have a baby to think about now."

"You're going to keep it? That's great."

"Yes, and strangely I don't feel trapped like I did before. Funny, really, now that I'm knocked up and homeless, I feel free for the first time in my life. I'm free of my mother, of Dormay, of worrying about whether Popeye will splash red wine all over the guests."

She laughed, then a frown flickered across her face. "And, I'm finally free of Joshua."

A tear sprang from her eye. "You know, he used to sneak out of his Brisbane boarding school and into mine sometimes, when we were teenagers?"

"Really?"

"Yes." She smiled sadly. "He used to call me his princess and say that Dormay was our kingdom. That one day we'd rule our own little world. I just laughed, I thought he was being dramatic. I never knew he meant it so literally, I never knew..."

She stopped, choked a little. "I never knew he'd kill for that."

Roxy sat down beside Helen and put an arm around her. "Of course you didn't. You can't blame yourself, Helen."

She brushed a finger under her wet eyes.

"I know, I know. Still, we created quite a monster, didn't we? My mother and I?" She sighed. "My poor mother. Chief Davara is releasing the body now, they're bringing her back to Dormay. We're going to hold a proper funeral this afternoon, give her a decent sending off."

"Good to hear."

"You know it's ironic. Despite what Doc said, my mother actually wouldn't have minded the way Joshua... did it. She really did love these people, their traditions. I think she would have liked being buried in the sand at her favourite beach, the way these people have been buried for generations. And she would have wanted to eventually be moved to their final resting place. So, we're taking her to the burial site on the other side of the island. We're putting her to rest with her people. The locals have asked if they can run the ceremony, the traditional way."

Roxy felt herself choking up. "That's beautiful," she managed to say.

"Will you stay for it?" Helen's eyes were imploring. "I can call the pilot, ask him to pick you up later?"

"Of course. I would be honoured."

"I have one other thing to ask you." She hesitated. "I know I have asked more than enough of you. But..."

"What is it, Helen?"

"I'd like you to come back, as soon as you can, to complete my mother's book."

This, too, caught Roxy by surprise. "You really want to do this?"

"It's what my mother wanted. Now it seems more important than ever. She deserves to have her story told, to not be remembered as the woman who was left in a ditch to die. I need you to tell her story the right way."

Roxy thought about this. "Again, Helen, I'd be honoured. But I'll need to interview the locals, and I'll need to interview you, to fill in the missing pieces. Will you still be around? When will you be handing it over?"

Helen stood up. "Oh I guess it will all take some time. I

have to organise a meeting with Mum's lawyer, the Lands Commissioner, get it all in place. Plus I'll have to spend some time training Maurice up for the job."

"Maurice will manage it? Really? So they don't want to sell the place and get on with their lives?"

Roxy was surprised.

Helen laughed. "No, I thought that too. But they dismissed the idea. Said they love the retreat, gives them all purpose, income. They're going to keep it exactly as it is, in honour of Abi. But they know they haven't got the expertise, and Popeye isn't interested, he's finally worked out he's too old. So they have asked Maurice to step up."

"Do you think he can do it?"

She shrugged. "I honestly don't know. But mother seemed to think so... so I should respect that. I should give him the benefit of the doubt. Besides, it's their island to mess with as they like. You can't believe how much of a relief that is, all of a sudden."

She opened the bedroom door. "So, we'll see you at the memorial service later? We'll be starting at the main beach around noon and heading off from there."

"Even in the rain?"

Helen laughed. "Especially in the rain!"

Downstairs, Roxy found Maya, Luc and Doc sharing a table inside the dining room enjoying a cooked breakfast as the rain bucketed down outside. Mary was back at her post and she smiled widely, confidently at Roxy as she settled her into a chair and enquired about coffee.

"I think I'll go the full cooked breakfast, too," said Roxy, "and a latte, thanks Mary." The waitress looked surprised, smiled and then disappeared again.

"Feels really weird," whispered Maya. "She'll be Lady of the Manor soon."

"And good luck to her," said Roxy.

"Here, here!" chimed Doc.

"So, Poirot, how do you feel this morning?" said Maya.

"Pretty smug?"

Roxy laughed. "Relieved, to be honest. I'm surprised you're even talking to me, after what I did to Wade."

Maya slapped her lightly on one arm. "Oh, don't be so silly! Wade'll con his way out of it before you know it! It's Joshua who's in real trouble."

She narrowed her beautiful blue eyes. "How on earth did you work it all out? I would *never* have picked him for a cold-blooded killer. Not in my wildest dreams!"

"To be honest, Maya, I didn't suspect him either, at least not for a while. But once I started to put the pieces together and get a clearer picture of his background, well, it just all clicked."

"What do you mean, 'his background'?" asked Luc.

She thanked Mary for her coffee, added two heaped spoonfuls of sugar, then took a tentative sip.

"I was confused right from the start about why Abi was so against Helen and Joshua being together. It didn't make any sense. I knew Abi loved Joshua, like a son, so I couldn't understand what she had against him as a potential son-in-law."

"Yes, she did seem to have it in for him," said Maya, contemplating this for a moment. "Oh, don't tell me—Helen and Joshua aren't related are they?! Not brother and sister, surely? How positively revolting!" She crinkled her perfect little nose up.

"Good question, Maya. I did wonder about that for a moment, too, and no they're not related." She shot Doc a quick glance. "But there was a connection between Joshua and Abi."

She took another, bigger gulp of her latte.

"Joshua first came to Dormay as a baby after his mother, Theresa, fell pregnant out of wedlock. We don't know to whom—apparently she refused to tell anyone, including her family—but what we do know for sure is that when she got pregnant she was working as a *haus girl* for a man named Jed Lilton."

She paused for the penny to drop.

"Lilton? Was he related to Abi?" asked Maya.

"He was Abi's first husband," interjected Doc. "And a miserable bastard at that. A philanderer, a brute, an all-round bad guy."

"That's right," said Roxy. "Not only did he slap Abi around a lot, but he used to sleep with all the local women, including his *haus girls*. That's why Abi left him and moved to Dormay. So I suppose when she heard that one of his *haus girls* was knocked up—in every sense of the word I don't doubt—she decided to do the right thing and brought her out to Dormay, too. That was Joshua's mum."

"Ah," said Luc. "So Joshua's father was Abi's ex-husband?"

"Actually, point of error," said Doc. "Abigail and Jed Lilton never actually divorced, God knows why! But yes, Abi believed that Joshua's father was Jed. She never knew for sure but she had her suspicions, she told me as much. There were some physical similarities, you see, between Jed and Josh, and they were both bloody hard workers you had to give them that."

"But Joshua is hardly a 'philanderer'," snorted Maya. "Barely looked twice at me."

She seemed almost disappointed and Roxy frowned.

"Count yourself lucky, Maya," she said, "because Joshua clearly had a violent streak which we all discovered far too late, and which I suspect Abi had sensed very early on. It was probably the reason she tried to keep the two apart. I can't know for sure, but I suspect Abi was worried that Joshua would not make a good husband. If he didn't end up being unfaithful, he might still have the violent gene. In any case she didn't want to risk it, so she tried to keep them apart. I think that was probably part of the reason she decided to give the island back to the locals—to separate Helen from Joshua once and for all. She was trying to protect her daughter, and it cost her her life."

"Poor, darling, Abi," Maya said, shaking her head.

She dabbed a napkin to her glossy lips. "Okay then, enough of all the sadness. A little birdy tells me the book's back on."

Roxy laughed. "Bloody hell, news travels fast around here!"

"Small towns, small islands, same diff'," said Maya. "So you staying on then, to do the book?"

"Not straight away, no. I have to get back home to Sydney first, sort a few things out."

Roxy thought then of her dear friend Max and of their first catch-up over wines at Pico's wine bar. It was once their favourite pastime, and she could not wait to do it again. She could almost taste the warm glass of merlot now as it trickled down her throat, her good friend staring across at her from his bar stool, smiling just as warmly. *Would they remain friends?* She wondered. *Or would she finally have the courage to take it to the next step?* If there was one thing this episode had taught her, life was too damn short to keep secrets and avoid your true destiny.

Perhaps it was time to put her heart on the line.

"So when will you be back?" Maya was asking, perhaps for the second time, and Roxy shook herself out of her reverie.

"Um, oh, pretty soon, I'd say. Next month maybe. Will you still be around?"

Maya scoffed. "What and give Wade more excuses to loiter about? No thank you, I'm filing for divorce—and please try and look vaguely surprised! I know we were never suited, just thought it'd be a lark, that's all. It's been anything but! I'll never pick a man twice my age again."

"What will you do?"

"Oh I'm getting back to the real world, sweetie. I'll head home to London for a bit, get back to my modelling, maybe even do a writing course!" She giggled. "I've already worked out art is most certainly not my forte."

"Speaking of which, what are you going to do, Luc?"

He offered her one of his breathtaking smiles. "Ooh, I am

leaving, too, *mon ami*. Marie-Simone wants me back in Paris, maybe I will try and come back one day to see Helen and the baby. I don't know for sure if eet eeze mine but you never know. I guess we will find out soon enough."

"Helen might be back in Australia by that time."

"*Oui*, then, if she likes, I will go there. But *non*, I can not stay here now. It is time for me to depart."

They all turned to stare at Doc.

"What about you, then?" said Maya. "You nicking off on the first available boat, too?"

He shook his head emphatically. "No, no, you can't get rid of me that easily. I'm determined to stay and help Helen get through this big change. She'll need someone beside her that she can trust, help her settle the place properly and move on. I owe that to Abi. And to Helen."

He winked at Roxy and she knew that eventually he would find the right time to tell his daughter what she needed to know.

"I'm sure Helen would love that," she said. "I guess she'll close it off to paying guests until it's sorted?"

"Hardly, my dear, she's got a boatload of Yanks showing up next week. Maurice is going to have to learn fast."

Maya giggled again. "Maurice! Running the place? Imagine it!"

They all sat back then and did just that. Already, Roxy could see the proud young islander welcoming wide-eyed foreigners to his land, showing them the places where his ancestors grew up, worked and played. She could imagine Popeye telling them real stories of the island's history, Mary presenting local dishes in this very dining room, the same dishes that were once eaten at the tables of her forefathers. Oh, indeed, Roxy could see a very beautiful, very bright future for Dormay and its people. And that, she decided, would be the perfect time to come back.

CHAPTER 21

As Abigail Lilton was laid to rest on the slopes of Abi's Point overlooking the airstrip and all those who would come and go, Roxy watched silently from the sidelines, under a wide umbrella, tears streaming down her face. The sky, too, wept long, torrential sobs in Abi's honour but the villagers remained defiant, their chins high, their eyes blazing with pride.

Abi's body, which had been wrapped in one of her colourful sarongs and decorated with fronds and frangipani, was placed gently into the rich, red soil along with an assortment of her favourite shells. Eventually Helen said a few words, then Maurice and Popeye stood up and spoke in their native tongue. She didn't understand a word of it, of course, but Roxy didn't need a translator to know that they were speaking of love and admiration, of gratification and a determination to continue on.

She knew, then, that Abi had already seen Dormay's future, had long ago believed in this island and its people. And she believed in Helen, and her ability to do something worthwhile with her life and the life of her baby. But it took her death for all of them to finally believe in themselves.

When Abi's body was eventually covered with the earth, the last of the flowers strewn across the top, the downpour suddenly stopped and a blinding ray of sunshine splashed across the island. They all stopped and turned to look at it, shielding their eyes and smiling.

Abigail Lilton was at peace at last.

~~~

ABOUT THE AUTHOR

C.A. Larmer is a journalist, editor, teacher and author of multiple crime series, stand-alone novels and a non-fiction book about pioneering surveyors in Papua New Guinea. Christina grew up in PNG, was educated in Australia, and spent many years working in Sydney, London, Los Angeles and New York. She now lives with her musician husband, boomerang sons and their very cheeky Bluey on the east coast of Australia.

Sign up for news, views and giveaways:
calarmer.com

www.ingramcontent.com/pod-product-compliance
Lightning Source LLC
Chambersburg PA
CBHW020720130726
47899CB00011B/587